"Laugh-out-loud funny. . . . Acosta's narrative zips along, keeping the pages turning faster than a salsa dancer."

—FreshFiction.com

"Darkly hilarious. . . . You'd have to be undead not to enjoy this book!"

—Julia Spencer-Fleming, Agatha Award–winning author of *All Mortal Flesh*

"A fun, snappy read."

—*Booklist*

"I couldn't put this one down . . . now I'm a fan."

—*Contra Costa Times*

"Fun and flirty."

—Julie Kenner, author of *Demons Are Forever* and *The Prada Paradox*

"Hilarious . . . intriguing plot twists . . . all the characters are worth watching."

—*Romantic Times*

"This book is a blast. It's funny, original, witty, romantic silliness that is pure genius!! Brava!! More! More!"

—Deborah MacGillivray, author of *The Invasion of Falgannon Island*

Also by Marta Acosta

Midnight Brunch at Casa Dracula
Happy Hour at Casa Dracula

"Will keep you up at night . . . hilarious."

—*National Examiner*

"Best Chick Lit Novel of 2007. Intelligence and fabulosity mixed into a delicious cocktail."

—Marcela Landres, *Latinidad*

HAPPY HOUR AT CASA DRACULA

An August 2006 Book Sense Pick
***Catalina* magazine's Top Humor Book of 2006**

What's a girl to do when she falls for a vampire and her ex-boyfriend wants to drive a stake through her heart?

"Page-turning excitement . . . wickedly snarky."

—*El Paso Times*

"A winner . . . quirky, surprising, and cinematic."

—*Star Democrat* (Baltimore)

"Clever and amusing."

—*San Francisco Chronicle*

"Will keep readers highly entertained until the final unpredictable destination."

—*The Birmingham Times*

"Stephanie Plum meets *Sex and the City* in this stylish, hilarious novel."

—Jennifer Cox, author of *Around the World in 80 Dates*

The Bride of
Casa Dracula

Marta Acosta

POCKET BOOKS

New York   London   Toronto   Sydney

POCKET BOOKS
A Division of Simon & Schuster, Inc.
1230 Avenue of the Americas
New York, NY 10020

First Pocket Books trade paperback edition September 2008

POCKET and colophon are registered trademarks of
Simon & Schuster, Inc.

For information about special discounts for bulk purchases,
please contact Simon & Schuster Special Sales at 1-800-456-6798
or business@simonandschuster.com.

Manufactured in the United States of America

10 9 8 7 6 5 4 3 2 1

Library of Congress Cataloging-in-Publication Data

Acosta, Marta.
    The bride of Casa Dracula / by Marta Acosta.
        p. cm.
    1. Hispanic American women—Fiction. 2. Vampires—Fiction. 3. Marriage—
Fiction. I. Title.

ISBN-13: 978-1-4165-5963-4
ISBN-10:   1-4165-5963-9

PS3601.C67B75 2008
813'.6—dc22
                                                              2008000908

In memory of Dr. Buddy Valentine,
most beloved friend and companion.

one

it's a nice day for a blood wedding

"I'm crushed, *crushed*, by your insinuation that I would purposely antagonize the Rules Committee," I said to the family attorney, Sam Grant. "I will treat those elitist bloodsucking bureaucrats exactly as well as they have treated me."

We were in the study, all manly, dark brown leather furniture and wood paneling and stultifying nonfiction books. I'd tried bringing in pretty chintz pillows and amusing novels, but Oswald, my fiancé and the owner of this house, had recoiled like Dracula from a flask of holy water.

Oswald now leaned back against the glossy mahogany desk and said, "Milagro, we all know that you like to poke bears, so stop trying to make Sam feel guilty."

He and his cousin Sam Grant were lean men with thick brown hair. They had nice broad brows, beautiful smiles, and even features. Sam, at six feet, was an inch taller than Oswald,

1

who had a delightful asymmetry to his grin and a gleam in his gray eyes. Oswald had changed out of his suit and was wearing jeans and a T-shirt from Buddy's Body Shop that said *Pounding, Sanding & Painting to Perfection Since 1963.*

Sam's features were gentler than Oswald's, and he had sincere, brown eyes. "Young Lady," Sam began, because that was their nickname for me. "I value and appreciate your, uhm, lively nature. But as your friend, I want you to have the full benefit of the rights and privileges that the Council can grant you when you become Oswald's wife, and that includes substantial financial benefits."

I held up my hand to stop him from once again extolling the mind-numbing virtues of no-interest loans and vacation time shares. "The only thing I care about is being allowed to attend your family events. Therefore, I will endeavor not to poke the bear."

Oswald's family, the Grants, and others from their original homeland had a genetic autosomal recessive disorder that made them sensitive to sunlight but gave them an excellent ability to heal from injuries. They never got sick and had an extended life span. They also had a craving for red food, including blood.

The Grant family referred to themselves as "having a condition," but others of their kind called themselves vampires. Centuries of persecution had forced them to hide their nature and form their own governmental organization, the Council.

I was one of them. Sort of, but not really. I'd been infected twice. The first time, I'd been accidentally infected with Oswald's blood, and I'd nearly died. The second infection left me stronger than Oswald and most other vampires. They could heal quickly from cuts, and I could heal from serious injury. They had terrific eyesight, and I could see in almost complete darkness. They were well coordinated, and my reflexes were faster than a teenage boy's. Best of all, I could bake in the sunlight until I got as toasty brown as a *buñuelo,* to no ill effect. I was a new, improved version of myself, Milagro 2.0.

Yet I was loath to call myself a vampire. After all, culturally, I was still a normal human *chica,* and it is culture that informs identity, isn't it? Oswald wanted me to accept that I was one of them, and he wanted the Council to put their official stamp on my membership card.

The Council resented my existence and acted as if I was trying to use a loophole to join their club. Some were wary of my status as the only known living survivor of a vampire infection, and others had a disturbing tendency to view me as a fleshy container of rare and intoxicating fluid.

I was sitting on the love seat next to Oswald's other cousin, Gabriel, who was in charge of the family's security. He was a small, lovely, redheaded man. He used the same expensive herb-scented multispectrum Swiss sunblock that Oswald favored.

Gabriel stopped twirling a strand of my black hair in his slim, pale fingers and said, "It's no use, Oz. She has that 'Where's the pokey stick?' expression on her face."

Leaning close to Gabriel's ear, I whispered, "No, I have that 'Poke me! Poke me!' expression," and we started laughing.

"I can see that we're interfering with your flirting," Oswald said wryly. "If there's anything you don't understand about the agreements . . ."

"I know how to read," I said. "I'll smile and sign the papers, and then I'll be an official member of the Society of the Living Undead and learn the secret handshake and get my discount membership to the gym."

Sam squeezed his eyes shut for a moment and then said, "Please, please, don't say 'living undead.' Please don't—"

"Don't poke the bear. I get it. Are we finished now? Because you know how cranky your grandmother gets if she shows up and I don't pour a cocktail down her gullet *stat*."

"I'm going to tell her you said that," Gabriel said.

Sam still looked worried, so I stood and went to him. "Allay your anxiety, Samuel. Everything is going to be dandy."

Gabriel followed me into the spacious kitchen, and he went to a window and pulled back one of the blue-and-yellow Provençal-print curtains to enjoy the view. The green fields of Oswald's ranch rolled to the base of forested mountains. The windows on the other side of the two-story sandstone house, which I'd come to think of as Casa Dracula, had views to my garden, more fields, and a small vineyard.

Before I'd met Oswald, I'd been living on quesadillas, patching together part-time jobs, and struggling to pay the rent while rats scrambled in the walls of my basement apartment.

I went to the drinks cabinet and pulled out bottles and the blender.

"Can I help?" Gabriel asked.

"Nope, I already took care of everything. Crudités and a dill dip with cocktails. Roast beef sandwiches with blue cheese dressing, roasted tomatoes, a salad, and a plum tart."

"You're quite the hostess these days." He turned from the view and said, "I'm glad Oswald bought this place. It's a treat to come visit."

"It's a treat for me, too, when everyone's here." I peeled and sliced mangoes, the juices of the ripe fruit making the knife slippery in my hand. "It seems so quiet most of the time. Especially now that Oswald is working more."

"I'm sorry about your dog."

I threw ice in the blender, sloshed in rum, curaçao, lime juice, and added the mango. I hit the froth button and the ingredients whirred together. I stared at the orange slush, trying to control my emotions, when I smelled a familiar burning odor. I quickly shut off the blender, then poured the icy concoction into tumblers and added grenadine to each glass.

When I trusted myself to speak, I said, "That's one of the reasons I don't mind leaving to meet with the Council. I'll have two days of sightseeing and shopping in a fabulous city I've never been to before, and I get to meet this mysterious cabal face-to-face."

"Only the Rules Committee, not the entire Council. Ian is out of the country."

"Or, as Oswald told me, 'At least *goddamn* Ian Ducharme is out of the country.'"

I had had a brief liaison with Ian, aka the Dark Lord, before I got together with Oswald. I had no idea what Ian actually did on the Council, and I didn't believe his explanation that he was called the Dark Lord merely because he'd inherited a boggy estate. Ian had given me an infusion of his blood when I'd been badly slashed by a rogue vampire, and that second infusion had given me my exceptional abilities. I still dreamed of the way his blood had burned on my open wound and how I'd bitten into his flesh to stop the pain.

"Were you hoping to see him?" Gabriel asked.

"He's very entertaining."

"And by 'entertaining' you mean he's smoldering?"

"That's what I said. And he *did* save my life."

"He could just as easily have . . . ," Gabriel began. "Someone at my level doesn't know all the Council's secrets, and I wouldn't let you go if I didn't believe you'd be safe at this meeting. But I agree with Sam and Oz: Don't poke the bear."

"I wouldn't even be doing this if Oz didn't want the Council's approval so badly. He still feels guilty about infecting me. But if he hadn't, I wouldn't have all of you," I said. "I wish he could come with me, but he's got surgeries scheduled." Oswald was a board certified plastic surgeon.

"Those breasts don't get augmented by themselves."

"I do not understand voluntary surgery."

"The world is full of mysteries. Like my grandmother and Thomas Cook."

Yes, he was talking about *the* Thomas Cook, the actor. We'd met him when I had a job rewriting a screenplay that got tossed aside. Thomas had a thing for older women, and men of every age had a thing for Edna.

Gabriel said, "I thought she'd be tired of him and pass him along to me."

"I'm telling your boyfriend you said that."

"He already knows! Grandmama should be with someone more . . . more worthwhile. Have you talked to her about him?"

"I tried. I said, 'Edna, how can you put up with such a nitwit, albeit a highly attractive one?' "

"What did she say?" Gabriel asked.

"She said, 'Because my grandson appears to be fond of you,' and I said, 'Ha ha and ha.'" I handed Gabriel the tray of hors d'oeuvres.

I carried the drinks and we walked out as Oswald's grandmother and her addled younger paramour came up the gravel drive from the direction of the guest cottage, aka the Love Shack.

Edna was dressed in a lilac linen blouse and skirt, and

looked fabulous for her years, whatever they were. Edna wasn't tall, but she managed to look down her straight, narrow nose at me with her exotic, glittering green eyes. Her silver hair was cut close to her excellently shaped noggin, and the skin around her eyes was delicate, like tissue paper that had been crumpled then carefully smoothed out.

Thomas looked as if he had dressed for a tennis match, circa 1920: white slacks, a white shirt, a cable-knit sweater flung over his shoulders, and dark sunglasses. His hair was sleek and jet black, and his copper skin gleamed. He looked as scrumptious as a caramel-and-vanilla ice cream sundae.

I'd had a crush on Thomas when he was Hollywood's newest Latino heartthrob and I was just a teenager. In person, he was a lot more irritating. He said, "Milagro, why are you just standing there like a lump? Does Edna have to get her own drink?"

Edna didn't even bother trying to hide her smile. "Thank you for being so considerate, Thomas," she said as she sat on one of the wicker chairs. When I handed her a glass, she looked at the drink and asked suspiciously, "What is this?"

"A Rancho Sunset. I invented it myself."

Thomas picked up a drink and took a chair next to Edna's. After a sip, he said, "Milagro was a terrible assistant, but at least she can make a decent drink."

"Bossing me around did not make me your assistant. I'm a writer."

"Then where are your books?" he asked.

Most of my income came from gardening jobs, but I'd put those on hold until after the wedding. My literary career had taken a downward trajectory after the failed screenwriting gig. I'd signed with an agent, but the last time I talked to him he told me, "There's no market for political horror novels. There will *never, ever* be a market for them. Call me if you ever decide to write something marketable."

I told Thomas, "For your information, I've got an interview tomorrow for a writing job. But the writing business is complicated."

"Edna sells everything she writes," he said.

In her youth, Edna had written novels, and recently she'd had success with her books on entertaining. She gave me an innocent look and said, "Not everyone is talented."

"Speaking of talent," Gabriel said, "Thomas, I remember when you used to model."

This led Thomas to launch into his monologue, "Thomas Cook: The Underwear Model Years." No matter how often I heard this thrilling tale of white cotton *chones* and fame, I found it enchanting.

As he was concluding his story, Sam and Oswald joined us. When Oswald stood behind me and rubbed my shoulders, I felt a marvelous zizzing, a delightful effect of my second infection.

Nothing extraordinary was said and nothing extraordinary happened, and yet I couldn't have been happier than I was here and now with Oswald and my friends, watching the sun slipping down behind the dark mountains. I was filled with *espíritu de los cocteles,* a mood of utter contentment, and I reached for Oswald's hand and kissed it.

He returned the gesture and said, "Where's your ring?"

My hand was bare. "On the kitchen counter. I was getting dinner ready." I hoped I'd left my engagement ring there. I had the habit of taking it off and leaving it around whenever I did any housework or gardening. "It's a nice evening. Let's eat on the patio."

The slate patio was on the other side of the house, surrounded by the garden I'd planted. I turned on the little fairy lights that wound around the trunks of the ancient oaks, and Gabriel lighted candles. The night smelled of damp earth, grass, early-blooming roses, nicotiana, and honeysuckle.

We brought out the food and opened bottles of pinot noir. It was like those evenings we'd had often when Sam and his family lived here, when Oswald and I stayed in the Love Shack, before Edna began going away for weeks at a time with Thomas.

After dinner, Thomas went back to the Love Shack to study a script. The actor had his own misunderstood genetic disorder and wasn't interested in what he saw as our boring perversion.

The rest of us walked to the large brown barn.

Since Oswald had been spending more time working, his dogs usually stayed with Ernesto, the ranch hand, at his one bedroom apartment at the front of the barn. The dogs heard us approaching and ran out to greet us.

I pushed back an ache of sadness and entered the dark, shadowy barn. One of the cats glided behind bales of alfalfa, hunting for mice. The barn had a rich, wonderful smell, and I could hear the animals moving about in the stalls.

Light came from under the closed door of a stall on the right. Oswald opened the door and said, "Evening, Ernie."

We followed him into the stall, which had been converted to a cozy den. Leather club chairs were set on a worn Persian carpet, and copper-and-mica sconces cast a warm golden light.

"Hey, Oz," Ernesto said. The compact muscled man had set everything up for our evening tasting. A bottle of dark liquid was on the sideboard as well as bottles of mineral water and wineglasses. "I got something different today. Emu."

"Emu?" Sam said.

"Tastes like chicken," Ernie responded and laughed. He poured a few tablespoons of purple-red blood into each glass and topped them off with mineral water. "I just got this sample. But if you like it, there's two birds for sale cheap."

I dropped into a chair and took a sip from the glass Ernie passed to me. After a moment of swishing it around in my mouth, I said, "It's not bad. A little too . . . uhm . . ."

"Floral," Edna provided.

"Yeah, well, the reason they're for sale is they got loose and ate someone's flower garden," Ernie said.

I was only half listening. The blood bloomed inside me, warm and invigorating. I gazed at Oswald and wondered how quickly I could get him into the bedroom. He caught my glance and gave me a crooked smile that cheered my heart.

Sam asked, "Young Lady, what are you going to do on the free day of your trip?"

"My friend from college, Toodles, is going to give me the insider's tour," I said excitedly. "She's been asking me to visit for ages."

"Toodles," Edna sniffed. "Who is this person, and do I want to know how she acquired such an unfortunate sobriquet?"

"I'm so glad you asked," I said. "Toodles lived next door to me sophomore year and we took 'Po-Mo Lit: Angst, Anguish, and Alienation' together." My education at a Fancy University (F.U.) had offered me many intellectually stimulating courses.

"I'm already captivated," Edna said.

"Of course you are. Toodles's real name is Kathleen Meriwether Hippensteele, but she smuggled her teacup poodles into the dorm and this nasty R.A. ratted her out. The headline in the campus paper was *Toodles, Poodles*. She has a tendency to use words with 'oo' sounds, and that cemented her nickname."

Edna said, "I shall never get those thirty seconds back."

"Just for that, I'm not bringing you back a snow globe diorama."

Edna rolled her eyes dramatically. She had a large and impressive repertoire of expressions, but she always returned to the classics. She said, "By the way, your future mother-in-law sent me her suggestions for your wedding registry."

Surprised, Oswald said, "Why did Mom send it to *you*?"

"She seemed to think I might exert some influence over the Young Lady." Edna slid her eyes toward me conspiratorially.

"Grandmama, you know Mom just wants to help."

"I don't think we'll need her suggestions," I said to Edna.

"Are you sure?" she answered. "No doubt her suggestions reflect the very pinnacle of suburban country club chic—mallard motifs and 'deluxe' bed-in-a-bag sets."

"Grandmama!" Oswald said. Then he smiled. "Okay, she did have a family tartan and crest designed for the den."

Gabriel said, "Big deal. My mom made me dress to coordinate with the wallpaper. And she wonders why I'm gay."

"You're only gay so you don't have to deal with women," Oswald said. "Coward."

"Speaking of women, I've got to get home to mine," Sam said, referring to his wife and daughter. "It's a long drive."

We all walked to the house. The stars had come out and shone in the blue-black sky. Sam said good-bye to us at the car park and wished me luck with the Council.

Edna went back to her addled paramour in the Love Shack and Gabriel adjourned to the family room to watch television.

Oswald and I walked through the large house, holding hands. He'd had a designer decorate it, and other than the kitchen and a small parlor, it was done in neutral colors and earth tones. We went up the staircase with its black wrought iron railing.

The master bedroom hadn't changed much since I'd moved in. It had hardwood floors, beamed ceilings, ivory walls, and Mission-style furniture. However, my necessities (books, makeup, baubles) cluttered surfaces. I spotted my yellow diamond engagement ring sparkling on the dresser. It was beautiful, but I felt odd wearing something so expensive in my daily life.

"Are you all packed?" Oswald asked.

"Almost everything. I wish you were coming."

He pulled me close to him. "Me, too. I'll take you somewhere wonderful when I can spare a few days."

I nuzzled his neck. "Good. At least we'll have tomorrow together."

He was unbuttoning my blouse when his cell phone rang. Glancing at the incoming number, he said, "It's my service. Sorry." They called only for urgent situations, so he had to take the call. When he hung up, he said, "It doesn't sound serious, but I'm going to check in with a patient. I'll just be a minute." He was still on the phone by the time I crawled in bed and fell asleep.

two

nice to gnome you

We got up early the next morning. Oswald went to the barn to talk to Ernie about ranch business, and I pulled on jeans and a T-shirt and went outside. The morning fog draped gracefully across the mountains, and the pale blue sky would shade to clear beryl by noon.

I cut a bouquet of pink-tinged, creamy heirloom roses, rosemary, and tulips and put them into a jar of water. Then I walked along the path that had been cut through the field, passing the compound that enclosed the swimming pool and walking beside the rippling creek all the way to the pond.

My dog, Daisy, had loved to swim in this pond and chase the frogs and birds. When I first came to the ranch, sick and angry and scared, the fluffy mutt had attached herself to me.

My mother Regina had never let me have pets, so having a

dog was a new and wonderful experience. Loving her was so easy. When I found the lump on Daisy's shoulder, cancer had already spread through her body.

Oswald and Ernie had buried her here and placed a boulder to mark her final resting place. Since she had died, I felt a hardness in the center of my chest, as if my feelings had collapsed into one small, dense place, a black hole of grief.

I replaced the wilted flowers on her grave with the new bouquet. "I miss you, Daisy. I miss you all the time." I blinked away my tears and returned to the house.

After showering, I dressed in a snug 1960s camel knit suit with suede panels. Vintage pointy black patent heels and topaz rhinestone earrings and a broach completed my look. I was slipping on my engagement ring when Oswald came in the room.

"Have I seen that outfit before?" he asked. He was wearing a dark blue suit and a pale blue shirt.

"No, it's new. New to me, I mean." I posed in front of him, stretching my arms to show the wonderful three-quarter-length sleeves. "I found it at the thrift store for only ten dollars and it fits perfectly."

"I'll say. It's hugging your curves as tight as a long-lost friend."

"I'm glad you like it."

"Is your bag packed?"

"Right here." I zipped the green zebra-print rolling case.

Oswald looked at it for a moment and then said, "You won't have any problem spotting that on the luggage carousel."

"That's why I bought it!" I said.

As he was taking our cases to the car, I packed my makeup and toiletries in a shoulder bag. At the last minute I went downstairs to a small parlor that served as my reading room. Hidden in the closet were presents from Ian Ducharme. I shouldn't have kept them, but he had such wonderful taste and I didn't know how to return them.

I pulled out a box with an unusual and beautiful ring, a red stone set in a gold band inscribed with symbols. I put the ring in my makeup case and went outside to Oswald's luxury sedan, which was parked beside my little green pickup.

"Let me drive," I said to Oswald and held out my hand for the keys.

"You drive yours and I'll drive mine. Besides, you speed."

It was difficult not to speed, since the limit seemed so slow to me. I got in the passenger seat.

Daffodils bloomed under the grand old English walnut trees that lined the drive. The electronic gate at the edge of the property swung open as we left Casa Dracula. Soon we were on the highway heading over the mountain. The winding road was shadowed by a thick growth of live oaks, pines, and manzanita. In places, the sheared red wall of earth seemed to lean over the road, and in others, the land dropped off into darkness.

Then the road opened up to the breathtaking view on the other side of the mountain. Below were green vineyards, stretching for miles, and a few of the original vintners' houses, white Victorians with mature palms out front.

I tensed as we entered the extremely expensive little town where Oswald had his offices, hoping that he wouldn't want to stop. But he drove right through to our favorite café-deli, where we bought lattes and cranberry scones for breakfast. Oswald also picked up some thick, old-fashioned red licorice ropes.

We reached the City an hour later. When I saw the skyscrapers, the hills, and the green-gray bay, I felt a thrill. We drove to Hotel Croft, and Oswald left his car with the valet.

The concierge assured us that our bags would be taken to our suite as soon as it was ready.

Then we walked down the street to the Grant family's favorite department store. The doorman was just unlocking the front door and the gift registry coordinator was waiting for us. She smiled and called Oswald "Dr. Grant" and me "Miss De Los Santos" as she guided us through the store. The store smelled the way expensive places do, like new, freshly cut grass, clean laundry, and inherited money.

Everything had the drenched color of a Polaroid photo, which increased my sense of unreality. Here I was in the City's oldest, most exclusive department store. The fabulous man beside me was my fiancé. When I glanced at myself in one of the walls of beveled mirrors, I saw a voluptuous and splendidly attired young woman who looked as if she'd stepped (in her pointy heels) out of a classic Luis Buñuel film.

I'd been here only once before, on one of the many occasions when I was broke and job hunting. I was sent into the basement to meet with a manager. There, among the crates and cardboard boxes, I'd been given a test on the care of silver. I was used to scoring well on tests. But the questions had baffled me. What was the correct temperature of water to rinse the dust from silver? Should silver be stored in linen, cotton, or flannel? The manager had said he was sorry, but there was no place for me at their establishment. What future was there for a girl who didn't know how to polish a soup ladle?

Now I had an off-balance, giddy sensation that I was about to break something very expensive. The rack of glittering crystal looked too precariously balanced, and I imagined skittering on the marble tiles, a shimmering shower of glass, and a gorgeous cacophony as everything crashed. Many decorative objects brought to mind fun words like "knickknacks," "bric-a-brac," "tchotchkes," and "doodads." Other items were tragically plain.

I dubbed the gift registry coordinator Mrs. Nice because she said "nice" incessantly. She now led us by a case with tiny little chairs made of gold and jewels.

"Furniture for posh elves," I said. All the price tags were turned discreetly away, and I flipped over the tag for a miniature ottoman. *"Que rico."*

Oswald turned and focused his clear gray eyes on mine. "What?" I asked.

"You've got that crazy expression. What are you thinking?" His brown hair was brushed back from his brainy brow.

I was thinking that I wanted to haul him to the linen section and have my way with him on the six-hundred-thread-count sheets exquisitely hand embroidered by Belgian nuns and orphans. "You shall learn later in tantalizing detail."

Mrs. Nice may have been listening, because I thought I saw her move her head just a smidgen, like a cat pretending it doesn't recognize its name. She had rimless glasses on a silver chain and looked like the librarian in my dream of heaven, where all books were shelved properly and there were no late fines.

She turned right at the narrow escalators and stopped at a display of china. "Would Miss De Los Santos like to select an everyday pattern?" The eyes behind her silver-rimmed glasses held a look of panic. Perhaps she was new at her job.

There were about ten different white plates, one hardly distinguishable from the next. But then my eyes were drawn to a cabinet that held a glossy red plate with a leopard-print rim in black and gold. "May I see that pattern?" I asked Mrs. Nice.

"Umm, Milagro, that isn't really . . . ," Oswald began, causing Mrs. Nice to hesitate.

"But it's so fun." I turned to Mrs. Nice and asked, "Isn't it fun?"

She glanced at Oswald and then said softly, "Very fun, yes, although a *classic* pattern might serve better for a variety of occasions."

"But everyone loves leopard prints," I said. "And red is a classic, too, like red lipstick."

"How about this one?" Oswald asked as he pointed to a white plate with a scrolled rim.

"It's nice, but it's not very fun," I observed.

"It's *very* nice," Oswald said.

"Yes, *very* nice," I relented. After saying "nice" all morning, the word began to sound strange to my ears. If "mice" was the plural of "mouse," perhaps "nice" was the plural of "noose." My old clubbing friends couldn't afford this store and had already sent me a fascinating catalog from the Womyn's Sexual Health Collective and Bookstore. I said to Mrs. Nice, "This registry is mostly for the Grant family, so I guess you can list the white pattern."

She heard the disappointment in my voice and said, "May I make a suggestion? Why not select the, ah, *fun* pattern as a tea service for special occasions?"

"That is an excellent idea!" I said. I could paint my nails exactly the same shade as the plates and have my friends to tea.

She and Oswald both smiled. Everyone was happy.

I lost interest in the store when I found they didn't even sell blenders. Thirty minutes later, we were registered for classic linens, classic dishes, classic towels, and other classic housewares. We said good-bye to Mrs. Nice, and Oswald took my hand.

As we went through the porcelain area, I saw a table with

figurines of dogs, and I stopped. There was a minute German shepherd, a corgi, a pug, a collie, and a golden retriever. None of them was as beautiful as Daisy had been.

"Baby, come on," Oswald said softly and led me outside.

I focused on the specks of mica glinting in the dark pavement. "I'm okay." I smiled to prove that I was fine.

"Are you really okay?" He tried to comfort me, kissing my temple and rubbing my back, but my grief was my own.

"Oswald, I'm always okay. I'm famous for being okay."

"After the wedding, we'll get a dog for you. Not to replace Daisy, because I know you can't replace her, but . . ."

I nodded. "You'll be late for your consultations."

He smiled and said, "Good luck with the interview."

"Thanks. Good luck with the boobs."

"Today it's noses and chins. See you soon." He popped on a pair of sunglasses and walked off.

I watched him until he turned the corner. It was easier for me here than at the ranch, because I didn't expect to see Daisy here. Besides, I loved city living. Plays, movies, museums, bookstores, and live music were all close by. New bars and clubs had opened, and my friend Mercedes's club, My Dive, was five minutes away. As I walked down the street, I enjoyed studying the other women, dressed in the casual-eccentric-chic style that was common here. Best of all, there was an ethnic and racial mix that I missed back at the ranch.

Influenced by Mrs. Nice's refined taste, I walked into a boutique and came out ten minutes later carrying a shopping bag. Inside was a white plastic miniskirt that had been on the clearance rack. When I'd tried it on it had been a little snug over my hips, but white plastic clothing was so mod London in the sixties, so classic. Like my dinnerware, it would go with anything.

I hailed a cab and told the driver to take me to the botanical gardens. During the drive, I contemplated my writing career. While I wanted success, I had to stay true to my artistic vision. Someday people would proudly display my cannibal zombie and monster novels on their bookshelves. In the meantime, I planned to take whatever paying writing assignments I could find. Pedro Nascimento, the man whose advertisement I'd answered, had said he needed someone interested in folklore and horticulture to help him write his memoirs.

A tiny wrinkled man in a white suit, white shirt, black-and-white patterned ascot, and a panama hat was standing at the entrance to the botanical gardens as my cab arrived. An old tooled-leather bag, darkened with wear at the edges, hung from a strap over his shoulder. I paid the cabbie and got out.

The gnome didn't come forward, but smiled broadly as I approached. "Hello," I said. "Are you Mr. Nascimento? I'm Milagro De Los Santos." I wasn't tall, but he was a few inches shorter than I and small-boned.

"Splendid girl, please call me *Don* Pedro." Oversized black-framed glasses magnified his huge brown eyes. "I did not ask for the title, but my students insisted upon bestowing this magnificent honorific on me!"

I was immediately charmed by this little bug's flamboyant way of speaking. He took my hand in both of his and gripped it firmly. The hair under the hat was silver, but he had a vivacity that made it difficult to determine his age. "It is so good to meet my Milagro! I knew from the moment I heard your name, 'Miracle of the Saints,' that you were the right person." He laughed. "The *write* person, get it?"

I laughed politely. People always tried to find symbolism in my name. My grandmother had insisted upon the name, believing that it was a miracle I'd emerged sound from my mother Regina's hostile womb.

Don Pedro said, "Let us ramble amidst the greenery and glory in this day." We went through the passage that led past the lecture hall and bookstore to the gardens. "I have read the stories you sent me, and I am in awe of your perfection for this assignment. Your academic credentials are unparalleled, and I can feel your potent spiritual connections to the animistic world."

He made me feel like a Rhodes Scholar, earth goddess, and mystic. "Thank you. I also wrote a screenplay last year on assignment, but nothing came of it."

"That is the infernal corruption of Hollywood! Above all else, I repudiate phoniness and pretense," he said sympathetically. "I was acutely touched by your passionate tale about the llama. You understand that the animal spirits are deeply tied to our own spirits."

I carried the llama story around like a dead albatross, a penance for a too hasty click of my spell-checker, which had changed *La Llorona,* the mythic wailing woman of Latino folklore, to *La Llama.* I no longer bothered to explain the mistake. "That story won an award."

Around us, the first of the spring flowers were blooming. "I love this place," I said. "My favorite area is the Australian section. All the plants are so strange and wonderful."

"You sense what the aboriginal people know—the pulsating soul of the plant and animal life. I have been to the Australian outback and taken a walkabout in the desert. I was ravaged by thirst when a lizard spoke to me, directing me to follow the flight of a flock of honeyeaters, and I did and found a crystalline pond. I praised the spirits, then drank fully of the freshwater and bathed my imperfect human body there."

"Really?" I said as I amended my assessment of him from fairly loony to completely loony.

"I was but a callow personage in an anthropology doctoral program when I had my first out-of-body experience while studying under a shaman in the Amazonian rain forest."

Absolutely Froot Loops. I wondered why he didn't use contractions when he spoke and if he was a native speaker of English. "Were you born here?" I asked.

He peered around nervously. "Did you hear that? I thought I heard someone. Or some*thing*!"

I heard only the leaves and branches moving in the breeze, and birds and squirrels scratching about. "No, I don't hear anything."

He kept peering around and said, "I have studied with the tribes of every continent and sat with quiet ecstasy at the feet of wise elders. May I be satisfied that you will act as my scribe so that I may share the lessons I have learned?"

What a loon. "I'd like that. Are you planning on publishing this memoir yourself?"

"Yes, I will give it as a little gift, *un regalito,* to my family and friends. I have students who may be interested in my spiritual journey."

"What do you teach?"

"I lecture on plants used for medicinal and ceremonial purposes. *Mira!*" He bent over to show me a dandelion growing on the border. "Here it will be violently ripped out and discarded as an unwelcome weed, but it can be boiled and used to treat high blood pressure, urinary complaints, and upset stomach. It makes a tender and piquant salad green, and the flower is the yellow of happiness and childhood."

"Ray Bradbury wrote a story called 'Dandelion Wine.'" I admired the cheerful flower. "It's about a boy's awakening to his own existence, the magic of everyday life."

Don Pedro was delighted. "Magic exists in every moment if we only open our eyes to see it."

I didn't mention that my new eyes could see in the dark.

A small wooden sign read *Central American Collection*. He gestured for me to sit on a bench nearby and then sat beside me. *Don* Pedro reached into his leather bag and pulled out a big envelope and a sheaf of papers bound with twine. "Despite all the wisdom I have gathered, I am still only mortal. I have become a *viejo* who is too proud to admit he needs help writing his memoir. I hope I do not insult you if I ask that you sign a letter of nondisclosure."

"Nothing to be embarrassed about." I quickly read the agreement, which said that I would not reveal my connection with the memoir, nor would I have any claims on the final book, beyond the agreed-upon payment. Sam had always told me not to sign things without checking with him first. "Do you mind if I make a quick call to my lawyer to ask about this?"

"If it will give you comfort."

"I'll just be a moment." I walked to the end of a path and called Sam. I described the project to him and read the pertinent paragraphs of the agreement.

"You don't mind not getting credit for your work?"

I imagined my F.U. creative writing peers howling with laughter if they discovered that I was reduced to penning a vanity book. "I'd like to keep this confidential, too. I've got my reputation as a serious literary writer to consider."

"If you think the payment is reasonable, I see no harm in

signing, but I recommend that you consult with your agent."

"My agent wouldn't even take a call about a self-published memoir. Thanks, Sam."

I returned to *Don* Pedro, and after I signed the agreement, he handed over the papers. They were a collection of handwritten notes, pages torn from wire-bound notebooks, printed essays, and newspaper clippings. He took a check out of his pocket. "Fifty percent now and the balance when you give me the transcendent completed manuscript by deadline."

I glanced at the check and saw that it was written out to "cash."

"I'll do my very best," I said.

Don Pedro patted my knee. "You are bursting with ripe womanhood. Do you have a boyfriend?"

I flashed my left hand to show him the large engagement ring. "I'm engaged."

"Ah, perhaps we shall meet on the astral plane of existence when I am not so old and you are not already taken." He then invited me to listen to him lecture in an hour, but said, "I'm afraid that I will not be able to acknowledge our new friendship. We must maintain secrecy about this project! I have enemies."

"What kind of enemies?" I asked in a neutral voice.

"There are those who seek to acquire my powerful juju! Those who would do evil with it, instead of good."

Star Wars fans were everywhere. I'd be sure to add a light saber into the story. I had turned my torso toward him, about to assure him that I would be careful, when I saw the oddest *shimmer* by the gnarled roots of a Central American banyan. I stared harder and saw the hindquarters of a dog slinking off into the shrubs. I hoped my eyesight wasn't going through yet another phase of weirdness.

Don Pedro drew my attention back by relating that he had once shape-shifted into a platypus in Tasmania. "I felt very macho with my thick, strong bill and my poisonous ankle spurs."

I promised to include this fascinating vignette in his memoirs. "Everyone loves a good platypus story."

"The platypus is an inscrutable and crafty creature," *Don* Pedro declaimed. He said he had to meditate before his talk in the lecture hall. "Milagro, I encourage you to follow your spirit guide when you write my story. I did not hire a journalist. I wanted an artist who could imagine the essential truths in my life story. Will you do that for me?"

I felt like a teenager who'd been given the keys to a Ferrari and told not to worry about the speed limit. "Absolutely."

three

i've got a beef (or don't have a cow)

While I waited for *Don* Pedro's lecture to begin, I wandered around the California Native Plants area. Something moved at the periphery of my vision, and for a moment I thought it was an animal. But I turned and saw a man bending over to tie his shoe by a huge gray-leaved shrub.

He straightened up, smiled at me, and said, "Morning."

"Morning," I said, admiring the tall man. He wore an olive shirt, jeans, and work boots. He had striking coloring, blue eyes, hair almost as dark as my own, pulled back in a ponytail, and olive skin. The word "hunky" came to mind. I wasn't prone to seafaring fancies, but I wanted to dress him up in pirate clothes and talk dirty pirate talk with him, full of "yar's," "ahoy's," and "Avast, here be my booty," and such. "Nice flannel bush."

"*Fremontia californica*," he said. "Or *Fremontodendron*."

"Is there a squabble about the name? Because *Fremontoden-dron* is too long for such a humble bush."

"I agree. But botanists love an argument."

"You must be a botanist, then."

"A plant biologist, but a horticulturalist, too." He had a nice grin. He had a lot of nice things. He made me rethink the whole concept of nice. "I'm Joseph Alfred."

I didn't know if this was his first name, or his first and last name. "Milagro," I answered. "I'm here for Pedro Nascimento's lecture."

"Are you into his 'spiritual' stuff?" he said with a smirk.

"I thought I might learn more about medicinal uses of native plants. Have you heard his shape-shifting stories?"

"Lots of idiots *claim* to shape-shift, sweetpea."

"Am I sensing some cynicism in you?"

"If I want crap, I'll buy a load of chicken manure."

"So why are you hanging out here if you're not interested in absorbing Pedro's wisdom?"

"I was supposed to meet someone, one of Nascimento's followers, but I guess she stood me up."

"She must be out of her mind," I said, flipping back my hair before I remembered that I shouldn't flirt with every miscellaneous fabulous guy that wandered my way.

"You have no idea."

We chatted about horticulture, and then he told me he was just visiting the City, too, and was in a "transition stage" with his career. I told him about my garden at the ranch and said that I'd looked into buying the empty nursery near the ranch.

"It's just the right size to have a variety of stock, and not too much to manage. It's a great opportunity, but I don't want to handle the actual business side of a business."

Before I knew it, I was late for the lecture. "I better get to the lecture." I reached out to shake hands with him.

His cornflower blue eyes lingered on mine, and he kept hold of my hand. "It's been a pleasure," he said, drawing out the word "pleasure," letting me know that he was ready for more.

In my previous, single life, I would have given him some subtle signal that I thought he was a fabulous specimen of male pulchritude, such as rubbing up against him.

"Bye," I said, a little disappointed that I'd probably never see him again.

By the time I slipped into the lecture hall, it was packed with hundreds of people. The vast majority of them were wearing colorful "ethnic" clothing without being "ethnic" themselves. They showed an unfortunate fondness for clumsy brown sandals.

Don Pedro yammered ebulliently about his terrestrial adventures with indigenous peoples. Each of these visits could be summarized thus: the Tribes immediately recognized that he possessed extraordinary spiritual depth; they held ceremonies that named him a chief; the most delectable maidens offered themselves to him; everyone enjoyed a meal of foods that had been gathered in the wild; they imbibed/smoked/snorted some natural potion that led to an evening of shape-shifting and mind-blowing revelations.

The audience was more focused than a lobbyist on a drunken politician. *Don* Pedro's knowledge of plants was disappointing. He claimed that the Aztecs had used *Copelandia cyanescens,* or Blue Meanies, to establish a state of communion with their gods. A former F.U. beau, devoted to exploring altered states, had informed me that that particular 'shroom was native to Australia.

I snuck out early, thrilled that I could completely fictionalize *Don* Pedro's memoir because there had seemed to be no border between fact and fantasy in the adventures he'd just recounted.

I hied myself over to the closest main thoroughfare to grab a cab. I was surprised to see Joseph Alfred closing the trunk of his car while the traffic zoomed by him. He moved into the street and was about to open the driver's door.

"Joseph Alfred!" I called, raising my arm.

He looked up, and when he saw me, he walked back around the car at the very same moment that a black sedan raced by, gathering speed as it approached. Joseph Alfred jumped out of the way and onto the hood of the car behind his, setting off a blaring alarm. There was a long painful screech as the black sedan scraped along the side of his car.

In the few short steps it took me to get to him, the black sedan was gone, hidden in the crowd of cars that followed.

"Are you all right?" I said.

Joseph Alfred slid off the car's hood to stand on the sidewalk.

After he finished a long stream of curses he said, "Huh? Yeah, I think so."

"Damn, that was close. Did you get the license plate number? We can call the police."

He blinked and said, "Forget about it."

"You could have been killed!"

"Nah, I don't think so." He smiled and said loudly over the car alarm, "I think she just wanted to scare me."

"She?"

"It was my bitch of an ex-girlfriend," he said with a shake of his head. "So where you going, cookie?"

"Back to Hotel Croft. I was going to grab a cab."

"Hop in. I'll give you a lift." He went out to the driver's side and I followed to examine the long, shallow dent. "This is gonna cost me."

"I can't believe how blasé you are about this." We got in his car and he merged into traffic. "You should bring charges against her."

"No way. She'd love the attention. Look, I don't feel like dwelling on it right now. Do you want to get some coffee or a drink?"

"I can't. I've got two appointments to interview wedding planners. My fiancé and I are getting married at the end of summer." "Fiancé" still sounded like a joke word to me, like "fricassee" and "fiduciary."

"All the sane ones are taken."

I was flattered that he considered me sane. "So why does your ex hate you so virulently?"

"Because she's a psycho." He let out a sharp snort of laughter. "I had to chew my arm off to escape that trap."

"Everyone has her quirks." What would he think if he knew about mine? "Was your girlfriend also a plant biologist?"

"She's in the medical field and was interested in my work on transgenic plants and recombinant DNA. I was checking out her body and missed the crazy behind the eyes."

"That will teach you to look at a woman's face."

"I'm a man. I can only focus on one thing at a time. Sometimes two," he said with a wolfish grin.

We were discussing bioethics when we arrived at the Croft. I thanked him for the ride, urged him to contact the police, but he just laughed and grabbed my hand, sending a little zing through me. "So when am I gonna see you again?"

"What part of 'engaged' didn't you get?"

"That's what makes you more . . . interesting." He turned

his body toward mine and continued grinning. "It's the chase. The rush of the deer bounding away, trying to escape. You wouldn't understand what a turn-on that is."

I looked down at his hand holding mine. Then I took my free hand and took his wrist and squeezed. Not hard enough to crush bone, but hard enough to see the surprise in his pretty blue eyes. "But you see, I'm not prey—I'm a predator. *Hasta la vista,* Joseph Alfred."

I hopped out of the car and sashayed merrily to the hotel entrance. The cute new doorman said, "Afternoon, ma'am," as he pulled open the heavy glass-and-brass door.

Ma'am! I felt a million years away from the impoverished girl who used to come to the hotel bar and nurse one drink for hours while gossiping with her friends.

The thick burgundy carpeting in the lobby was pleasantly squooshy underfoot. I got my room key from the front desk and then entered the elevator. I remembered the first time I'd been upstairs, lured by Oswald on a false premise. He'd wanted information about my sleezoid ex-boyfriend, and I'd convinced myself that he was interested in my writing. Neither of us had been what the other expected.

The mirrored doors of the elevator slid open and I walked to our suite. It was the same one Oswald always reserved, decorated in masculine coffee colors of mocha, latte, and espresso. The outer room had views across the City to the bay, and the bedroom beyond was plush and comfortable.

It was well past lunchtime and I was starving. I kicked off my stilettos and then called room service and ordered cranberry juice and an extra-rare burger. At the ranch we kept animal blood in stock, but rare red meat and red drinks were enough to stave off my cravings for a day or two.

31

Within seconds, there was a brisk rap at the door. I'd said, "Barely cook the burger," but this was amazingly fast service.

I opened the door, and Nancy, my best friend from F.U., breezed in. Her blond hair was in loose curls to her shoulders and she wore an apricot blouse with a sea green cotton skirt and flats. Lithe and petite, she looked as full of mischief as a newly paid sailor on shore leave.

"Hi, honey pie," she said, giving me a hug. She threw her straw tote onto the sofa and picked up the phone. "Champagne and a fruit platter, please. No honeydew. *Merci.*" Hanging up the phone, she smiled at me.

"I'm confused," I said.

"Have I not taught you anything? Honeydew is never ripe enough. Escrew honeydew."

"Eschew," I said.

"*Gesundheit.*" She dropped into an armchair and swung her legs over the side.

I sat on the chair opposite her and said, "I'm confused because I wasn't expecting you. I have a couple of appointments today."

"*I'm* confused because you set up appointments with wedding planners and didn't tell me. Luckily, I saw Gigi Barton at a gala for needy hermaphrodites or something, so naturally your name came up, and Gigi told me what you were doing today."

I hadn't told Nancy because she thought weddings necessitated expenditures on a par with the annual GDP of a midsize nation. "I didn't want to bother you. I know how busy you must be, trying to get pregnant."

She made a *pfft* sound. "That was Todd's financial consultant's idea, but he never had to take his hoo-ha's temperature three times a day and only do it doggy-style to have a boy. I hired my own financial planner, who says I can wait. I have a pergola of opportunity to guide you. Where's Oscar?"

"Oswald," I said. My relationship with Nancy had gone through difficult times, especially since Nancy's husband and I despised each other. On the one occasion that she'd met Oswald, she'd interrogated him on plastic surgery innovations while contorting her face with her neatly manicured hands. "Oswald is doing consultations today, and I seriously doubt you can influence the gender of a baby by using a certain position."

"Don't be silly, Milly. It's got an amazing fifty percent success rate. Don't try to change the subject. I bet you want some weird little ceremony in Mercedes's scuzzy nightclub where you quote odious poetry while a hippie plays the bongos."

"Mercedes renovated the club. It's swank and swell."

"You don't deny the bongo music and bad poetry!"

I would have objected further if I hadn't already suggested a nightclub wedding, only to have Oswald burst out laughing. When he'd relayed his mother's elaborate plans, I realized that I needed professional help.

Room service arrived, and Nancy grabbed the tab and signed my name with a flourish. She lifted the cover off the food plate, took one glance at the blood soaking the burger's bun, and said, "Major eewh. This isn't even cooked."

"I like it rare." While Nancy poured champagne, I took my food to the table and bit into the hamburger. The salty rich juices from the organically raised, grass-fed, nearly raw beef filled my mouth. Warmth hummed through my body.

"This is the perfect daytime drink," Nancy said, and I froze, thinking that she'd read my mind. But then she handed me a flute of champagne. "You can drink gallons and never get sloshed."

"How true." It was especially true for me: I could drink turpentine and not feel a thing. I wished I could tell Nancy about my condition, but she wouldn't understand. "Nancita, I'm happy to have your advice, but there's no way I'm having an extravagant, exorbitant wedding."

"Why not? Is not Dr. Oscar picking up the tab?" she asked. "Have you even told your parents yet? Not that they'd care."

"It's Dr. Oswald. No, I haven't told them yet."

"Dr. Oscar's funnier. Your mother Regina is a sociopath. It's a miracle you're only a little slutty instead of completely bonkers like those baby monkeys who are raised with a metal doll instead of a real monkey mommy."

"We can thank my grandmother for saving me from unmitigated skankitude," I said, and then sighed. I'd loved my small, brown *abuelita,* who had raised me until I was ten. "It would be different if she was alive. A wedding is supposed to be a family celebration, but how can I celebrate when my mother Regina will be there looking at me like . . . like she does? Oswald says I have to invite them anyway."

"You absolutely have to invite your parents. You'll invite my husband, too."

"Toad and I have a mutual animosity for each other."

"Toad? I like that. It doesn't matter. This isn't all about you." She went to my new shopping bag and lifted the plastic miniskirt. *"Muy* interesting."

"Since when do you know any Spanish?"

"Oh, darling, everyone's using Spanglish. How else would you communicate with household staff?" My friend looked me up and down. "Fab ensemble, and the broach really makes it work. Broaches are shockingly underused."

"Thanks. I put it there to cover a moth hole."

"But you want to show the wedding planner that you have an edgy contemporary fashion sense. Go change into this skirt. If she comes, I'll entertain her."

Nancy was being surprisingly helpful. "Okay."

I took the skirt into the bedroom and closed the door. I changed into a stretchy black T and tugged the white skirt over my hips. It seemed tighter than it had been at the boutique. When I went back to the other room, Nancy had turned on the stereo and was dancing by herself to an old swing song.

"Good, she's not here yet," I said.

My friend took hold of me. "Todd hates dancing. He thinks it leads to liberal politics and free-trade restrictions. How do you and Osgood dance together?" She tromped on my feet.

I winced and said, "Like angels on clouds." But Oswald and I weren't very good at partner dancing.

"Your *lover* was a fabulous dancer, all oozy sex," she said. "Why don't you marry him?"

"Oswald is my lover, and I *am* marrying him."

"No, I mean the *lover* you brought to my wedding. Lord Ian."

Old beaux, already insubstantial in character, had faded in my memory as quickly as badly dyed cotton in the wash. But I recalled Ian's face, his voice, his touch just as clearly as if he'd been groping me yesterday. Sex with Oswald was joyous and fun. Sex with Ian had been exquisitely pleasurable and highly unsettling.

"One, Ian's not my lover, two, how come you can remember his name, but not Oswald's?"

"*A*, I know you had the dirty, dirty sex with him. *B*, I

couldn't tell if I was terrified of him, or wanted to submit completely to his will. *C,* I wish you wouldn't talk in outline form because it reminds me of school, and I miss school."

I had recalled the dirty, dirty sex more times than I was going to admit, even to Nancy. "Ian's amusing company, but not exactly marriage material." He was the kind of man who would slash someone a hundred times as revenge for one cut I'd received. He was the kind of man who had human thralls service his various sordid whims. "Speaking of school, I'm seeing Toodles on my trip east."

"*J'adore* Toodles, but I think that if she takes off her pearl necklace, her head will fall off. Let me see your ring." Nancy turned my hand to examine it. "Brilliant-cut canary stone with lateral diamonds in platinum. Compare and contrast." We held our left hands together. "You bitch, it's bigger than mine. I'm going to tell Todd we've got to upgrade."

"You know, I hate to say anything in Todd's favor, but he *did* take you on a long honeymoon to Tahiti."

"Where are you honeymooning?"

"Oswald can only take four days off and we're going to Baja." Oswald would be performing cleft-palate surgeries for the poor during the day, and we'd frolic on the beach at night.

"Baja isn't Bali," Nancy said as she gave me a final twirl and let me go.

I turned down the music and stared out the window. "You'd think this wedding planner would call if she's running so late."

"She's appallingly irresponsible." Nancy joined me and we stared down at the street below. "But so are you, waiting all this time to hire someone. Have you even ordered your dress yet?"

"The wedding isn't until August. I've got almost four months."

"Shame on you! When you're planning a wedding, you don't

have months, or weeks. You have days and hours. Right now you have a mere one hundred and seventeen days to put together the biggest event of your life."

"It's too daunting. I'm totally daunted. Oswald's mother thinks it will be a nightmarish carnival of mariachis, chili pepper string lights, and taco tables, and I'll wear a gown made of purple polyester lace. Why does she think I'm tacky?"

"You're a lavish girl, and people mistake subtlety for style, when it is no such thing. I'm developing an entire thesis around this. Chapter titles will tell you what *isn't* style, such as 'Monochromaticism Isn't Style.' "

Leaning my forehead against the glass, I said, "I wanted a *simple* ceremony. But at least we've got a location I like."

I told her about the winery we had booked as the wedding location. It was just inland from an exclusive seaside town that had long been a favorite vacation spot for vampires because of its boutiques, fine dining, golf courses, and summer fog. "They grow amazing dahlias, too, and they're going to take care of all the flower arrangements."

"Do you have *any* ideas that aren't gardening related?"

"A few, but can you believe how late this planner is? I'm going to call her."

"Darlink, if she can't be bothered to show up, she's not the right person. Let's go out and about."

"No, I have another wedding planner coming for an interview right after her," I said. "This whole thing is maddening. Why can't it be simple?"

"That is the second time you've said 'simple' in the last thirty seconds. Simplicity is not elegance; it is a lack of imagination. Please refer to Nancy's Theory of Style." Nancy refilled our champagne glasses and sat down.

"You're quite the deep thinker when it comes to all matters frivolous."

"*Muchas gracias.* Now, here's what I think. It would be the most genius thing ever if I was *la* mistress *de* wedding."

I stared at her earnest face for a minute before I said, "No, no, and also no."

"Yes, yes, and also yes. You know I'm fantastic at parties."

"You're fantastic at *going* to parties. It is a distinction with a difference."

"I'm fantastic at all party-related activities. I did almost all my own wedding, since my planner was an imbecile." She sneered, "P.U."—the F.U. nickname for the acclaimed public university. "Besides, I've always dreamed of being a fabulous trendsetting career woman in a pencil skirt."

"Since when?"

"Since I finished decorating the house and guest quarters."

"You'll spend too much money. It's still no."

She glared at me. "Milagro, I always keep within my budget. Why are you so determined to be so cheap with Oslo's money?"

"Oswald. I'm not marrying him for his money."

"But you're not marrying a poplar, either."

I couldn't argue with that, but I found other points of disagreement, and we were having a heated debate when there was a knock on the door. I glanced at the clock. Either the first wedding planner had finally arrived, or the second one was early.

Nancy was as swift as she was silly. I was fast, but I had an ottoman in my way and my plastic skirt didn't have enough give to allow me to jump. We reached the door at the same time, and Nancy pointed to the window and said, "What's that?"

When I followed the direction of her glance, she shoved me. I regained my balance by yanking at her arm, and we were still tussling when she managed to open the door.

"Thank you, but room service already came," she said sweetly. She was trying to close the door when I got hold of the edge and pulled it open.

The wedding planner who stood there was a very neat and petite young man.

"I'm here for my appointment with the bride-to-be." He turned from Nancy to me. "Ms. De Los Santos?"

"Milagro," I said.

Nancy said, "Sorry, but Ms. Los Dos Knockers has already hired me for the job. Thank you for caring and sharing."

He glared at me and snapped, "Thank you for wasting my time!" Then he stormed off.

I could have stopped Nancy from closing the door, but I thought it wouldn't be wise to murder her in front of a witness.

"Why are you sabotaging me, Nancy?"

"Because I'm perfect for this job. I've helped organize many nonprofit galas. I know all the best caterers, florists, and photographers. I know the right people to print *Milagro and Orville* in gold English script on tiny ribbons. I know that Mylar balloons are Satan's party decoration."

I kept objecting until Nancy said, "If you give me Orloff's mother's phone number, I will keep her off your back."

And that's how Nancy got her first real job and I got stuck with her as my wedding planner. When she left, I decided to call the wedding planner who'd missed her appointment. "Hello, this is Milagro De Los Santos."

"Yes." The voice was cold, almost hostile.

"I was waiting for you today, but I guess you got held up. I just wanted to say that I've hired someone else."

"Are you on drugs? Because you already told me that when I came for my appointment today." She hung up on me.

Sneaky Nancy. I tried to convince myself that I could handle a crazy-ass bitch as my wedding planner. Alas, my world would soon be undone by a swarm of crazy-ass bitches.

four

a separate piece of luggage

While I waited for Oswald to return to the hotel, I looked through *Don* Pedro's papers. I spread them out on the floor and attempted to sort them. They were not quite the rantings of a madman, but definitely the musings of a nutcase. Shape-shifting was the running theme, and that interested me because I'd once written a story about a young woman who uses her ability to shape-shift to defend the poor and wrongly accused.

I looked through the magazine clippings. One sentence caught my attention: "Boiled dandelions have been used to treat high blood pressure, urinary problems, and digestive complaints. They make a deliciously piquant salad." *Don* Pedro had stolen his tribute to the weed.

The door opened, and Oswald came in carrying a small aqua bag. "What are you doing in the dark?" He turned on the lights.

"I was so engrossed, I didn't even notice."

He stepped around the papers and handed the bag to me. "Here, for you."

I saw the label. "Jewelry? Oswald, you didn't need to."

"It's not jewelry, but I thought, well . . ."

Inside the aqua bag was an aqua box tied with a creamy white ribbon. I opened it and saw a silver penknife resting on white cotton. It was monogrammed *To MDLS with Love, OKG*.

"Oh, it's very nice," I said, feeling guilty. I hadn't let him cut me and taste my blood since I'd been attacked last year on the night of Nancy's wedding.

"If you ever change your mind," he said. "No pressure."

So why did I feel as if he'd just brought another woman home and asked for a threesome? Except that he didn't want anyone else—he just wanted all of me. I put the lid on the box.

He shrugged off his jacket and went to the minibar. "How did your meetings go?"

"There's good news and bad news and good news and bad news. Which do you want first?"

"You choose," he said and took out a bottle of water.

"Bad news, Pedro Nascimento is as nuts as wearing stockings with sandals. Good news, I got the writing gig. I'm sworn to secrecy that I'm ghosting it, though. Bad news, Nancy is going to be our wedding planner." I saw the look on his face, so I quickly added, "Good news, she's very good at organizing social activities, and she knows my style."

"She's a complete ditz."

"No, she only cultivates the appearance of being a ditz because nobody likes smart girls."

"I like smart girls."

"I know you do." I held out my hand and he pulled me up. "But you're an anomaly."

"Most men like smart girls. But they don't like girls who tell them they're stupid," he said. "Now that you've got a wedding planner, don't you think you should tell your parents that we're getting married?"

"Uhmm." I yanked the white plastic skirt down over my thighs and tried to smooth out the creases. "Do you like my new skirt?"

"I'm mesmerized by it."

"It's kind of a classic, don't you think?"

"Uhmm," he said. "Do we have to go out tonight? The last time we came here, you made me listen to accordion music."

We'd gone to Mercedes's club to hear a sizzling klezmer-Cuban alternative band. I loved Juanita and Her Rat-Dogs, but the band's genius had eluded Oswald. "Didn't the club look great?"

"There was a serious infusion of money," he said. "I hope Mercedes didn't take on too much debt."

"Oh, no, she said she has a backer." Mercedes was not chatty, especially about her finances, so I hadn't expected her to reveal the identity of her investor.

I ran my finger over the lovely curve of Oswald's lips. "We don't have to go out *now.*"

Faster than you could say *"hamburguesa con papas fritas"* we were undressed and on the floor, pushing my papers aside. I marveled at Oswald's sleek, firm limbs, and I loved the way he smelled, of himself and herby sunscreen.

Oswald's mouth was warm and hungry on my wrist, heading as he always did for the vein there. I twisted my body until I could run my tongue up his thigh, sucessfully diverting his attention. Turning my head, I saw skyscrapers against the dark sky. "Anyone with binoculars can see us."

"Then we better put on a good show," he said and rolled me back onto the carpet. In a few minutes I had completely forgotten peeping toms, crazy memoirists, and wedding planners.

Later, when Oswald got up off the floor, he glanced at his arm, and I saw the bruises there.

"Oz, I'm sorry. I guess I got carried away."

"It's okay. They'll be gone soon." And as he spoke, the bruises began fading.

But I knew that I'd probably hurt him. I hated that I still wasn't able to gauge my strength. I hated hurting him. "I'm sorry," I said again "I'll be more careful."

He reached over and helped me up. "I don't want you to have to be careful with me, babe. Let me finish up a few things and we'll go out."

"You've got more work?"

"It'll take thirty minutes, tops. Wouldn't you be happier if you had something to really focus on? You seemed on track when you were getting your teaching credentials."

I'd *thought* I wanted to be a teacher. I'd thought I'd just waltz into a classroom and begin yammering about the books I loved. But I'd been disheartened by the complicated process of getting teaching credentials and the bureaucracy that regulated teaching. "Oswald, the horticultural landscape department was right next to the graduate ed program. It was a message to me."

"You don't believe in omens."

"I do when they're convenient." Before we headed into another excruciating discussion about Why Milagro Should Have a Practical Career Plan, I said, "Okay, I'll occupy myself while you finish your work. Then we'll take a sudsy bath and then we'll go out."

"That works for me."

While Oswald pulled case files out of his briefcase, I wrapped myself in a thick terry hotel robe and pulled a new composition book from my suitcase. On the black-and-white speckled cover I wrote, "Nancy's Theory of Style." I spent the next half hour scribbling down everything I'd ever learned from Nancy, beginning with her axiom that taste is not style.

We did take a bath, but somehow we never left the hotel suite. Later, as we curled up in bed, I said, "I'll be glad when I can finally be done with the Council. Poor Sam's been negotiating with them forever, even with Ian supporting us."

Oswald's body tensed and then he said, "Goddamn Ian Ducharme."

I rolled on top of him so I could look right at him. "When are you going to stop being jealous? When we're married with kids, are you still going to assume Ian wants to seduce me away?"

"I don't know. Whose kids are they?"

"Ha ha and ha. You want jealous? Talk to me sometime when I'm thinking about your hands on some naked woman."

"Not woman. Patient. Naked patient."

"A technicality. If I ever thought you were interested in another woman . . . ," I said. That dark, dense, sad place in my chest tightened and tugged, threatening to pull other things into it.

"You're the one I love," Oswald said and pulled me to him.

I hid my face in his shoulder and held him tight, but not too tight.

The next morning, after we'd had breakfast, I packed my things and we checked out of the hotel. My flight was in the evening, so I was having a girl's day in the City. I left my suitcase at the hotel and stood with Oswald out on the street while the valet got his car.

He put his arm around my waist. "Have fun, but be careful."

"I'm signing papers with a bunch of stodgy administrators." He still looked worried so I added, "I'll be careful, Oswald." I took my engagement ring off my finger and handed it to him, saying, "You keep this safe for me."

I waved good-bye as he drove off, and then I window-shopped on the way to my salon for a haircut and mani-pedi. While I waited for my appointment, I chose a red-purple nail lacquer that was the same shade as blood in a vial. The hair stylist trimmed my hair but kept it long.

Mercedes's club was a pleasant walk from the salon. On the way there, I stopped in a corner grocery and bought ham, cheese, pickles, and French rolls. The club was on a run-down block, but new businesses were moving in. The club's plain black exterior had been repainted and there was a new discreet sign in red neon that said *My Dive.* The doorman wasn't on duty yet, and the girl at the ticket booth unlocked the door for me.

The interior still smelled of fresh paint. Thick, new, dark blue velvet drapes hung on the stage, and new tables and chairs circled the dance floor. The dressing rooms and Mercedes's office were behind the stage.

My friend was at her desk, in a Juanita and Her Rat-Dogs T-shirt and Levi's. She wore her hair in dreadlocks for practicality, and her pretty cocoa complexion had a sprinkling of darker freckles across her nose.

"Hola, mi amiga," I said. "I brought sandwich fixings."

"Excellent," she said. She took the grocery bag from me to the credenza, where she had a panini press. "This city is supposed to be a food capital, but I can't get a decent Cuban sandwich."

"I remember when you used to use an iron to make them," I said as she layered meat with slices of pickle on the rolls.

"Those were good. Gabriel told me they're nervous about your meeting with the Council."

Mercedes was the only person who knew about my relationship with the vampires. She'd become friends with the Grant family and connected with Gabriel on a computer-hacker level.

"I'm just smiling and signing papers. I'm going to see my friend Toodles on my trip."

"Toodles," Mercedes said. "One of those trust-fund, rich-girl nicknames. I know a few places you should go for good Cuban food and music."

"Toodles already has our whole visit planned. But maybe you and I could take a trip together and you could show me all the best clubs."

"Sure, why not? If it won't interfere with your . . . what is it you do, exactly?" Mercedes had inherited her parents' immigrant work ethic and thought writing wasn't a real job.

"I just got the commission to ghostwrite the memoir of a world-renowned academic. I can't say anything about it, however, because of a confidentiality clause." I told her about registering for wedding gifts at the ritzy department store.

"You're not expecting me to shop there, are you?"

"Oh, please. I have a catalog for the Womyn's Sexual Health Collective and they have a gift registry. Oswald keeps going to the page with the pink fur handcuffs. I don't know if he wants them for him or for me."

"*Too* personal, *mujer,*" Mercedes said. "I'm getting you a blender. Not just any blender, but the Margaritanator 3000."

"That's *exactly* what I want! You're psychic."

"Yeah, that and Gabriel told me you destroyed another one," she said. "The Margaritanator 3000 is for commercial use, and even you won't be able to kill it."

We enjoyed our toasty sandwiches and talked about music for the wedding. While we thought Juanita and Her Rat-Dogs were fantastic, Mercedes suggested bands that had a broader appeal.

As I was leaving, my *amiga* gave me a big *abrazo* and said, "Anything comes up, you know my number."

I kissed her cheek and said, "I had it tattooed on my *colita* in case I ever get hit by a truck and get amnesia."

I took the red-eye flight out, leaving late in the evening and arriving in early morning. When I went to the baggage carousel, I spotted my green zebra case the moment it came out and grabbed it up while others jostled to identify their boring black luggage.

Oswald had booked a room for me at his favorite hotel, a posh place smack in the heart of things, and insisted on paying for it. I could ponder my discomfort with our vastly different economic circumstances while I soaked in the marble Jacuzzi.

Navigating the subway in a big city made me feel cosmopolitan and capable. When I got out on the street, I studied all the stylish women so I'd know what to buy when I went shopping with Toodles, who was meeting me at the hotel. Guiding my rolling bag through the crowd was challenging, especially since I kept staring up at the tall buildings and signs and trendy urbanites instead of looking where I was going.

The boutique hotel had a Deco glass awning, and the doorman tipped his hat as I wheeled my bag into the carpeted lobby, which was as hushed as a monastery.

The middle-aged clerk at the front desk smiled pleasantly and said, "Good morning. May I help you?"

"Hello. I have a reservation and an early check-in."

"Certainly. Under what name?"

"De Los Santos, Milagro."

But he couldn't find a reservation under my name or Oswald's. I produced my confirmation information to no avail.

"That reservation was canceled," the clerk said and told me that no rooms were available.

The concierge was called over to help. When the situation was explained, she gave me her card and said, "If you can't find anything else, come back late tonight, after eleven. We hold a few rooms for emergencies. Tell the on-duty clerk that I sent you. We can give you a room at half off."

I didn't mind waiting for that kind of discount. "Thanks. I appreciate it." The concierge offered to let me leave my bag in their luggage room. After I gave my bag to the luggage attendant, I turned and saw a preppy young woman coming toward me. "Toodles!"

"Milagro!"

We hugged and stepped back to look at each other. I remembered Nancy's remark when I saw the pearl necklace at the open collar of Toodles's blue pinstripe blouse. She wore navy corduroys and brown flats, and her curly brown hair was pulled back. Toodles seemed plain initially, but her sweet expression and plump body became very pretty with familiarity.

"Do you want to go up to your room?" she said.

"My reservation got canceled somehow."

"Oooh, noo! My brother and his messy friends are crashing at my place, but I'll kick them out."

"Don't do that! The concierge said I could get a room here

after eleven, so I'll do that. I don't want to waste any of our time together."

"Are you sure?"

"I'm totally sure."

"Goood! I've got a whole day planned and reservations at an *amazing* restaurant after your meeting."

I'd told Toodles that I had a meeting at 6 P.M. with my fiancé's relatives and implied that it was about a pre-nup, knowing she'd be too polite to pry.

We raced from monuments and landmarks, to department stores, to museums. We had so much to do that we ate lunch at a hot dog stand. I kept seeing things that I'd seen in movies and on television, so my experience was one of mingled recognition and wonder.

Toodles and I were sitting in a dark old bar that had been frequented by writers we'd studied at F.U. I told her about Nancy's new career. "You'll see her in action at the wedding. She's developing something called Nancy's Theory of Style, a rigorous, analytical approach to fashion."

Toodles's laugh turned into a very unladylike belch. She covered her mouth and looked surprised. "Oh, dear. My stomach is feeling a bit ooky." She rushed off to the ladies' room.

Her face was flushed and glistening when she came out ten minutes later. "I feel terrible that I'm ruining your day."

"You feel terrible because you're sick. I've had an incredible day and now I'm going to get you home." I ushered her out to the street. A cab was just dropping off someone and I grabbed it for her.

As I handed her in, she said, "You've *got* to use the restaurant reservation. Promise! I'll be better by tomorrow."

I had just enough time to catch the subway back to the

hotel. I gave the luggage attendant my ticket, collected my bag, and went to the ladies' room in the lobby. I'd had a lot of experience using toilet stalls as dressing rooms and knew just how to twist and turn to get into a structured black jacket and hip-skimming skirt. I swapped my flat shoes for peep-toe heels that showed off my pedicure.

I brushed out my hair and as I was redoing my face, I spotted the red stone ring in my makeup case. That one small item was the finishing touch my outfit needed.

five

bear with me

I'd planned on checking my case back into the luggage room but a horde of tourists was monopolizing the clerk's time. I pulled my bag out to the street, and one of the wheels got caught in a grating and froze into place, forcing me to drag the bag behind me. I caught a cab, and we inched forward in heavy, noisy traffic. Thirty minutes and less than a mile later, the cabbie pulled up to an older skyscraper.

The security guard in the lobby checked my ID and then directed me to the twenty-fifth floor. I hauled my bag into the elevator and smiled when I saw a plaque for Presidential Properties. The vampires who had immigrated to America adopted presidents' names to camouflage their origins, and every one I'd ever met had been wild for real estate.

The doors opened to a starkly elegant lobby with white-and-black marble floors and amber walls. White marble columns framed doorways, and the minimalist furniture was black and chrome. Three huge abstract paintings hung on the walls. I dragged my case to the reception desk.

An elderly woman with gold-rimmed glasses sat there, and her engraved green-glass nameplate read *Mrs. Smith.* I was reasonably sure that there hadn't been a president named Smith, so I guessed that she was a Normal.

She glanced at my badge and snapped, "You're five minutes late. The committee is waiting."

Don't poke the bear, I thought. "I'm sorry for the delay. Traffic was insane."

"The conference room is downstairs." She stared at my bag and said, "You may put *that* in that closet."

I dragged my case to the closet, and then followed Mrs. Smith to the elevator. When it arrived and we got in, she pushed the button marked *B2,* the second level of the basement. She held a ring of keys and jingled them as we rode down.

The elevator opened into a gloomy room lined with hissing and clanking machinery. Pendant lamps cast anemic circles of light. Mrs. Smith led me down a narrow aisle.

She unlocked a door at the end of the room, and once I had gone through, she locked it behind us. We walked through a storeroom to another door. She unlocked this one, too, and again waited for me to pass through before locking it behind us.

We were in a dank, narrow hallway that was even more dimly lighted than the rooms we'd just walked through. We walked and walked and I realized that this was not a hallway but a tunnel. I felt a rumbling and guessed the subway was nearby. At the end of the tunnel was an old-fashioned cage elevator.

We got in and the gate closed with a loud clank. Mrs. Smith turned the crank handle to the right and we slowly and creakily descended until the elevator stopped with a heavy thud.

Mrs. Smith opened the gate and I stepped out. We were in a cavern. Glittering chandeliers illuminated an area like a stage. Beyond their glow, the cavern was pitch black. An enormous carpet in rich shades of scarlet lay on the brick floor. The cavern had a fantastic arched and tiled ceiling, and there were arches over the large wooden doors on a far wall.

A massive table of white-veined red marble was centered on the carpet. Six men sat at the table. They had the generic anonymity of prosperous businessmen: dark suits, graying hair, and regular features. In front of each was a bottle of mineral water, a glass, and a small carafe of deep red liquid.

The man at the head of the table stood and said, "Welcome, Miss De Los Santos." His face was calm, his hazel eyes were sharp as a ferret's. He had a narrow nose and a dimpled chin that gave his face character.

"Hello." Despite the astonishing setting, my eyes kept going to the dark liquid, and the man saw that.

He turned to my escort. "Thank you, Mrs. Smith."

She nodded her head and I heard her footsteps retreating, and then the creaking of the elevator as it rose.

The man said, "Please take a seat, Miss De Los Santos."

I sat at the empty chair in front of the last setting of beverages and willed myself to be patient. Cranberry juice had controlled, but not sated, my thirst. I looked around the table at the other men. A few stared at me as if I were a prize bug and they were amateur entomologists, eager to stab a pin through me for a display. Others seemed annoyed at having to be there.

"Miss De Los Santos, we have received the Grant family's

petitions to grant you rights within our community, but we would like to review the details with you personally." He clearly pronounced every *r*.

"And you are?" I asked.

"I'm Mr. Nixon." He saw my expression and said, "It *really* is my name," but I didn't believe him.

I picked up the carafe and smelled it. It had a strange aroma, not human, but not like the blood of any animal I'd tasted before.

"It's llama, Miss De Los Santos, since we learned that you won an award for a story about a llama."

Not that damn llama again. But the thick liquid had a fresh, sweet, copper scent that made my mouth water. "How thoughtful." I poured a teaspoon of blood in my glass and filled it with water. The taste was a little odd, grassy like lamb, with a not unpleasant stronger note. It was definitely better than emu. It warmed me and I instantly felt more alert. "What is this place?"

A man who'd been eyeing me with fascination explained that it had been built when the first subway had been built, over 150 years ago. "If anyone noticed the additional construction, they forgot about it. Or died."

I suspected that the doors led out to subway lines and other exit passages. This was where the vamps would come in an emergency. I felt a twinge of sympathy for a people who always had to worry about their safety. I said, "Sam Grant told me that I would be signing the agreement that we already reviewed."

"Yes, you will," said Mr. Nixon. "But first we'd like to hear your story in your own words. Let's start at the beginning. How did you first meet Oswald Grant?"

Don't poke the bear, I thought, and I recited a brief version of my experiences: my initial infection; kidnapping by a crazed ex-beau; and my more recent encounter with a rogue vampire and the extremist Project for a New Vampire Century.

Nixon said, "You've got an ally in Ian Ducharme, but that's to be expected considering your *special* relationship."

"He did save my life after that attack. But if you are referring to our friendship, we don't even keep in touch. If you mean more, you are mistaken."

"We are a little unclear on exactly how Ducharme saved you, Miss De Los Santos. He doesn't usually take an interest in Normals."

"Basic first aid," I lied, remembering the taste of Ian's blood. "I can't speak for what interests Ian. He seems to like parties and expensive cars."

"Hmm," Mr. Nixon said again. It was a dissatisfied "hmm." "I find it hard to believe that you're willing to keep this situation a secret from your own family."

"I have no family other than my parents, and they ignore my existence. There are no phone calls or birthday cards."

"Even if that isn't a problem, do you really accept fully what it will be like to live as one of us? To live in secrecy, to have a partner vulnerable to sun poisoning, to have a craving that disgusts and repels people, to have enemies who treat you as less than human?"

He looked around the room, and the other men nodded sadly. He said, "You don't share our vulnerabilities and your DNA tests don't show our anomaly. You'll want a family of your own. If you miraculously manage to conceive, it's highly unlikely that you'll carry to term. Our rule against intermarriage was not made to protect us—but to protect spouses and children. There's no greater pain than having a child die."

There was such sorrow in his voice. I said, "The Project for a

New Vampire Century found historical evidence that those rare survivors, like myself, can have children. I promise you that Dr. Grant and I take this as seriously as you. We have discussed all these issues extensively."

He smiled apologetically and said, "We have only a few more questions. This is of a somewhat delicate nature. We request that you and Dr. Grant cease all physical relations until you are officially married in our ceremony. If possible, you should move out of his house."

I grabbed the pokey stick. "Other engaged vampires shack up all the time!"

"We sometimes overlook the regulations, but your situation is different and we must adhere strictly to our traditions."

"Why am I not surprised that I'm held to a different standard?" I said. "And what did you mean by 'our ceremony'?"

"In addition to your public marriage ceremony, you'll have a traditional wedding ritual. Sam Grant told us how much you wanted to participate in our ceremonies, and what better time than your own marriage? We'll assign an associate to guide you through the requirements and preparation."

"You mean a wedding planner?"

"Yes, I suppose. We're in the process of filling that position since Mrs. Smith has retired from those duties."

I felt as if I'd had a narrow escape. "Fine, so long as you don't try to siphon my blood for the wedding toast."

The men all laughed, but I wasn't sure if it was a "how silly" laugh or an "I can't wait" laugh.

Mr. Nixon said, "We just have one more matter to attend to before we conclude. Why don't we take a ten minute break?"

I asked if I could make a few phone calls, and Mr. Nixon suggested I go upstairs. Mrs. Smith returned and escorted me back to the reception area of Presidential Properties and then sat at her desk pretending not to eavesdrop.

I called Oswald. I could have told him about the hotel fiasco, but I had more pressing matters on my mind. "You can't believe what the Council wants. They say we can't cohabitate or have sexual relations until we're married!" I watched Mrs. Smith to see if she would react. She shoved a file folder in a drawer. "What do you think about that?"

"I don't like it, but I don't want to give them any excuse not to approve your rights. We can do other stuff." He began listing all the interesting and perverse activities that he believed fell outside the strict definition of sexual congress and said, "Ask them if those things qualify."

Laughing, I said, "Let's make Sam ask them that just so we can see him blush! And I'm not moving out. I'll take the downstairs bedroom."

"I'll sing serenades outside your window. How was your day?"

"Great, other than this. Toodles is a brilliant tour guide. Did you know that you don't really have to go through an entire museum, you can just visit the gift shop?" I was telling him about the fantastic restaurant I'd be going to when I heard Mrs. Smith making "ahem" noises.

I looked at her and she barked, "The break is over!"

"I've got to go back to the meeting, Oz," I said. "I'll call you tomorrow. I love you."

"Love you, too, babe."

Mrs. Smith took me back to the cave, where the Rules Committee was already seated. I joined them and said, "I've talked to Oswald and we agree to your terms."

"Excellent!" said Mr. Nixon. "Now there is just one last

thing." He passed a piece of paper to the man beside him, who passed it to me. "Your signature on our Oath of Loyalty."

I skimmed the page and one phrase jumped out: "do hereby renounce all allegiance to any other nation." I was angry. "Sam didn't see this or he would have discussed it with me. I'm not giving up my citizenship."

"We don't expect you to renounce your citizenship in any *public* way," said Nixon soothingly. "By all means, keep your passport and ID. This is for our own . . . assurance."

My first instinct was to say, "No." My second instinct was to say, "Hell, no." "I'm not signing this." I pushed the paper back toward him.

"Think about it. After all, this country has not exactly welcomed *your* people. They'll always see you as a second-class citizen because of the color of your skin and your name."

"That may be true, but what matters is my love for this country and its ideals. Those ideals are clear to anyone who reads my writing."

"Consider this, then: Affirm your loyalty to us, and we'll give you a substantial grant so you can dedicate yourself to your art. We'll also use our considerable resources to promote your work." He smiled and added, "Do you ever wonder how books get on the best-seller lists? Wouldn't you like to see your book at the top of those lists?"

Yes, I had wondered. "I won't change my mind."

"We don't need your answer now." He picked up the loyalty oath and placed it in his folder. "Return home and discuss it with the Grants. It's been a treat to finally meet you."

I poured the rest of my llama blood in my glass and tossed it back undiluted. "Nice meeting you, too," I said and stood.

Mr. Nixon came over to shake my hand and when he looked

down at my hand, his expression changed. "Where did you get that ring? Did Dr. Grant give it to you?"

"It was a prize at the amusement park. Good night."

Mrs. Smith was waiting in the elevator for me. As I was about to step in, I heard a muffled cry. I turned back and asked, "What was that?"

"What was what?" Mr. Nixon answered.

I listened and again I heard the wail. It seemed to come from behind one of the closed doors in the shadows of the cavern. "Someone's crying out."

He shook his head and said, "Crazies and drunks live in the tunnels, and we often hear them. Sound bounces and echoes down here—it's very disorienting. Have a good evening."

There was a loud rumbling of a subway train and I listened, trying to locate the source of the crying sound, but Nixon was right: the noise bounced off the walls.

I went back upstairs with Mrs. Smith, got my suitcase, and then returned to the lobby of the building. The meeting had run long, and I decided to go directly to the restaurant. After getting directions from the security guard, I walked to the subway, dragging my suitcase behind me. When the train rattled and screeched to the platform, I wondered if the Rules Committee could hear it in their cave.

I got off the subway and as I walked toward the restaurant, incredible aromas wafted toward me on the cool evening air. Chic people clustered out front and there was a buzz of excitement. I hauled my bag inside and saw a huge two-story space in rich caramel shades with chocolate leather banquettes and chairs.

The maître d' smiled as he glanced down, obviously impressed by my cool suitcase. "Good evening."

"Hello. I have a reservation for Kathleen Hippensteele."

He looked at his reservation book. "I'm sorry, but I don't see that here."

"It might be under Meriwether. Or Toodles."

He examined the book again. "Here it is. The reservation was canceled."

Was this a vast conspiracy? "That must be wrong. Would you please check again?"

He gave me a tight smile and picked up the phone. He murmured in Italian and then hung up. "We call to confirm all reservations and the gentleman that answered at, uhm, Toodles Poodle Emporium said the lady in question was indisposed."

Toodles's brother must have answered. "I see. I can wait for a table, a table for one."

"The first availability we have is, let me see, for Sunday brunch in eight weeks."

I felt like screaming, but I thanked him and left the restaurant. I stood on the sidewalk, not feeling cosmopolitan or capable, but alone and absurd.

A Town Car pulled up to the curb and an extremely tall, extremely thin, extremely chic young woman got out. Her platinum blond hair hung to her waist and her blue eyes were heavily made up. Her dress was a scrap of cloth, and she wore an iridescent wrap around her bony shoulders. I bet her dinner reservations never got canceled by nitwits.

I picked up the handle of my rolling bag and began dragging it away.

"Young Lady," said a deep voice behind me, "don't tell me you're leaving already."

The skin at the back of my neck prickled.

I turned to see Ian Ducharme standing outside the car while the tall young woman leaned against him.

six

stop gherkin me around

Ian wasn't handsome, but he had an undeniable charisma. He was of only average height and appeared stocky—but underneath his always impeccable attire was a muscular, powerful body. His dark brown hair curled when it was longer, as it was now. He had a swarthy complexion, hooded eyes, a strong nose, and a compelling Cheshire Cat smile.

I was so relieved to see a friendly face that I grinned wildly. "Ian! Don't tell me this is a coincidence."

He came forward, his familiar spicy cologne bringing back memories. When he kissed my cheeks, the blood beneath my skin rose to the surface, leaving it hot and tingly. This physical reaction was new and different from the usual tasty fizz of energy I got from people, and it was different from the fizz I'd received from Ian when we last met.

"None of our meetings are mere coincidence, *querida.*" He

looked at the girl, who was gazing away at nothing in particular. "Milagro, this is Ilena. Ilena, this is my friend Milagro. Milagro's engaged to a distant relative."

It was true that Oswald and Ian were related, since all the vamps came from the same genetic strain that dated back hundreds of years.

"Pleasure," she said with a slight accent. She held her thin hand out so languidly it was like shaking hands with a piece of rope. Her eyes skimmed over me and found nothing of interest.

"How did you find me?" I asked Ian.

"Mrs. Smith told me you were coming here."

"Is that old bat your spy?"

"The dear woman was concerned about you. Have you eaten?"

"Not yet. They don't have any tables available."

"A good meal will revive you." He took the suitcase from me and signaled to his driver, who came to his side. "Let's put this away for now." The driver lifted my bag into the trunk of his car. "Come along, Young Lady."

We went back into the restaurant to the maître d's station. *"Buona sera,* Roberto," Ian said as he shook hands. He was palming money to the man. Ian was an extravagant tipper, a trait that made him beloved by wait staff and valets throughout the known world. "I hope there's a place for us tonight."

"Ah, *Signor* Ducharme! But one moment!" The man rushed off. "I'll see what I can do."

Ian turned to me. "Why didn't you tell me you were coming?"

It was not as if I ever called him. "I thought you were out of the country."

Ilena said, "Ian is always with the airplanes."

"Traveling bores Ilena," he said, putting his hand on her narrow back.

Jealousy slimed out of some dark, dank place in me. I squashed it like a snail.

"Is work," she said, and I wondered if she was an in-flight hooker. She had a subtle golden tan and her skin was almost translucent. I thought you could hold her up to the light, like a porcelain cup, and the intricate network of blood vessels and organs would be visible.

The maître d' came back and said, "If you would follow me."

On those occasions when I'd been with Ian, we usually got special treatment, so I was surprised when the maître d' led us past the main room and toward the back of the restaurant. He walked through the swinging doors to the kitchen.

More than a dozen workers were toiling over hot ranges, where intensely fragrant steam billowed. Pans clashed and food sizzled. Plates were dropped with a loud clatter on stainless steel counters under heat lamps. There was a sense of organized chaos as the men worked, shouting in a patois of English, Italian, and Spanish.

"Here you are." The maître d' gave a game-show-hostess wave toward a table crammed into the corner of the kitchen. A Latino busboy was hastily setting it for six.

"Thank you, Roberto," Ian said graciously to the maître d'.

The maître d' left just as a waiter appeared with a bottle of red wine. "Pally will be with you in a minute."

I saw Ian looking at the ring on my finger. I said, "I didn't want any muggers to be tempted by my engagement ring."

"Once on subway, a man try to steal my makeup kit," Ilena said flatly. "I kick the onions and he is crying like a pig baby. It was Chanel samples I send to my sister."

The waiter poured the wine, dark as blackberry juice, into our glasses, but Ilena held her hand over hers and said, "Water with lemon."

After the waiter left, Ian asked me, "Is this table all right?"

"They put the Mexican girl in the kitchen to eat with the help," I commented, noticing a few Latinos working around me. "But the food smells like heaven."

Ian grinned as if I'd said something funny, but the food *did* smell incredible. He lifted his glass to me and drank.

I sipped the wine. It tasted of berries and earth. I wanted to bathe in it.

"I don't like the eating," Ilena commented. "Always the same, in the mouth, out the body. What is point?" She gazed with open hostility at the basket of freshly baked breads that had just been placed on our table.

"The point, my dear Ilena, is pleasure," Ian said as he passed the bread basket to me. "How is Edna?"

"Still full of spit and vinegar and leaving the ranch far too often with her addled younger lover."

"I adore that woman."

Ilena's eyelashes flickered despite the heavy weight of mascara on them. "Who is woman you talk of, Ian?"

"A dear old friend, darling," he said.

Someone bellowed, "Ducharme! You filthy bastard!"

We turned to see one of the kitchen staff hurtling toward our table. Ian stood and the tall, gaunt man flung his arms around him. His sandy hair might have been hacked off with a cleaver. He looked as if he'd been very handsome about a thousand parties ago.

"Pally, so good to see you again."

"Where the hell have you been? We tried to call you when

Rafe and I went fishing for glass eels. You missed a helluva fry-up." While Pally was talking, he glanced at Ilena and her water, and took a lingering look at me as I bit into a thick rosemary bread stick.

"I'll make it next time," Ian said. "You've met Ilena, and this is Milagro, visiting for a few days."

Pally took Ilena's hand and gave it a shake—"Good to see you again"—and then he stood before me with his arms out.

I made the mistake of letting him hug me, and he enthusiastically ground his body against me. A few of the guys in the kitchen hooted and whistled. "You feel like a girl who likes a good meal."

I extricated myself and said, "Does your boss allow you to molest customers?"

"Only the succulent ones." He licked his lips lasciviously and the others laughed, but I was sensitive to people seeing me as an item on a menu. Pally grabbed Ian's wine and drank it in two large gulps, then wiped his mouth with the corner of his white jacket. "I gotta get back to work. I'll send some chow over and some friends are gonna sit here, too, if that's cool."

"But of course," Ian said.

Ilena let her wrap slip down to the chair and slightly rotated her left arm so that I could see the purple and ochre bruise on the inside of her elbow. When she was sure that I'd noticed it, she leaned against Ian. His hand went to the bruise, and his thumb stroked the mark. Satisfied that she'd claimed her territory, she said, "Ian, no one sees me here. I will be at bar for nob-hob with pretty boys and girls."

"Have fun, darling." When she was gone, Ian said, "How have you been?"

"Good. Busy. I've been writing, and then there's the wedding at the end of summer." Oswald and I hadn't discussed the guest list and I didn't know if Ian would be invited.

"You'll understand if I don't offer my congratulations."

"Not really," I said. "You've obviously moved on with your new thrall."

"Ilena isn't a thrall. She's what you might call a compatriot. Her people have been allied with ours for ages."

"But she lets you take blood from her."

"Don't be jealous, darling," he said in his rich, sonorous voice. "I'm not."

Before I could respond to his ridiculous comment, Pally's other friends came into the kitchen and joined us. Soon we were all talking away. The woman, who wore a perfect little black dress, said, "Ian, how is your sister?"

Cornelia Ducharme, who'd been adopted by Ian's family, was high-maintenance and low-tolerance. She'd been furious with me when I discontinued my role as Ian's love poppet. The vampire world being a small one, she'd had some sort of relationship with Oswald, but I didn't know if it had gone beyond socializing.

Ian said, "Cornelia is very well, thank you. She's coming into town soon."

The woman said, "Wonderful. I want to introduce her to a friend of mine. He's just her type."

Probably Type O, I thought, and Ian said, "I'll tell her to call you."

Ilena returned from the bar, somewhat enlivened, and I was shocked to learn that she was not in fact an international airline hooker, but a model. She contributed comments to a discussion about the international monetary fund that was completely over my head, leading me to suspect that she must be an idiot savant.

Plates of food and bottles of wine arrived at our table. There were cured meats, grilled fish, spring vegetables, and delectable, barely seared lamb and venison. Small plates of pasta appeared, curved orecchiette and luxurious pappardelle.

Pally, whose job seemed limited to cleaning spills on the edges of plates before they were sent out, kept offering his opinions to the chefs. They were surprisingly tolerant of him, especially since he frequently left his station to hang out with us.

I excused myself to go to the ladies' room, and when I returned, Pally caught me in the hallway and said, "I like that caboose you're hauling, *mamacita*. Wanna party with me later?"

He had a strong carnal appeal, and I thought he'd be a fantastic, drunken, lusty, messy lay, all orgasms and crazy laughter. "I'm not available."

"You mean you and Ian and Ilena . . . We could all have a good time."

"Pally, how do the dishwashers say 'bleach' in Spanish?"

"*El* Clorox. Why?"

"I'm going to ask the dishwasher for a bottle so I can pour it into my brain," I said, laughing as I pushed past him.

The meal concluded late, after Pally joined the dishwasher to croon a love song in Spanish and we'd finished a plate of tiny almond cookies and drunk liqueur the color of garnets.

As we left I saw Ian's Town Car was out on the street. I said, "Ian, thank you for dinner. It was incredible."

"You're welcome. Pally liked you."

"I liked him, but I can't believe he gets to have his own parties at work. Every time I tried to bring a little life into a workplace, I got fired."

"What would you like to do now?" Ian asked.

"I've got to go back to a hotel and see if they have a room for me. My reservation got canceled."

"I wondered why you were carrying around that case. Come stay at the Council's house. We're the only ones there now and there are several guest rooms," Ian said.

He'd said "we." Was he living with Ilena?

Ilena said flatly, "Is good house. Excellent plumbing with very much hot water."

I liked hot baths. Besides, what if I went to the hotel and they told me again that no rooms were available? "Okay, thank you for offering."

"Good," Ian said. "Let's have a nightcap first."

Ian had the driver take us to a small jazz club. We sat on bar stools lined against the back wall and listened to a modern quintet. The sound was so beautifully balanced that I said to Ian, "Mercedes would love this place."

"She's the one who told me about it."

I remembered that they'd discussed music when I'd introduced them, but didn't recall them talking about this place.

I hadn't slept much on the plane and I'd had a long day. When my eyelids began drooping, Ian suggested we go home. The driver took us to a tree-lined street and stopped in front of a white stone Beaux Arts mansion with arched windows trimmed in black. A tall black wrought iron fence surrounded the property, and enormous black jardinieres held boxwood topiary. Flames burned in antique gas lanterns over the entrance.

Inside the front door, a two-story entrance led to a circular staircase made of black marble. Ilena did one of those slinky model walks up the stairs and I followed her. Ian came behind us, lifting my bag so that it didn't bang on the stairs.

I saw a living room with paneled walls and traditional furniture, and a formal dining room. Ilena walked down a hall and up another flight of stairs. On the landing of the second floor, she said, "Good night, pretty little chubby pickle."

I stood there stunned, trying to decipher if she had meant that I was pretty *and* a little chubby, or pretty chubby.

Ian put his arm around her scrawny waist and said, "I'll be just a moment."

Ian and I went up the next flight of stairs. He walked down a hall and opened a door, "Here you are."

The guest room was charming, with pink-and-white linens on the four-poster bed and a beautiful floral-patterned rug. A vase of pink and white tulips graced the mirrored vanity table.

I asked, "What did Ilena mean by calling me a pickle?"

"It was a compliment. She has a very high regard for pickles." He was trying not to smile as he lifted the suitcase onto a bench at the foot of the bed.

"No one has a very high regard for pickles. Where is she from, anyway?"

"Her parents are in the diplomatic service and she's lived in many countries." He came close, then leaned in and kissed my neck in an intimate way that set off those strange sensations. "Sleep well, Young Lady."

He left the room and closed the door. He'd once told me to dream of him. It had been like a spell, or a curse, and I hoped that he would stay the hell out of my dreams tonight.

I turned my thoughts to many irksome matters, the first of which was the Rules Committee's no-boinking edict. I'd also have to deal with some nasty vampire wedding consultant. Finally, the Committee wanted me to sign the loyalty oath. I kept my mind on everything but Ian and Ilena in their bedroom doing whatever it was they did together.

The next morning I awoke feeling more cheerful than I had in ages. It took me a moment to figure out why: I hadn't expected Daisy to come waggling up to me in this strange place.

There was a knock on the door. I pulled the comforter up and said, "Come in."

A woman entered, carrying a tray with a silver pot, a red beverage, and a croissant. She looked like Mrs. Smith, but much younger and smiling. "Good morning, miss."

"Good morning. It's just Milagro."

"I'm Ms. Smith. Would you like a bite?"

I didn't know if she was joking or not. "I'd love coffee. Are you related to Mrs. Smith?"

"She's my mother," the woman said as she placed the tray on my lap and poured coffee from the silver pot into the cup. "Our family has served the Council for several generations. Does sunlight bother you?"

"Not at all."

She smiled. "I always ask. Everyone has varying degrees of sensitivity. Although some seem to fuss for the sake of tradition." She opened the drapes over three bowed and arched windows. "Lord Ian and Ilena have gone out, but he said you're to take the car if you like. He'll be back this afternoon."

"I think I'll explore on my own." I looked around the room for a clock. It was almost eleven.

"If you need anything, I'll be in the office on the main floor."

I thanked her and she left the room. I tasted the juice. It was tart-sweet blood orange. I had just bitten into the croissant when my phone rang.

"Hi, Milagro, it's me." Toodles coughed at the other end of the line. "It wasn't food poisoning. I've got the flu. Did you get a decent room at the hotel? I'm sooo sorry."

"It's fine. Actually, I ran into a friend of my fiancé's family and I'm staying with him and his girlfriend," I said, thinking of how aboveboard it was.

"Good! I wish I could have gone out to dinner with you. I've wanted to go there for ages. Was everything perfect?"

"Oh, the reservation got canceled."

"Just a sec." I heard her yelling, "Did you cancel the reservation yesterday? What?" Then Toodles came back on the line. "My brother is horrible. I'm soooo sorry!"

"It's okay. The place was packed, but my friend knows one of the kitchen staff, a guy named Pally, and he let us eat *in* the kitchen."

She coughed so severely I thought she would choke on her outrage. "You ate at the chef's table with Paolo?"

"His name's not Paolo, it's Pally. I think he's the garnish inspector. Friendly guy, and the food was amazing."

"Pally's his nickname and he owns the restaurant! People would kill to eat at his table." She coughed violently.

When she finished hacking, I offered to pick up some chicken soup and visit, but she told me to enjoy myself in the City. "I'll see you at your wedding!" she said, and I felt glad that I'd have a few old friends on my side of the aisle.

Oswald was an early riser, so I called him. "Hey, babe."

"How'd the rest of your evening go, babe?" he asked.

"There was one glitch," I said, trying to sound breezy. "The hotel insisted that I'd canceled my room, but they were nice enough to offer me a midnight check-in special."

"Are you there now?"

"No, I'm at the Council's house," I said. "Ms. Smith has been very kind."

"It's a beautiful old place," he said.

"It's pretty fab. Ian and his girlfriend, Ilena, are here, too. They invited me to stay when they found out about my situation."

I waited and then he said, "Goddamn Ian Ducharme. What's he doing there anyway? Why didn't you go to the hotel?"

"I was tired and didn't want to deal with the hotel. Look, Oswald, I didn't have to say anything about Ian, but I think we should be honest with each other, don't you?"

"I don't trust him with you."

"I'm not asking you to trust him. I'm asking you to trust *me*, Oswald. Besides, Ian and his Euroslut-slash-model seem very happy together."

After a few seconds, he said, "I'm overreacting, right?"

"Not compared to the way I feel about the Council's latest condition." I ranted about the loyalty oath and then I told him I was sightseeing on my own today.

Then I called Mercedes and told her about the meeting and the vampires' underground lair. "I could have sworn that I heard someone crying out from behind one of those doors."

"I know this hacker who's obsessed with the tunnel system," she said. "He's been making a subterranean map of the City for years. He even tracks rat populations to discover tunnels."

"You know how I feel about rats, ugh. Do you think he could figure out an alternative way to get to the vamp nest?"

"Persecuted peoples tend to have escape routes," she said. "Give me the address." I gave her the details and she said she'd call me as soon as she learned anything.

I went downstairs to tell Ms. Smith I'd be out. She was in a small office off the hall leading to the living room.

"I should be back in a few hours," I told her as I looked at the old sepia-tinted photos of the house and neighborhood on the walls. "Have you worked for the Council long?"

73

"For about ten years now. I'm always happy when Lord Ian comes to visit."

"Does he stay here often?"

"Not often enough. Although we spent a lot of time together when . . . But you know all about that unfortunate situation with the Project for a New Vampire Century and his house arrest."

She meant the time the Council had reprimanded Ian for slicing up the man responsible for the attack on me. "So he was here with you and not in *other* quarters? I thought the Council might have a place to detain someone in their underground chambers."

She smiled and said, "You must have read *The Count of Monte Cristo.* But I'd heard you liked books. You're quite well known in our circles, you know—the only known survivor! I wish I could become one of them like you."

"Being a vampire is overrated," I said. "It's better to be able to enjoy the sun, have kids, and live as a normal."

"You've only been one for a short time. You'll learn to appreciate the advantages of having the condition."

"I don't really have a choice, do I? See you soon."

"Bye, Milagro. Enjoy your afternoon."

This was advice that I could follow. Now that I had mastered the subway system, I set forth to visit interesting neighborhoods, marveling at how familiar and yet how different everything was. I was people-watching at a sidewalk café and drinking a strawberry smoothie when my phone rang.

A man's voice chirped, "Miraculous one, I dreamed about you last night!"

"Hello, *Don* Pedro. I hope it wasn't a scary dream."

"I shared *hoasca,* a sacred herbal tea, with enlightened

friends, and we journeyed together to the spirit world. I saw many things. I saw you opening your moist new wings!"

"I was a butterfly emerging from a chrysalis," I said, amused.

"No, your wings were dark and webbed like a bat's! You flew out of a black cave, into the sky, and there were three—no! There were four creatures watching you, but sometimes they had faces like people. One loved the beautiful bat, one watched guard over the bat, but two others wanted to crush her. I sensed much danger and desire and knew I must warn you to be careful!"

As dreams went, that was a doozy. "Thanks for the warning, *Don* Pedro. Is there anything else?"

"Yes, I am sending some recordings of my seminars to you. You will find them invaluable as you write my memoir."

"I appreciate your thinking of me."

What a loco peanut. His silly dream lingered in my mind though; perhaps my vanity was insulted by the comparison to a flying rodent. It was even worse than being called a pickle.

Putting his nonsense aside, I visited a renowned botanical garden and was delighted to find some varieties of plants that I'd never seen before. While I was in the Shakespeare garden, I watched a photographer taking pictures of a bride in a sumptuous wedding gown as she posed by a rose-covered arbor. Her mother and friends fussed around her and they were all laughing and happy.

My mother Regina and I would never share such an intimate moment. But I did have friends who cared about me and I needed to buy them presents. So I made a pilgrimage to Nancy's favorite department store and admired the intriguing window displays before entering the enormous building.

The ebony-and-white staircase that swirled upward through

the open well of the store was dizzying, as were the shining glass counters and the mirrors. I went to the directory, thinking that I might visit the bridal salon, when my phone rang.

"Mil, it's Nance. Where are you?"

I told her and she said, "Don't you dare look at wedding dresses with Toodles! She'll exert her ghastly preppy influence and make you buy a princess A-line dress that would be horrific on you."

"I'm not with Toodles. She's got the flu. What gifts should I get my friends?"

"Beautiful scarves are the perfect gift. They pack well, accentuate any ensemble, fit everyone, and they're timeless. One good accessory forgives a multitude of fashion sins."

"Any tips?"

"Cashmere or wool for the gentlemen, and silk for the ladies. Get mine in sea-foam to accentuate my eyes." She waxed idyllic about scarves while I found my way to men's accessories.

"So why did you call, Nancita?" I said as I pulled out a slate gray cashmere scarf for Oswald. I grabbed a cinnamon brown merino one for Sam and a malachite green one for Gabriel. The prices were shocking, but these men had always been generous with me.

"The invitations arrived. They're gorgeous, the color of homemade vanilla ice cream with most-excellent scrolly black writing. You need to address them by hand. How's your cursive script?"

"Fabulous. Did you know that I can copy any writing sample?"

"Forging is such a useful talent. I want to see you as soon as you get back. We have so much to do. Must run. Smooches!" she said and ended the call.

I realized that I didn't have a gift for my host, Ian. I picked up espresso brown deerskin gloves that seemed right for him. In the women's accessory department, I found scarves for my girl-friends and a gossamer silvery summer shawl for Edna.

It was a long walk to the Council's house, but I wasn't espe-cially anxious to get there. I saw a lot of people walking their dogs. I hoped the flowers on Daisy's grave hadn't wilted.

When Ms. Smith answered the door to the house, she said, "Lord Ian is in the library. Let me show you the way."

seven

don't vamp so close to me

Ian was standing and talking on the phone as I entered. I drifted to the other end of the long wood-paneled room to give him privacy. The books, mostly histories and biographies, were in several languages, and I tried to make out the titles as I ran my finger along the spines.

Then I saw a row of books written in the awful alphabet that was used in ancient vampire texts. I drew my hand away from them.

"Did you enjoy your day, Young Lady?"

Ian was standing right behind me. His dark eyes caught mine, and I said, "You could have told me that Pally was the restaurant owner."

He grinned. "We didn't have much time to talk last night. We didn't even discuss your meeting with the Rules Committee."

There were only inches between us. I turned back to the

books and took a step away as I pretended to read a title. "I descended into the vampires' subterranean lair like Persephone into Hades. The jackass who called himself Mr. Nixon wants me to swear my eternal fidelity to the vampire nation by taking an Oath of Loyalty. This wasn't part of the agreement that Sam reviewed."

"So you ate your pomegranate seed, but now you are not content to be queen of the underworld?" Ian asked.

"They weren't asking me to be their queen. They were asking me to renounce my American citizenship. Besides, I don't agree that it is better to reign in hell than serve in heaven," I said.

"I can't imagine you happily serving anywhere."

"Let us return to the topic of *los vampiros*," I said. "Sam is going to be irked that they brought me out here, coach airfare by the way, and slapped on this outrageous request for a loyalty oath."

"Did they ask for anything else?"

I was sure that his administrative toady, Mrs. Smith, had told him about the celibacy requirement.

"Nothing else," I said. "But as I was leaving, I thought I heard someone in distress down there, a voice crying out."

He shrugged, "Possibly one of the denizens of the subway, but they can't intrude on our catacombs from their tunnels."

"That's what Nixon said. Where's your girlfriend?"

"Ilena's on her way to Geneva."

So I was alone with him. "A modeling job?"

"Not this time. She also works in international finances, advising on private sector development."

"She's a model *and* a financier?"

"Yes."

"Of course she is." Many of the vamps were overachievers,

so it figured their longtime allies were as well. "She seems very, uhm, practical."

"And quite stunning, don't you think? I'm terribly fond of her."

"I'm so glad that you've found someone who suits your lifestyle." I wasn't entirely successful in keeping the sarcasm out of my voice. "Jet-setting, bon vivanting, soirees, international orgies, all that."

"You've summed up my existence in its totality." He was smiling, but not amused. "You're probably much happier isolated in the country."

Before I could stop myself I said, "My dog died, Ian. Daisy died." I hated the thought of her out there in the field alone. The pain rose again, at the base of my throat, and I put my hand there.

"Oh, my dear girl," he said. "I'm so sorry."

I swiped at my eyes.

He pulled a handkerchief out of his pocket and handed it to me. Then he placed his hand in the center of my chest, the part that held the pain. His warmth infused me, taking the edges off the pain. I didn't know if Ian was playing some vampire parlor trick on me or, worse, if I was responding to his comfort.

He took his hand off me and moved toward the library table. "Would you like to go out? Indulge in a little bon vivanting?"

I nodded.

"I have some business to take care of first."

"That's fine. I'll just get ready," I said.

I went up to the guest room and took a long shower, sampling the interesting bath products. When I was living on my own and broke, I'd use a bar of soap until it was a sliver so thin I couldn't hold it any longer. I'd melt the slivers together to make a lumpy new bar, a trick my *abuelita* had taught me.

A rose silk dress was the prettiest thing I'd brought, and Ilena's so-called compliment still stung. I slipped it on over my prettiest panties, bra, and slip. Staring in the foggy mirror, I agreed with Pally's assessment. I wasn't a chubby pickle—I was a succulent babe. I blow-dried my hair so that it fell smoothly over my shoulders, and used a rosy lip gloss and an extra coat of mascara.

I slid my feet into high-heeled slingbacks, which gave me four additional inches of height, if not the freakish height of a model.

I picked a pretty shawl for the evening chill and went downstairs. Ian was waiting for me in the living room. He stood as I came in. He'd changed into an elegant black suit and a snowy white shirt. His hair was still damp and he smelled of that marvelous cologne.

"Young Lady, you look lovely. Shall we?"

It suddenly felt like a date. We exchanged good-byes with Ms. Smith and went to the car out front. The driver opened the door for us and we got in. I asked, "So when does Ilena return?"

"Soon, or I shall meet up with her," Ian said. "I thought we might start at an artist's reception."

The reception was held in a converted warehouse on the waterfront. The late afternoon light filled the loft and I felt amazingly cosmopolitan when I ran into an F.U. acquaintance who was a friend of the painter.

The room got crowded and the conversation grew louder as people tried to talk over the music. As the sky darkened, I got that rush I always got at night in a city, anticipating all the possibilities. The people who came out at night were more exciting, more adventurous, more glamorous.

Then Ian and I went to a cocktail party in a stunning white and mirrored penthouse apartment. The host was a well-known author and when Ian told him that I was a writer, he asked, "What are you working on now?"

"A commissioned project based on ethnobotany and folklore, two of my interests. I've also written novellas paying homage to the writing of Mary Wollstonecraft Shelley. They're about the monsters that lie within us."

"Sounds interesting. Have your agent send me a copy."

Before I could tell him that my agent had dumped me, the author got pulled away by a guest. No matter. I would send him a copy of *Uno, Dos, Terror!* and he would see that I was a serious writer.

As guests moved on to the next social engagement, Ian said, "Are you hungry? Do you still like to dance?"

"Yes to both questions."

"There's a place I've heard about," he said. He called his driver to bring the car up and we went out to meet it.

The driver took us through a run-down neighborhood of brick houses and farther on to an area with boarded-up buildings and broken windows. Ian asked the driver to stop and said, "We can walk the rest of the way."

We stepped out of the car, and Ian took my arm and led me through a dirty littered alley. I became aware of delicious aromas and the faint sound of salsa music when a sturdy mixed-race young Latino came down the alley toward us. He was so busy talking on his phone that he bumped into Ian.

In a second, Ian had grabbed the kid and slammed him up against a wall, lifting him so high the kid's feet couldn't touch the ground.

"Ian! It was just a bump," I said as the kid was rapidly objecting, apologizing, and cursing in English and Spanish. He was about twenty, dressed in knockoff designer jeans, a T-shirt, and a cheap leather jacket.

Ian reached into the kid's jacket and pulled out a wallet. "I believe this is mine," he said, still holding the kid up against the wall.

"Ian Ducharme, let that boy down!"

Ian released the kid, who dropped heavily to the ground and immediately tried to run off.

My arm shot out and I grabbed the back of the kid's jacket, wrenching him backward. *"Uno momento, por favor,"* I told him.

"What do you plan to do with him?" Ian asked. "Call the police and wait for hours? Why don't we just drain him of blood and leave his lifeless corpse in a Dumpster?"

"Ha ha and ha, Ian." The kid was twisting and struggling to escape and I told him, "Behave or I'll rip your leg off and use it to beat some manners into you. What's your name?"

"Frankie," he said dejectedly as I dragged him along toward the delicious aromas. "You're strong for a chick."

"Crazy strong, emphasis on the crazy," I said. "I'm Milagro and this is Ian."

"Where we going?"

"There's a Cuban restaurant here," Ian said, which set Frankie off into another struggle to escape.

While I tussled with Frankie until he was convinced that I was both serious and stronger than he, Ian watched and chuckled.

"Aren't you going to help?" I snapped at him.

"Yes. Frankie, don't muss the young lady's dress. It's a favorite of mine."

The alley opened to another alley and I saw the restaurant.

The rich aromas and throbbing music came from a small, jungle green wooden building without even any signage. We went inside and the small cramped tables were filled with people eating meals off paper plates. A fortyish woman in an apron shouted, "Frankie! Where you been? Get back outside."

"Yeah, *mami,*" he said. Turning to us, he said, "I gotta get back to work."

I was so surprised that I let him go, but we followed him through the restaurant and out the back door. The backyard was illuminated by strings of colored Christmas lights. On a small platform, a sizzling hot band played tropical rhythms. Several couples, as supple and gorgeous as leopards, danced on the patio. At the back of the yard was a roaster made from cement blocks, and on a plywood table, a roast pig was being carved by a tiny man. Frankie went to the man and took over his duties.

We sat at the only empty table, and Frankie's mother came to us. There was something very familiar about the chubby, exasperated woman. "You want the special? Something to drink?"

Ian told her to bring us whatever she thought we'd enjoy.

She was surprisingly incurious about our relationship with her son, but when she returned with two heaping plates of food, she said, "Frankie break into your car or something? Dinner's on the house and he'll pay you back whatever he owes."

"Not at all, ma'am," Ian said. "We saw him on the street and asked for directions. He was kind enough to help us."

She said, "Really? Huh!" and then, "Okay, then I'll run a tab for you."

We drank fruity punch made with red wine and rum and ate tender, citrus-marinated roast pork with *mojo, arroz,* and fried *plátanos.* As I listened to the blast of the trumpets and the beat of the timbale, I had to admit that Oswald's mother and Nancy weren't so very wrong about me: I would love to have a wedding in a place like this, a place that fed all my senses.

Ian said, "Shall we?" He led me into the crowd of dancers and took me in his arms. I reveled in the delicious warmth and the tingle that came from the places where our skin touched. I wondered what that sensation would feel like on other parts of my body, a thought I shouldn't be having.

Ian's face came close to mine, his lips so near my neck that I could feel his breath. He pulled me tight, and my hips moved in rhythm with his. I felt as if I could anticipate his moves, and I wished I could dance with Oswald like this.

When the song ended, Ian smiled at me. "I've missed the way you smell."

"Like dinner," I said.

"Like no one else."

The crowd began clapping and shouting. I looked to the stage and saw the trumpeter pulling Frankie's mom up. As she untied her apron and smiled, I said, "That's Juanita! I saw her singing at My Dive!"

She began to sing a romantic bolero, too romantic for my situation, which was standing beside a continental smoothie who had put his arm around my waist. Someone tapped my shoulder and I felt as if I'd received a death row reprieve from the governor. I stepped away from Ian and turned to see Frankie.

The young guy was shuffling his feet and mumbling, "So I'm sorry. No harm, no foul. Let's move on."

"Good idea, but how should we do that? Why were you stealing when you've got a job?"

He shrugged. "I'm trying to get a little money together so I can get out of here. Maybe go to California and meet me some California girls."

As a California girl, I was deeply and sincerely touched.

Ian said, "An admirable goal."

"I can't believe your mom is Juanita," I told Frankie. "I saw her playing with the Rat-Dogs."

"That crazy band," Frankie said. "Who wants to listen to klezmer and salsa?"

"I do. She's following her heart," I said. "What do you think you'd like to do with your life?"

"You know, work in a club. Or cook, maybe."

I opened my evening bag and searched through my wallet until I found Mercedes's business card. "Give Mercedes a call. She might be able to help. Tell her your mom's Juanita and Milagro told you to call."

Frankie was staring at the card as we left the restaurant.

I said to Ian, "He's just going to go out and rob again, isn't he?"

"So I'd wager, Young Lady. Would you like me to check up on him later?"

"That would be nice."

"I would only do it for you," Ian said, and then he called his driver, who met us a block away. As I sat in the backseat of the car, I stared out the window, hoping I would be able to remember it all.

We neared a river and I saw a bridge sparkling with lights. "It's so beautiful. This country is so beautiful." I suddenly felt sad. "Nixon, or whoever he really is, told me that I'd never be fully accepted as an American."

"Nixon's a sly one. He's playing upon your weakness—your desire to be accepted." Ian turned to me with a smile, his teeth gleaming white in the darkness of the car.

"There's nothing wrong with that. It's a normal human desire."

"My dear girl, normal and human isn't enough for you."

"No, normal and human isn't enough for *you*. I would be delighted with normal and human," I said, but he had made me feel better.

When we got back to the house, Ian asked, "Would you like to see the garden? It was designed to be enjoyed at night."

"I'd like that. I've only seen the tops of the trees from my window."

"Come then." He led me through the hallways to a breakfast room with French doors opening onto the backyard. He flipped a switch and lights glowed on the stone paths.

As we walked into the garden, I inhaled the fragrance from aromatic herbs that were planted in formal circles. We walked into a small grove of ancient birch trees with papery white trunks. In the center of the grove was a small amphitheater with two concentric rows of marble benches. Ian said, "When our people first lived in this house, they held ceremonies here. It's one of our oldest sites in this country."

"The birches are beautiful," I said, listening to their long graceful branches swish and whisper in the light breeze.

Ian took a gold penknife from his pocket and I held my breath as I wondered what he was going to do. Then he cut three switches from the trees, folded the knife, and put it away, and began braiding the switches.

"You know how to braid?"

"I used to braid my sister's hair."

I watched as he twisted the birch branches into a wreath. He placed it atop my head and then took my hands. The warmth and tingling spread throughout my body and I was aware only of Ian—his brown eyes so dark they looked black in the shadows, his aquiline nose, and the sense of power that emanated from him.

"You've never heard our language spoken correctly." He began speaking softly in the strange language. From his mouth, the words had a compelling, lyrical quality.

"I'll teach you," he said. He uttered some words, and I repeated the sounds, surprised that I could pronounce them.

I felt the blood rising in my skin, almost as if it was moving toward Ian. I thought I could hear the blood flowing in his veins. I wondered what it would be like to bite into his flesh, to once again fill my mouth with his intoxicating blood. "What does it mean?"

"It means that my blood is your blood, my life is yours," he said, moving close. "Don't go back, Milagro. Stay with me."

I stepped back, pulling my hands away. "Why do you do this? You know that I love Oswald, and he loves me."

"He may think he loves you, but he's been in love half a dozen times since I've known him. He's addicted to your blood."

"That's impossible. I don't even let him drink it anymore. I haven't since . . ." I hadn't craved Oswald's blood since Ian had given me his own. "I love him."

"You're mistaking your love for his family with love for the first vampire you had sex with."

"But Ian, *you* were the first vampire I had sex with—and I don't love you. It was just sex, a meaningless fling." The words sounded far harsher than I'd intended, and I said quietly, "What would we have had anyway, Ian? A few weeks of partying until the next Ilena came along?"

"I would be by your side, Milagro, and you would be the

woman you're meant to be." There was anger in his voice. "The longer you stay with Grant, the more he'll try to make you into a conventional, ordinary wife, and you'll both grow to resent each other."

"You don't know me, or what I want in life." I wanted a home, family, love, a normal life.

"I knew you the moment I set eyes on you. I knew you the moment I tasted you. I know you every time I touch you and feel something I feel with no one else."

"You can't know someone that way." I pulled the beautiful red ring from my finger and held it out. "I shouldn't be wearing this. Please don't send me any more gifts." When he didn't take it back, I let the ring drop to the ground.

I ran inside and up the stairs to my room and shut the door behind me. My hands were shaking as I took the birch wreath from my head.

eight

home is where you hang your bat

I had a restless night but had finally fallen asleep. There was a knock on my door. "Come in," I said. I didn't know if I hoped it was Ian or not.

Ms. Smith came in with a breakfast tray. "Good morning."

"Good morning," I said.

She placed the tray on my lap. "The driver will be back in time to take you to the airport this afternoon. Lord Ian asked me to tell you good-bye for him."

"Ian's gone?"

"He left early to meet Ilena." Ms. Smith went to open the drapes. It was a beautiful morning. "I'm glad he's found someone after all he's been through."

"What do you mean?"

She looked puzzled. "You know about his parents?"

I shook my head.

"Not everyone is meant to be a parent," she said kindly.

"My mother Regina wasn't." I doubted that Ian's parents could have been more unfit than the woman who'd filled a kiddie pool to the brim and left me in there alone as a toddler.

"He's always been so responsible, even when he was a boy. He insisted they take in Cornelia. She was such a beautiful child, you can't imagine, but frail and traumatized after her parents' deaths."

"She seems so confident now." When I tried to imagine Ian and Cornelia as children, I envisioned them in miniature form.

"He brought her out of her shell, and now that he's found someone special, we hope that Cornelia will find someone, too."

Just as she seemed about to say something else, to confide in me, my cell phone rang.

Although Ms. Smith still smiled, her expression became more closed. "I'll leave you to your business."

Mercedes was calling. "I've got some info for you."

"Talk to me."

"My subway expert knows of a few locations, including one near the address you gave me, with suspiciously high electrical usage and other odd things. He thinks there's an abandoned tunnel there, one that's not on any known maps."

"Does he know any possible routes to this hypothetical tunnel?"

"He's got a few ideas, but he's never actually tried to get in that area. Milagro, what are you thinking?"

"I'm thinking that I might do a little spelunking. Where does your pal think access to the tunnel may be?"

She told me and added, "Don't do anything too stupid. A lot of crazies live down there, too."

"Worry not about my safety, O brown damsel."

"I'm not worried about you getting hurt," she said very quietly. "I'm worried about you hurting someone."

I worried about that, too. "I only whack people upside the head when they deserve to be whacked upside the head."

I dressed in my black suit so I looked like any other competent and capable city girl. I told Ms. Smith that I was going out for a walk and I'd be back in a few hours, and then I took off to find the vamp cave. On the way to the suspect address, I saw a manila envelope at the top of a trash bin and picked it up.

The building was in the middle of a block, brand spanking new, stainless steel and glass, and I was able to go right by the security desk, carrying my envelope as if I were delivering something. It was only when I got in the elevator that I saw that the button to the basement required a key. You didn't need an F.U. degree to guess that the stairway access to the basement would also be locked.

I had been unceremoniously let go from enough jobs to know that the majority of workers were sadly in need of interesting diversions. I unbuttoned my blouse until the lace from my bra peeked out.

Returning to the main floor, I surveyed the three security guards stationed around the lobby. An appealingly beefy guy with his hair cut close to his head was sitting at a desk in the corner and wearing a suit with the firm badge. I strolled over to him and smiled. "I need to talk to your supervisor."

His hazel eyes took in the view and he returned my smile. "I'm the supervisor. What do you need?"

I inched closer to him and dropped my voice. "I need to get to the basement. I left something down there."

"Access is restricted," he said.

"Tell me about it. I left my key down there."

"Who gave you a key? Who are you?"

I'd always been an ace at pop quizzes even when I hadn't studied. The trick was to choose the most likely answer. Who was most likely to be at the top of any vampire power structure?

I said, "He likes it when I call him George. Or President Washington. I'm Honey, his *special* friend, but he'll be mad at me if he knows I forgot the key."

The security guard wanted so much to believe my story, but he had to ask, "Why don't you go through the Presidential Properties building?"

"Mrs. Smith spies for all the wives, you know. Some women want to neuter men," I said and leaned low to give him maximum diversion. "But I admire masculinity. I *honor* it."

The security guard swallowed. I was about to say that George Washington liked it when I dressed in a trilby hat, see-through plastic platforms, and nothing else, when the security guard said, "I can let you downstairs. You want a flashlight?"

"You're fabulous!"

He opened a desk drawer and took out a big metal flashlight. We went into the elevator and he sorted through his key ring, selected a small key, and inserted it in the lock. Then he pushed the button for the basement.

When the door opened to a dark basement he said, "Do you want me to come with you?"

"I'd love you to *come* with me," I said huskily. "But then Mr. President would have to fire you. I know the way."

I walked into a hallway. The rooms off it were filled with machinery and office furniture. I glanced in one room filled with cleaning supplies and was about to leave when something caught my attention.

Against the wall was a rack of hats and a shelf with bottles of expensive sunblock. A few seconds later I discovered a hatch in the floor under a blue industrial rug. I opened the hatch and saw a ladder leading down into darkness.

I climbed down the ladder, feeling chilly dampness. It led to a narrow corridor. It was so utterly dark that even I couldn't see. I turned on the flashlight and slowly made my way along the corridor, at the end of which was a narrow, low-ceilinged stairwell.

By the time I had walked down three sets of stairs and along as many walkways, I had lost all sense of direction. I wondered how much farther down I had to go, but there were no more stairs. I turned a corner and saw grayness ahead. I had arrived at the vampires' lair.

It had looked impressive with the lights on. Now it just looked spooky. The darkness seemed to shift and move like a living thing. I wanted to know what was behind the arched doors. The one closest to the marble-topped conference table opened to a large lounge area, complete with sofas, a television, and a kitchenette filled with unmarked vials of blood. There was a full bathroom off this room. A vampire rumpus room, I thought.

The next door was locked. At the far end of the cavern was another door, unlocked. I opened it and saw three small cells behind iron bars. Chains were bolted to the walls by the bare mattresses. In one cell there was a half-filled plastic cup of water, as if someone had been there recently.

I'd taken too long already. I'd seen enough, so I hurried back the way I'd come along the corridors and up the stairs. As I climbed up the ladder and saw the dim light from the open hatch, I felt a rush of relief.

I pulled myself out of the hatch and stood up.

Mr. Nixon was standing there. "I was just about to send out a search party for you, Miss De Los Santos. People have gone down into the tunnels never to be seen again."

"I don't doubt it. How'd you find me?"

He pointed upward and I saw a small camera in the corner of the room. "I should be asking you how you found this building."

"I just sensed it," I said, trying to sound sincere. "Sometimes I just *sense* things. How often do you keep prisoners down there?"

"The person you heard was not a prisoner. He's one of our own, a schizophrenic and a danger to himself and society. We were in the process of transferring him to a secure mental health facility where he'll receive the best care available."

I couldn't tell if he was lying or not. I hadn't met mentally ill vampires, but I had met fanatical ones. "Maybe he's just a danger to *your* society."

"You of all people should understand that there are very real dangers to us. I'm not going to apologize for taking action to protect our safety."

"Do your prisoners have any rights?"

"Of course they do, but we won't sacrifice our own safety for kindhearted but misguided ideals."

"And if you make mistakes? If you act precipitously and innocent people are hurt?"

"Safety has a price."

"Benjamin Franklin said, 'Those who would give up essential liberty to purchase a little temporary safety deserve neither liberty nor safety.'"

"That quaint notion would render us vulnerable to our enemies." He sighed and shook his head. "I wish it were otherwise, and though I'd like to discuss this with you, I had to leave a meeting to come here, and they're expecting me back. May I escort you out of the building?"

I nodded and we went back upstairs. As we passed the security officer, I winked at him.

Out on the sidewalk, Mr. Nixon said, "Until we meet again, Miss De Los Santos." He turned and walked toward the Presidential Properties building.

As soon as I was a few blocks away and confident that no one was following me, I called Mercedes and told her what I'd found. She said, "You already knew they had their own criminal justice system."

"Sure, but those cells really freaked me out. Maybe I'm paranoid, but I think one was meant for me."

"Your friends wouldn't let that happen."

"What if they didn't know?" I asked. "Oh, you'll never believe who I saw last night! Juanita of Juanita and Her Rat-Dogs. She's got this incredible restaurant and her house band is smokin'."

"That's the place I was going to recommend to you. Your friend Toto took you there?" Mercedes asked, puzzled.

"Not Toodles. I went with Ian. Juanita's son, Frankie, tried to steal Ian's wallet. I gave Frankie your number, and if he calls, you should know that besides his criminal tendencies, he makes this to-die-for, fork-tender roast pork."

"Talking to you gives me a headache. I'm hanging up now."

It was exhilarating to be above ground again. I walked all the way back to the Council's house, enjoying the sky above me.

When I checked in at the airport, the clerk told me that my seat had been upgraded to first-class. Ian had thought about me, even though . . . I'd left the leather gloves with Ms. Smith and asked her to give them to Ian. I don't know why I always felt as if I had unfinished business with him.

Once I was settled into my roomy seat and the flight attendant had served me a Bloody Mary and taken my meal order, I stared out the window. I had a vague continental-whorish feeling, but it wasn't a *bad* feeling. I wanted to be back at the ranch. I wanted the wedding to be over and for Oswald and me to be living happily ever after already. I wanted not to feel guilty about Ian, although I couldn't quite figure out why I did feel guilty.

My mood lightened as the miles passed, and soon I was taking advantage of first-class luxuries. I watched a movie, ordered every red drink on the menu, and stared out the window at the country, *my* country. The plane arrived in the early evening, and I was thrilled to see Oswald waiting for me. I threw myself into his arms and said, "Did you miss me?"

"A lot."

The broken wheel had completely fallen off my green zebra-stripe suitcase, and Oswald took it from me and carried it by the handle. "I'll get you good luggage," he said.

"I only need the wheel fixed. This bag really makes a statement."

"Uhmm."

As we went to the car, I told him about the things I'd done the day before, but I didn't mention that Ian and I had gone out alone. I would have told Oswald if he'd asked. I was describing the Council's underground lair, which he'd never seen, when I noticed that we were taking an odd route. "Where are we going?"

"I've got a surprise for you."

Generally, when men told me they had a surprise for me, it was a bad thing. But Oswald was so cheerful that I didn't want to ruin his mood.

We drove into the City and he pulled into a garage in an area that had first become popular with artists and musicians, who lived there cheaply in violation of zoning laws. Speculators had quickly moved in to kick out the artists and create "live/work lofts," which they sold for big money to professionals. Oswald parked in a space marked *Visitors* and slapped his *Physician* placard on his dash.

I said, "Is someone having a Botox emergency, or an implant implosion?"

"You're a funny girl."

"Who lives here?"

"You ask too many questions." We got out of the car and he took my arm and led me to an elevator. He used a key to open it, and we went up to the fourth floor.

"Is it a surprise party?" I asked. "Because I want to freshen my makeup."

"It's not a surprise party." Oswald used a key to open a door to an empty loft space. "Come on in," he said.

Perhaps he had borrowed a swanky bachelor pad. But the loft was the exact opposite of a love nest. It was a hopeless nest.

Tall windows, which provided a view of other converted warehouses, were the best feature. The place had been renovated at a time when pink and gray checkerboard patterns were fashionable. Cement flooring showed under the torn, dirty, industrial carpet. A kitchen area with old black appliances was marked off by glass-block columns.

"What do you think?" Oswald asked.

"It's very period, isn't it? I can practically hear Blondie and see girls with big shoulder pads snorting cocaine."

He opened the door to a gray and black tiled bathroom. "It hasn't been touched since then, but there's a lot of potential here."

Potential for a New Wave retro party maybe. We'd invite a few hundred of our closest friends and fire up the Margaritanator 3000. "Uhm, yes, I'm sure there is."

"I was going to save this for later, but . . ." He held out the key to me. "This is my wedding present to you."

My fingers closed around the key. "What?"

"Once the Council gives you full rights, you can apply for a no-interest loan and remodel it," he said happily. "You can sell it and reinvest the money if you want, but I think you should rent it out and let it appreciate."

This was too much for me. "Oswald, I don't know anything about renovations or construction."

"That's why this place is perfect. It's a small enough project for you to learn."

He looked so excited and expectant that all I could say was, "Thank you, Oz. It's incredibly generous," and give him a big kiss, even though I felt as if I'd just been handed the leash to a wolverine wearing a diamond collar, something valuable that was certain to bite me in the ass.

We spent another thirty minutes in the loft, Oswald making suggestions about remodeling and me saying, "Really? Hmm." I finally said, "Oswald, this seems very time-consuming. What about my writing?"

"You can still write. But you won't have to worry about it as . . . as a career," he said.

"According to the Council, if I sign their Loyalty Oath, I won't have to worry about money at all."

"Let's talk about that at dinner. Then we can head home."

We went to one of our favorite restaurants, a tiny place where all they served was soufflés and the waiters were as capricious as cats. We shared a gruyere soufflé and a salad.

"It's amazing to me that just this morning I was on the other coast. It was like being in a foreign country, where everyone was speaking my language," I said. "Everything looked different in real life."

"Three-dimensional?" He smiled crookedly, and my heart went out to him even though he'd given me unwanted real estate.

"Yes." The candlelight brought out the beautiful angles of his pale face. When I touched his cheek, he took my hand and kissed it. "Oswald, I don't like this new provision about loyalty. I'm an American."

"Treat it like dual citizenship. But you already know that if the government finds out about us, our civil rights will mean nothing. We'll be extradited as fast as they can get us on secret flights out of the country." He was quiet for a minute and added, "It isn't as if we don't know where you stand. I'll talk to Sam about it."

"What is the real name of that guy who called himself Nixon?"

"I don't know. I've never even been to the Council's headquarters. It's all very secret. The fact that they allowed you there was a big step for them." He said, "Goddamn Ian Ducharme could have told you Nixon's real name."

"Yeah, well, I didn't ask." I stared at the cornichon garnish on my plate. "His model-slash-international-finance-expert girlfriend, Ilena, called me a pickle. Supposedly it's a compliment, but I don't see how being called a pickle can be complimentary. You don't think I look like a pickle, do you?"

He laughed. "No, but you do get yourself in them. Was she blond?"

"How did you know?"

"It's one of your many hot button issues."

"If it is, and I'm not admitting to anything, it's only because this society has dictated that blond is the ideal of female beauty," I said. I slid down a little in my chair and covered a yawn with my hand.

"You're tired."

"I am, but not *that* tired." I put my hand over his and played with his long fingers. "About the celibacy, it's a really stupid requirement. Don't you think it's really stupid?"

"It's completely stupid. The only reason I agreed is to force the Council to come through on their side of the bargain. Full rights is insurance for you, babe. If anything happened to me, the Council would have to take care of you."

"Don't even talk like that, Oswald! Nothing's going to happen to you. I'd never let anything happen to you." Just the thought of it made me panic.

He smiled dryly. "I'm the one who's supposed to be looking after you, Milagro."

nine

that's what (crazy-ass) friends are for

The ride home always seemed to take too long, and I was always happy when we finally got off the mountain and were back on the flat highway that stretched straight ahead. Home was only a little farther, and soon we were driving past the electronic gate and along the drive.

The dogs came bounding up to meet Oswald's car. Except for Daisy. The pain in my chest had faded after Ian touched me but it hadn't vanished, and I blinked back tears.

The dogs escorted us to the car park, and when we got out, they leapt happily. Oswald unloaded my suitcase, and I looked across the field to the cottage where his grandmother lived. Only the porch light was on.

"Where's Edna?" I asked.

"She decided to go on Thomas's film shoot with him."

"Oh, I was hoping she'd be here to go over wedding ideas with Nancy and me tomorrow."

"While you were gone she said something about not getting involved with the planning," he said. "Her exact words were, 'I'll let the Young Lady battle it out with your mother and see who rises from the dust.'"

"She thinks she's so funny," I said as we went through the mudroom and into the kitchen. "You can just take my bag into my old room," I said, referring to the comfortable maid's room next to the kitchen.

"Why don't you stay in our room and I'll take one of the guest rooms upstairs?"

"If I can't sleep with you, I'd rather be down here. I like the view of my garden."

"Okay." Oswald took my bag into the room behind the kitchen. I followed him and turned on the lights as he put the case down on the sunken but comfortable old bed. There was a beat-up wooden desk by the window, a big overstuffed chair, and a private bath with a wonderful clawfoot bathtub.

"It's stuffy in here," I said and went to open the window. The window was jammed, though, and opened only about six inches. I could have forced it, but I was afraid of breaking the sash.

"Must have warped," Oswald said after failing to push it up more. "I'll ask Ernesto to take care of it."

"Don't worry about it. I know he's got more important things to do." I hated making extra work for Ernesto. "If it gets too warm, I'll use a fan."

"Do you want a nightcap?" he asked.

"I'd love one," I said as I followed him to the kitchen. "But I feel like I need to stretch my legs. I'm just going out to the pond."

I changed into my sneakers and went outside. I liked the breeze, the bright stars in the indigo sky, and the sounds of night. I picked up my pace and ran the rest of the way to the pond.

Sitting on the rock that marked Daisy's grave, I talked aloud to her. I told her how much I would always love her, how beautiful the evening was. And I suddenly realized that I felt different. The pain in my chest was gone. I wasn't remembering how the light in her eyes had dimmed as the life went out of her. I was feeling happy at the memory of how she used to jump into the pond beside me.

Then I saw something that made me start: Daisy was coming toward me from around the pond. No, it was a dog, but not one of ours, who'd been put in the dog run for the night. Besides, this dog was much bigger, some kind of large shepherd-Lab mix.

It came toward me cautiously, with a lowered head.

"I hope you're not rabid," I said. "Not that it would matter if you bit me, but I'd resent it."

The dog wagged its tail.

"Come," I said, and it came to stand before me. It was a male with a thick coat of grayish, black-tipped fur. He had no collar and wasn't neutered, neither of which was uncommon out in the country.

I scratched his head for a few minutes. "I used to come here with my dog, Daisy," I told him. "She was the best dog ever. I'm sure you're fabulous in your own way, however."

He set his head on my knee and looked up at me as if he understood. "It was lovely meeting you. We've both got to get home, though."

Then I jogged across the field to the house.

Oswald was waiting for me as I came to the back door. "Sorry I took so long," I said.

He smiled at me, and then his expression changed. "Milagro, I want you to walk very calmly into the house."

"Why?"

"Because there's a wolf behind you."

I turned and as the dog came to me, Oswald jumped and knocked me over, putting his body between me and the dog. The dog stood still now, straight-legged, looking larger and vaguely, well, wolflike.

"Oswald!" I sat on my fanny and dusted off my knees. "It's just a dog. Here, fellow."

Oswald lunged to grab the animal, but it was swift and ran around him to me. I put my hands on either side of its long face. "Good boy." He wagged his tail and I looked up at Oswald.

I stood up and said, "Sit." The dog sat. "Down." The dog lay down. I looked at Oswald and said, "See? No collar, but trained, someone's pet. Do you recognize him?" The animal rolled over, exposing his belly for a rub.

"No. Maybe Ernie knows what local idiot bought a purebred wolf. I hope he hasn't gotten to any livestock yet."

"'He is mad that trusts in the tameness of a wolf, the health of a horse, a boy's love, or a whore's oath,'" I recited from Shakespeare, but when I finished, the words seemed more sad than cynical to me. "He's just a dog."

"No, he's not. I'll put him in one of the stalls, and tomorrow we'll find his owner. Someone paid thousands for him."

"I'll take him, Oz."

"No, let me," he said. "He's dangerous."

But I was already off with the dog at my side, and I called back, "I will handle this."

When I led the dog or wolf, whatever, down to the barn, I saw the fur on his back rise at the scent of the animals. "You behave or I will kick your hairy behind."

I grabbed a few treats from a bin in the tack room and tossed them in an empty stall. He followed the treats in and I shut the door behind him. "Night, dog." I heard a brief whine from behind the door.

Ernesto's cozy one-bedroom apartment was at the front of the barn. When I knocked on the door, he yelled, "Come in!"

He was now playing a video game. "Wassup, *chula*?"

"I found a dog out by the pond and I put him in one of the empty stalls."

"Why didn't you throw him in the kennel?"

"Oswald says it's a wolf, but he looks like a shepherd mix to me."

Ernie smiled under his suggestive handlebar mustache. "Oz knows a wolf from a dog. I wonder if the family's ever had wolf's blood."

"You are not going to siphon that dog!"

He looked disappointed and then told me that one of his latest girlfriends had sent a pack of homemade tortillas for me.

"Marry that girl," I said as I took the tortillas and went back to the house.

Oswald was at the big kitchen table with two glasses of cow's blood and water. "Did that animal give you any trouble?"

"Not at all. He's a very nice *dog.*" I picked up a glass and drank it quickly, feeling it relax and refresh me. "Better hide the blood. Nancy's coming tomorrow and she'll go through the fridge."

"You said she doesn't cook."

"She doesn't, but she took a mixology class and has the delusion that she's going to invent the perfect cocktail."

"I told you she's a ditz." He leaned over and kissed me. "I'm going to miss sleeping with you. Not the actual sleeping part. But it's only three months."

"Nancy says that the wedding is practically upon us and that we shouldn't think about the time in months, but in days. It's one hundred and something."

"Someone should explain to her that one hundred is a bigger number than three." He bent over and kissed my forehead. "Night, Milagro."

"Buenas noches, mi amor."

He went upstairs to our bedroom, and I went to my new quarters. After I crawled into the clean sheets, I did a compare-and-contrast with Oswald and Ian. It was no contest. Oswald was better looking. He was a very well respected professional. He did charity work for the poor. He was loving to his family. He was kind and good. He was fabulous at sexing me up.

Ian wasn't handsome, though he did have an undeniable molten-lava quality. He didn't seem to have a job, and I didn't believe that handing out huge tips to valets counted as philanthropy. His sister, Cornelia, adored him, but she was out of her tiny little mind. He was a fabulous lover if you liked someone who was always in total control, but the imbalance of power had disturbed me. I was fairly sure that he wasn't a good man.

But if he hadn't saved my life, I wouldn't have it to give to Oswald.

My professor of "Female Transgressives and Dissent in Russian Literature" would have been able to explain my lingering feelings about Ian, but she would have made me write a fifty-page essay afterward.

The next morning, I got up early and dashed off to the barn. Ernie was at the chicken coops right next to the barn. My pet chicken, Petunia, had decided to move here from my garden and she was pecking and chirping contentedly.

Ernie looked at me and said, "What did you do with that wolf?"

"What do you mean?"

"There's nothing in that stall."

Even though it was unlikely that Ernie would miss a large animal, I went into the stall and checked. It was empty. When I came back out, I said, "How'd he get out?"

"*No sé.* The door was closed."

"Huh, must be an escape artist." One of Oz's dogs could open a sliding door. "Maybe the wind shut it behind him."

"Maybe."

I felt unexpectedly disappointed. I returned to the house just as Oswald was leaving for work. "That dog got out of the stall somehow. He's gone."

"That saves us the trouble of taking that animal to the shelter."

"I thought you said it was a good idea for me to get another dog."

"Yes, a dog, *Canis lupus familiaris.* That creature is *Canis lupus* without the very important *familiaris.* Besides, he already belongs to someone." He glanced at the clock and said, "Gotta run, babe. I'll be late."

No sooner had he left than I heard the front door open and a high-pitched "Yoo-hoo!"

Nancy was wearing matching pink gingham shorts and top, like a kindergartener with a fashion-forward mother. On her shoulder was a huge lilac woven tote and she carried a package wrapped in white paper.

"Hi, Nance. How did you get in?"

"Orwell let me in the gate on his way out. I left early to beat the traffic." She handed me the tote and wandered through the rooms on the first floor. "Very nice, but where's the *you* here? Nothing here looks like you."

"Do you want some coffee?" I asked, leading her toward the kitchen.

"What do you have that's yummy?"

I showed her the restaurant-quality espresso machine that I had never used and the flavored Italian syrups in the pantry.

"Outstanding. Let's invent something," she said. She wrangled with the espresso machine while I offered suggestions and made French toast. Soon we had foamy cups of a coffeelike beverage on the table in front of us, where Nancy had placed the package.

"What's in there?" I asked.

"Open it and see."

I unwrapped the white paper and saw flowers. Celadon green and deep plum hydrangeas, antique roses in rich mauve, and burgundy callas were arranged in a brown twig basket. Silk ribbons of pink, plum, violet, and pale moss were wound around the handle of the basket. "They're stunning."

"Do you like the colors?"

"Absolutely gorgeous. Where did you get those callas?"

"I am so revered at the flower market that they practically curtsy when I show up," Nancy said. "That's the color scheme for your wedding."

For the first time I felt a little thrill at the idea of my wedding. "But aren't they a little autumnal for a summer wedding?"

"Even though I think seasonal themes are so tired, these chartreusey and plum shades are totally right for a warm-weather wedding in wine country."

Nancy pulled two boxes from her monstrous tote. "Here are your invitations."

"How did you get these done so fast?" I said as I opened the boxes. A yellow invoice sheet was folded over the stack of beautiful, thick ivory cards. I ran my finger over the graceful black script, feeling the imprint of each letter.

"A lady always has a good printer, a good caterer, and a good waxer. I upgraded from those save-the-date cards you sent out and had them done on letterpress."

"They are beautiful . . ." I opened the invoice and stared in shock. Surely the decimal point for the price was in the wrong place.

Nancy snatched the sheet from me and said, "They're worth every penny. I'll send Ogden the invoices on a monthly basis." She reached into her tote, pulled out a binder, and opened it. "Here's what I've worked out so far."

When I reached for the binder, she slapped my hand away. "No, not until you call your mother Regina."

"What do you want me to call her?"

"Don't be funny." Nancy took her phone out and dialed a number. "Can you believe that I still remember your number from college days?"

"Nancy!"

She smiled at me and said, "Oh, hello, Mrs. De Los Santos, this is Nancy, Milagro's friend." After a pause she said, "Yes, that photo of me in the society column was wonderful. Charity events are the last refuge for evening gowns." There was another pause and she said, "Milagro is right here and she'd love to talk to you."

Nancy jammed the phone into my hand. I considered using it to bang her repeatedly on the noggin, but I'd miss her too much.

The last time I'd talked to my mother Regina, I'd given her

my new address and phone number. I hadn't even received a birthday card. "Hello, Mother," I said.

"Yes," she said coldly.

"I hope you and Dad are doing well."

"We're fine. Milly, I don't have time for talk now. I've got an appointment with my aesthetician."

My father's landscaping business had taken off at about the same time I'd gone away to F.U., and since then my mother Regina had funneled his profits into maintaining and overhauling her emaciated carcass. "I don't want to keep you, and we can talk an—," I began, but Nancy kicked me with her pink slip-on. "I wanted to tell you that I'm getting married, and I'd like you and Dad to come to the wedding."

There was a pause before my mother Regina said, "So you're pregnant? If you get married quietly at City Hall, you won't humiliate me by walking down the aisle with a huge *panza* showing."

"As much as I look forward to having children because I know nothing would make you happier, I am not pregnant. I am marrying my fiancé, Oswald. Dr. Oswald Grant. I told you about him. He's a plastic surgeon."

"Why would anyone like that marry you? You live in a fantasy world. I blame it on those books, all those made-up *stories.*" She hissed out the word as if she were saying "all that syphilis" or "all those scorpions."

I turned to Nancy and mimed my feelings in a series of creative gestures. Then I said, "Yes, it's every girl's fantasy, marrying someone as wonderful as Oswald." I told her the date and location of the wedding. "Oswald hopes that you will be there, and Nancy is really excited about seeing you, too. Good-bye, Mother."

I handed the phone back to Nancy. "She thinks I'm pregnant and making the whole thing up."

"Your mother Regina is most heinous. Let's talk about something happy-making. Your dress."

"You're not going to try to stuff me in a sheath, are you?"

"I'd stuff you in, but those cannonballs of yours would shoot right out." She handed me the binder. "Pick your favorites."

I opened to the section marked *Gowns,* expecting to see wedding dresses. Instead there was a compilation of pictures: old line drawings of models in couture, celebrities, even teenagers in prom gowns. The amazing thing was that most of these dresses were suitable to a girl with curves.

As I looked through the pictures, Nancy said, "What did you and Toodles do?"

I mentioned that I'd met one of our F.U. acquaintances at a gallery opening, talked to a famous author, and sat at Paolo's chef's table.

Nancy narrowed her eyes. "Toodles never traveled in those circles. She was more bridge-with-the-alumni club."

"Paolo, but we call him Pally, made a pass at me," I said quickly.

"Did you *do* him? Does he have a giant salami-like—"

"Nancy!"

"But it's okay to *do* someone on vacation. It's one of the Three Major Exceptions. Exception One is doing someone you've done before. Exception Two is doing someone on vacation. And Exception Three is doing someone because he's so scorching hot you'd be crazy to miss the opportunity."

I kept looking down at the pictures in the binder. "You don't really believe that, do you?"

"The trifecta would be to go on vacation and run into someone you'd sexed up before who's scorching hot."

I got a creepy feeling that Nancy had suddenly developed psychic abilities. "Does your husband share your philosophy?"

"Todd." She said it like a four-letter word. "It doesn't occur to him that I'd want to have sex with anyone but him because his pedigree is so superior."

If there wasn't so much antipathy between Todd and me, I would have talked to her about any problems she was having with him. I regretted the barriers that had come up between us over the years, although her marriage to a pompous ass had been more optional than my accidental vampirishness.

"Oswald gave me a loft last night as a wedding present."

"*Es verdad?*"

"*Es* totally *verdad.* You could have knocked me over with something small and light. An oil-blotting tissue."

"All I got was a mixed portfolio of high-tech stock."

"Oswald wants me to remodel it and rent it. I'm sure it's a good idea."

"Then stop looking like he gave you a vacuum cleaner. I'll help you remodel it. I'm a genius at that stuff. I've got that vision thing."

I turned a page of the binder and saw a stunning photo of Sophia Loren in a satin cocktail dress. "She looks like a goddess," I said. "Why are you showing me dresses I can't have?"

"O ye of belittling faith. You haven't even asked if I've called your future mother-in-law. I have, and she adores me. She will come straight to me for anything and I will steer her in the direction of light, sense, and all that is fabulous."

Nancy and I spent a few hours going over wedding details.

She thought of things that would never occur to me and went through all my needs on an elaborate checklist. Then she said, "Don't you have a swimming pool here?"

I took Nancy to the pool compound. She was very impressed by the retractable roof and I was happy to have company who could enjoy the sun with me. We stripped down and splashed in the nude, and by the time we returned to the house, we were drowsy with sun and warmth.

The worst—calling my mother Regina—was over and Nancy seemed to have everything in control. I was feeling hopeful about the wedding when Nancy kissed me good-bye and left.

ten

don't go staking my heart

It took me four trips to carry my essentials from the master bedroom to the maid's room. I settled my writing gear on the old wooden desk. I crawled underneath and found where I had scratched my initials. Using the end of a paper clip, I added Daisy RIP with the date. She used to sleep on the bed beside me, my first friend at Casa Dracula.

I made a cocktail (calf blood, mineral water, a dash of Tabasco, and a squish of lime) and sorted through my pile of mail. A white envelope held a terse rejection letter from an agent: "The material you submitted does not fit our needs at this time."

I tossed it into the recycling bin and settled in a chair with the latest edition of the *Weekly Exposition*. One of my friends was a stringer for the tabloid, so I'd subscribed. His brilliant story about a senator's love baby with a Venusian princess was very inspiring and made me eager to begin working on *Don Pedro's* project.

Since I intended to fabricate most of the story, I'd begun to think of it not as a memoir, but as a *fauxoir*. I began plotting out the astonishing tale of a boy born in the jungle whose great spiritual gifts are immediately recognized. I had a peanut butter and jelly sandwich and grape juice while I worked.

When Oswald came home at about nine and found me in my new digs, he gave me a kiss and said, "What are you doing?"

"I'm working on my special project. Are you hungry? Do you want me to make you a sandwich?" This was how things had become when we didn't have guests here—we were careless about our hours and meals, especially since Oswald worked longer and longer hours.

"Thanks, but I already ate." His eyes looked worn out, with bluish shadows under them.

"You're tired. Do you want to watch a movie tonight? Or I can give you a massage."

"I've got some more work to take care of. How was your day?"

I wanted to tell him that he worked too hard, but that would only lead to an unsatisfying discussion. "Nancy is an event-planning genius. We went over all the wedding arrangements, and we already have a color scheme."

He had an "I'm trying to be attentive" expression, but I could tell he was preoccupied. "That's good."

"Yes, cream, spring green, and shades of plum."

"Sounds good, but don't make it too dramatic."

"Do you mean 'Mexican'?"

"If I meant Mexican, I would say Mexican," he said with a grin. "I mean that I prefer more subtle color schemes."

"Subtlety is not style," I said. "Nancy's taste is impeccable.

Also, she spent a crazy amount on letterpress invitations." I got up from my desk and stretched.

"That's okay, but I'd appreciate it if you and Nancy could spare me the gruesome details."

"Are you giving us carte blanche?"

"I'm giving you credit card blanche. My mother's going to start launching her assault soon enough, and I've got to rest up in case I need to throw myself on a grenade."

"Ah, Nancy's already spoken to her. Your mother loves her." Oswald looked skeptical. "I even told my mother Regina today," I added.

"Did you really? Good for you."

"She thinks I'm making the whole thing up because I read too many books."

He laughed and kissed the top of my head. "I'll be in the study."

I went to the family room, which felt too big and empty, and watched a show about celebrity weddings. The program divided the total wedding cost by the length of the marriage. Ordering a ten-foot-tall cake seemed to spell doom for any relationship.

I called Nancy and told her to turn on the show. "Are you watching? What do you think of that leather bustier?"

"She looks like a streetwalking ho! But check out her pretty tiara."

"I love tiaras. Can I wear one?"

"Not unless you're Hollywood trash or royalty. Otherwise it is Not Done. You might be able to wear one if you marry your lover. Doesn't he have some title?"

"Yes, it's 'doctor.' "

"I mean Ian Ducharme. Gigi says he's a lord."

"He told me it was a prize-with-purchase. An ancestor bought a bog and got the title." Bogs made me think of peat, and peat made me think of gardening. "Will you make sure the flowers on my cake are organically grown, but bugless?"

We dished until the show was over, then I ran out to the pond. I pulled out the weeds that had begun to sprout between the rocks around Daisy's grave. I occasionally glanced around, hoping to see the new dog, but he didn't show up. I hadn't realized until she was gone how much I'd relied on Daisy's companionship.

The next morning, I had a good block of time to work on *Don* Pedro's memoir. Because he was a florid speaker, I wrote his story in extravagant purple prose. I began each chapter with a tidbit of mystical nonsense, such as, "The passageway to true transmutation can be achieved only by grasping the wings of the august condor and guiding it into the raging gorge of our fears."

When I was writing like this, I forgot everything else. I could practically hear *Don* Pedro speaking as the words flowed from my mind to my fingers on the keyboard. When I'd asked *Don* Pedro where he was from, he hadn't answered, and none of his documents had any early biographical information.

I thought he should have an exotic background. I wrote that he was born in Belize, because I knew they had jaguars and that pirates used to hide in the coves there. I wrote that *Don* Pedro was born at the same moment that the village shaman died and a magnificent jaguar appeared on the roof of his palm frond hut. There was a rumble of thunder, a flash of lightning, and the animal vanished as mysteriously as it had appeared.

The story raced along. I was just figuring out how to incorporate the discovery of cursed pirate booty when Oswald's office manager called to tell me he wouldn't be home for dinner again. "Complications with a patient who'd lied about her medical history. They never learn."

"Do you know how long he'll be?"

"You know how these things go, hon. Could be another two hours, could be six."

I was alone again. I blasted some music and worked until the sky darkened. Then I changed into my warm-up pants and went outside. I ran on the path around the perimeter of the property. I was by the creek when I saw a dog coming toward me. It was my pal from yesterday.

He joined me and stayed at my side while we circled the fields. I could hear his gentle panting and the padding of his paws on the soft soil. I slowed to a walk at the pond. "The return of *El Lobo*," I said aloud. "That would be a good title for a story." The creature's ears went back and his mouth opened in the way I always thought of as smiling.

I sat at Daisy's rock and the dog lay down at my feet. It was funny how comforting a companion could be, even one that didn't talk. A shooting star appeared in the sky, and I wished that the wedding would go wonderfully and that the groom would be ecstatic with his bride. In hindsight, I should have been more specific.

When I got back to the house, the dog looked at me. "Okay, come in," I said, even though I knew Oswald wouldn't be happy. The dog joined me on the sofa in the family room as I flipped through television stations. "I think I'll call you Pal. Is that okay?" His tail thumped on the sofa.

The dog stayed with me as I watched an old spy thriller starring Cary Grant and Ingrid Bergman, but then he heard something outside and went trotting off to the front door. I opened it and listened. There were only the usual sounds of the wind rustling the branches and a dog barking in the distance. Pal looked back at me and ran off into the night.

"*Vaya con Dios,* Pal." I watched until I could no longer see him, and then I went to bed.

When Oswald came down to breakfast the next morning, I said, "The dog came back."

Oswald kissed me and then poured a cup of coffee for himself. "That 'dog' looks exactly like an Eastern timber wolf. I don't know if it's even legal to keep them." He sat beside me and said, "Can you call Animal Control today to see if someone has reported one missing?"

"What if I want to adopt him?"

He sighed. "The shelter is full of dogs that could use a good home. And you could pay attention to some of the dogs we already have."

"Those dogs like you and Ernie better. But Pal has a connection with me."

"How are you going to feel when that creature rips up one of the lambs or attacks the horses?"

"I took him to the barn and nothing like that happened."

"Nothing yet."

Our discussion degenerated into an argument that involved failed attempts to domesticate wolves (Oz); allusions to Romulus and Remus and the birth of Western civilization (me); saintly dogs awaiting adoption (Oz); kismet (me); claims that if I had a real job, I wouldn't get preoccupied by wild beasts (Oz); snipes that even feral animals paid more attention to me than Oz (me).

The words "Type-A mama's boy" and "immature, irresponsible dreamer" may have been uttered. Doors were slammed. It was a very exciting way to start the day. It had taken me a while to get used to the idea that an argument didn't mean the end of the relationship. I was riding high on self-righteousness when I realized that we wouldn't be able to have make-up sex that night.

The next few weeks assumed a pattern. Oswald left early and came back late. I wrote with such fervor that the hours flew by. In the evenings, Pal would show up for my run and to hang out. Nancy didn't seem to be calling me very much about the wedding, but when she did, she operated with such efficiency that we were able to quickly finish business and move on to important gossip.

Neither Oswald nor Ernie was ecstatic about my dog. But they made inquiries and didn't hear of anyone missing a wolf, or any new predatory attacks, so they relaxed a little.

We all relaxed a little. Which was why I didn't run in circles screaming and rending my clothes when the Council's Rules Committee mailed a note telling me that they were sending their new wedding coordinator to meet with me. She would arrive tomorrow and stay with us for a few days.

"I hope she doesn't interfere with my writing," I told Oswald. "I've got a deadline."

Oswald commented that I hadn't been back to the loft to see about renovations. He'd bought me books on real estate investing. I had looked at them—not read them exactly, but I'd opened the books and picked out individual words. I was disappointed to learn that amortization had nothing to do with *amor*, and equity wasn't about social consciousness. I'd always heard that men in relationships eventually revealed horrible things about their perverse passions, but I'd assumed that meant suggesting bizarre sexual acts. This real estate issue could not be resolved with a slap of Oswald's hand and an "Only in your dreams!"

"I'll study those books later," I told him. "Should we put this wedding person in your grandmother's cottage?"

"You know how Grandmama is about her things."

"I suppose we can put her in the room next to yours, Oz, if you don't mind."

He shrugged. "Whatever you think is best."

I spent an hour preparing the guest room for the vamp wedding coordinator. I changed the linens, and put a vase of 'Kathleen' hybrid musk roses on the dressing table and several new magazines in a rack by the bed. The guest bath was clean, with a new bottle of shampoo and new bars of honeysuckle-scented soap. The stairs might be difficult if she was elderly or frail, but we would deal with that if the problem arose.

That night I felt antsy, not just because of our expected guest but also because Oswald and I were finding it increasingly difficult to live boink-free. We kept grappling deliciously with each other and then he'd break away guiltily as if he'd caught himself doing something awful.

"Oswald, no one would know . . ."

"I'm not taking that risk," he said. "I'm not going to jeopardize your situation with the Council."

"If I told you that you could cut me, would you change your mind?"

His pupils widened and he pressed his body against me. "We can do that without the sex," he said. The excitement made his voice catch, and that made me recoil. It wasn't Oswald's fault that he wanted my blood. Of course he wanted my blood. He was a fricking vampire. "No, you were right, Oz. Let's wait."

The next day, Oswald wished me luck with the wedding co-ordinator and said he'd be home early and would pick up things for dinner.

Ernie brought a demibottle of rabbit blood from the barn. "Everyone seems to like rabbit," he said. "I've got some nanny goat, too, if she wants that."

I fussed around the house, getting more nervous by the minute. When the buzzer sounded, I pressed the button that automatically opened the front gate, and then took a last look in the hallway mirror. My hair was pulled back and I wore a blue pique cotton shirt and black slacks. I was too tan, but still presentable as a vampire bride.

I walked outside as a pearly white luxury sedan came down the drive, sun reflecting on the windshield. The car stopped and the driver's door opened. A woman dressed in a white linen shell, topped with a sheer jacket, and white cigarette slacks got out. Her dyed ebony hair was cut in a severely chic bob, and her sunglasses were huge. A beaten gold collar was displayed on her long, bony neck.

She was striking and beautiful, if you thought beautiful meant skeletal, overly made-up, and well-dressed.

She held out her long, thin arms like a raptor about to plunge and attack. Her scarlet lips opened into a smile and she said, "Aren't you going to kiss me hello, Young Lady?"

My brain shortwired. After a second I said, "What are you doing here?"

"The Council sent me here to help you plan your wedding. It's my new job!"

Like a zombie, I walked into Cornelia Ducharme's perfumed embrace. On the outside I was smiling, but on the inside I was screaming.

eleven

my bff (bestest frenemy forever)

Cornelia seemed to have forgotten all the nastiness of her last departure from the ranch, but I had not. I was also acutely aware that her brother might have told her of our recent, uhm, socializing.

When my mind began to function again, I extricated myself from her hug.

"Be a dear and get my bags, would you?" She opened the trunk of the car and took out a small makeup case. "I'm dying of thirst. Where's that gorgeous fiancé of yours?" she said, her voice fading as she walked to the house.

She had three large cases in what looked to be white alligator. I pulled them out of the trunk, wondering exactly how long she planned to stay. The heavy suitcases banged against my legs as I carried them into the house.

I took the bags upstairs, wondering if it was too late to switch Cornelia to a room farther away from Oswald's.

She suddenly appeared behind me and said, "So wonderful to be back here again. I'll fix us some drinks, shall I?"

When I heard her footsteps going down the stairs, I slipped into our bedroom, closed the door, and called Oswald. His receptionist answered, and I told her that I had to talk to Oswald right away. "It's urgent."

It took him a minute to get to the phone. "Milagro, I was in with a patient. Is this really important?"

"My brain is frying with disbelief. Cornelia's here and she says that she's our wedding consultant. Did you know anything about this?"

"Cornelia Ducharme? You're kidding!"

"Yes, Cornelia Ducharme. Why would they send one of your old girlfriends here?"

"She wasn't my . . ." He let out an exasperated breath. "I can't deal with this now. Can you try to be civil to her until I get home?"

"You owe me, Oswald K. Grant."

"I know I do."

When I went downstairs, Cornelia was opening and closing the kitchen cabinets. I said, "Those suitcases aren't really white alligator, are they?"

"White alligator is endangered," she said, which did not answer my question. She closed a cabinet door. "I'm useless in these places. Wherever is Edna?"

"She's away with her young actor friend."

"Ah, she is my role model. I don't suppose there are any delectable young actors here?"

"No, but there are some extremely appealing cowboy types." I stopped before describing the beauty of worn Wranglers on a taut butt since I didn't want to encourage Cornelia to go hunting for a snack.

"I think it's just amazing that you and Edna know how to cook things."

"Who wants to eat a fresh kill raw?" I added a "ha ha" at the end to show I was sort of joking. I arranged mineral water, ice, limes, and the demibottle of blood on a tray. "Is rabbit all right?"

"If that's all you have." She ran her long, manicured finger down my cheek and I stared into her heavily mascaraed eyes.

"It's all I have for *you.*"

She had a merry laugh. "You're still a fierce little thing, aren't you? What I wouldn't give for a taste!" She strolled away. I picked up the tray and followed her to the living room.

When we were seated there, she sipped her drink and said, "I realize that we may not have parted on the best of terms."

"You called me a common Mexican girl."

"Did I? Well, there's nothing wrong with that."

"No, there isn't," I agreed. "And now you're here."

She patted my knee. "We'll have a wonderful time. I asked for the job when I heard that the first wedding scheduled was for you and Oswald. Consider this my gift to you."

First the loft and now this. What ever happened to people giving a nice pair of salad tongs as a wedding gift? "In a perfect world, I would let bygones be bygones. Sadly, I live in a reality-based world. What I want to know is, are you here to ruin my wedding? Have you decided to try to sink your claws into Oswald?"

"Young Lady, how can you say such things! I want nothing

more than to see you happily married to the man you love. That's why I'm here."

"Are you telling me the truth?"

"I swear on my parents' watery graves."

"Cornelia, if you make any attempt to get at Oswald, I will make your life a living hell," I said. That business concluded, I said, "So, how've you been?"

"Wonderful. I just spent a few days with Ian and Ilena," she said. "Isn't she incredible? They make the perfect couple."

Ilena would have told her about meeting me, I suppose. "She's very striking," I said. I hated asking Cornelia for a favor, but I blamed myself for this situation—well, myself, Toodles's illness, overbooked hotels, and Oswald's own jealousy. "I'd appreciate your not discussing your brother in front of Oswald. He has this attitude . . ."

"That Ian still fancies you?" She laughed. "Oswald wouldn't worry if he'd seen Ilena. After all, she's a plastic surgeon's ideal, isn't she? Long legs, perfect features, platinum hair, so stunning and thin."

I'd been reassured and insulted so prettily that I couldn't complain. "Why don't you tell me about the ceremony? As you might have heard, I've had some bad experiences with the old rituals."

"Yes, it was all the talk at one of the Nixons' croquet parties." She poured more blood into her drink, tasted it, and made a face. Cornelia looked down on animal blood, but it was the staple that most vamps used, and ours was especially good. "I'm here now because it's best to start on the folk costumes now so there's no rush. The ceremony itself is the old mumbo jumbo. You're such a smart girl, you'll have no problem memorizing it quickly. It's a lovely ritual, quite innocent and romantic."

Cornelia could be an amusing companion, if you had a liking for amoral, promiscuous, and adventurous Eurotrashy types, which I apparently did. "I'm fairly sure we have different definitions of innocent," I said, but couldn't help smiling.

"Possibly. I called Pepper on the way up and told him we'd meet in a little while. He said he would be enchanted to see us again."

I doubted that Ernest "Pepper" Culpepper, biker and former purveyor of home-crafted pharmaceuticals, had ever used the word "enchanted" in his life. I'd met Pepper on Cornelia's last visit, and we'd kept in touch. "I'm rather surprised that you remember him."

"I always remember delightful people."

While I really liked Pepper, Oswald discouraged me from visiting the biker's favorite watering hole alone. But I wouldn't be alone if I went with Cornelia. "Sure, we could go hang with him."

A visit with Pepper required a different ensemble. I changed into jeans, a vintage CBGB T-shirt, and red heels. I clasped wide silver bracelets on my wrists, made my hair big with a generous amount of product, and drew on dark eyeliner. Glancing in the mirror, I thought I looked great. I looked like myself.

Because Cornelia wasn't Ian's biological sister, she didn't have his (and my) resistance to booze. "I'll drive," I said. "Alcohol doesn't really affect me."

"You got that from Ian?" she said. When I nodded she added, "How sad. It's one of life's pleasures." She handed me the keys.

I drove north, to the small town of Lower Sky. Pepper was leaning against the wall of his favorite hangout, swigging from a longneck bottle of beer. He wore his usual costume: black jeans, a Harley T-shirt, and a black leather vest. He was wearing his beard in three braids with beads at the end. He gave us an infectious gap-toothed grin when we walked up the sidewalk, and then he swept us up in his beefy arms.

We exchanged greetings and grabs. He went for a clutch of my bottom, and I felt up his biceps. "Nice guns. You working out, Pepper?"

"Yeah, there's a new gym in town. Me and the boys all got memberships."

"You must be a vision in Lycra workout clothes," I said.

He snorted a laugh and led us inside the honky-tonk. Pretty soon everyone was buying rounds for everyone else. The waitress said, "Long time no see, sugar. Where's your man?"

She meant Ian, but I said, "They're all around, hon," which made Pepper laugh.

A few of the guys got handsy, but Pepper would thwack them on the shoulder and they'd lay off. It saved me the trouble of walloping one and then explaining my ungirlish strength.

"Whatchu been doing, Milagro?" Pepper asked. "You too good for us these days?"

This was a complex question about socioeconomics and ethics that I could not answer succinctly, so I didn't. "You know I always enjoy your company."

"Pepper, your beard is absolutely wonderful," Cornelia said. "Will you take me for a spin on your hog?"

"You betcha. Let's down a couple drinks first."

Time flies by when you're hanging out with bikers shooting pool, drinking Wild Turkey, and playing Southern rock on the jukebox. I had joined in a chorus of "Sweet Home Alabama" when I heard my phone ringing.

It was Oswald. "Where are you?"

"Hi, Oz. We're with Pepper."

Cornelia took the phone from me. "Darling, I can't wait to see you. Milagro and I will leave right away!"

We really would have, but navigating our exit was somehow delayed. As Pepper was finally walking out with us, he said to Cornelia, "When am I gonna see you again? And your bro?"

"You'll see us at Milagro's wedding. You've got to promise to save me a dance."

Pepper tilted his head, setting the braids of his beard swinging. "You getting hitched?" he asked me.

"I'm making an honest man out of Oswald."

"Glad you're not trying to do that with me!" Pepper said. "So it's Oswald you settled on? Send the invitation here."

"I'll do that," I said.

When we finally got in the car and I was driving home, Cornelia leaned back in her seat and said, "I'm glad I was wrong."

"What do you mean?"

"I thought you'd become a dull little Country Mouse."

I felt the stab. "Who told you that?"

"Why else would you register for gifts at that dusty old department store? Not that there's anything wrong with that—the Grant family has always been very upstanding and respectable. They'd appreciate your new *maturity*."

"The gift registration was for Oswald's relatives, and there's nothing wrong with growing up."

"There's a difference between growing up and giving up, Young Lady." Instead of elaborating, she began talking about the wedding ceremony. "The Council will appoint someone to perform the service. There's a sweet young fellow who applied to officiate ceremonies, but he's having problems with the language."

"I always thought it sounded like a robot chewing metal," I

said, trying not to think of the way the words had sounded when Ian spoke them to me. "Can't we have it in English?"

"You can ask Sam to submit a request for you, but you may want to appear more accommodating."

"Reciprocity would be nice. The Council treats me like I've got cooties."

When I explained the curse of cooties to Cornelia, she started laughing. I knew she was a terrible person, so why did I have fun with her? I remembered Ms. Smith's description of her as a child, and I felt a wave of empathy for the scared little girl she'd once been.

Oswald was sitting on the terrace as we drove up. He looked annoyed. Cornelia got out of the car and dashed into his arms, crying, "Oswald, you sexy creature!" and he broke into a smile.

They did the kiss-kiss thing, and then she held him at arm's length. "Darling, you get better looking every time I see you."

"And you look beautiful, as always," he said. "I wasn't expecting you, though."

"I asked the Council not to say anything, because I wanted to surprise you." Cornelia and Oswald shared an old-friend-well-met smile that made me all too aware that they'd known each other long before I'd met them. Cornelia was always flirtatious. I didn't mind it around Pepper, and now I tried to control my suspicions as I edged up next to Oswald.

I slipped my arm around his waist and said, "I'm sorry we're late, Oz. We were hanging with Pepper and . . ."

Oswald didn't stop smiling, but his expression shifted fractionally in disapproval.

Who was he to judge Pepper, just because of Pepper's more freewheeling, frequently criminal lifestyle? I pulled my arm back.

"The food's staying warm in the oven," Oswald said. "Why don't we eat?"

He'd picked up food from the posh deli near his clinic: chicken in a tomato-caper sauce, smoked red pepper soup, a salad, and a berry tart. Now I felt bad that he'd rushed from work to the market and hurried home while we were learning to shoot dice and screaming, "Mama needs a new push-up bra!"

I asked, "Cornelia, have you been seeing anyone?"

"No one special," she said with a sideways glance at Oswald. "Most men seem so . . . so very ordinary. Even our kind have lost touch with their instincts." She sounded almost wistful, but it lasted only a moment. "Oh, la! The country air makes me so sentimental."

"You wouldn't want all men as 'instinctual' as Pepper anyway," I said.

"Don't be so sure," she said.

Oswald said, "That bar isn't a very safe place for women by themselves."

"How sweet of you to be so protective of us," Cornelia said, "especially since I know that Milagro can take care of herself so terribly well."

"That's not a reason to go looking for trouble," Oswald replied.

"Then we won't," she said. "Oswald, when I was in Gstaad, several of my friends were raving about your work. Tell me everything you've been doing."

Oswald was happy to do so in great detail. Cornelia asked questions so informed they seemed to indicate personal experience with cosmetic procedures. Not that you could tell with vamps, who aged well and healed smoothly.

I saw Oz's happy face and wished I could be more interested

in his profession. Unfortunately I associated it with my mother Regina. I tried to listen now, but found my mind wandering. I was thinking about the next chapter of *Don* Pedro's story when I heard a series of short, sharp barks.

It had gotten late and I'd missed my run. "Excuse me," I said, standing up. There was an extra piece of chicken I could take to Pal.

"One of your many dogs?" Cornelia asked.

"Somebody else's dog," I said. "But he comes round in the evening."

"He's not a dog," Oswald said. "I'm fairly certain that it's an Eastern timber wolf."

Cornelia turned to me. "Really? May I see him?"

"Come on." I picked up the chicken breast, getting sauce all over my fingers. Cornelia hadn't a spot or smudge on her white clothes.

We all went out the front door and I called, "Here, boy." I scanned the fields and a moment later I saw him loping toward us. He stopped about twenty feet away, looking wary. "Come," I said, and I moved toward him, holding the chicken aloft. "Got a treat for you."

He approached slowly, keeping watch of my companions.

"Milagro," Oswald said, but then Pal gingerly took the chicken from my fingers. He swallowed the meat in about one bite and then carefully licked the sauce from my fingers.

"See, he's a good fellow." I scratched the area between his ears. He took another look at us and loped toward the cover of trees.

"A magnificent creature," Cornelia said. "I can't remember the last time I had wolf's blood, Oswald. Can you?"

"I'd rather have his than the other way around."

"Neither of those situations is going to happen," I snapped. "Pal is better behaved than most people I know."

Oswald said, "Sure, if you're talking about people like Pepper's crowd. But I'm the one who's legally and morally responsible for everything that goes on here, and I don't like you encouraging that animal to come around."

I was furious that he didn't trust my judgment. "So my human friends aren't good enough, and neither are my canine friends! I didn't realize that I'd become incapable of making my own decisions." I walked angrily into the house, seeing Cornelia's amused expression, and I shouted over my shoulder, "And in conclusion, you can go to hell, Oswald."

While I was putting away the food and dishes from dinner with much banging and stomping, I realized that this was perhaps not the best display of marital compatibility we could have set forth. Well, I couldn't help that Oswald was behaving like a complete jackass.

I kept expecting him to come into the kitchen and apologize. But he hadn't by the time I'd cleaned everything. I glanced at the clock. Where were he and Cornelia? They hadn't come back into the house and they weren't on the terrace.

I stepped outside and looked toward the barn. Lights glowed there. They'd gone for a nightcap in the tasting room. Why did I feel excluded when I was the one who'd stomped off?

I spent a few hours reading and writing, expecting them to return at any moment. I felt foolish and worried despite the fact that Oswald hadn't shown any inappropriate interest in Cornelia.

I closed the door to my bedroom and called Winnie, Sam's wife. Sam answered groggily. "What is it, Young Lady?"

"I need to talk to Winnie."

"She's sleeping. Can I help?"

Sam wasn't exactly the sort of person I naturally confided in, but he was trustworthy and smart. "The Council appointed Cornelia Ducharme as the wedding consultant. She's here now."

"Oh," he said. It was a weighty "oh." He'd had his own close encounter with the she-devil.

" 'Oh' exactly. Sam, could the Council have done this just to break us up?"

He chuckled. "I can't see the Council entrusting Cornelia to do anything like that," he said. "She's actually a good fit for the job. It's not a big commitment, but requires someone who's social and comfortable with all branches of the family."

"Why would she even want this job?"

"Maybe she wanted some independence. The position has an expense account and great perks." In the background, the baby began crying. "I've got to go," Sam said. "I'm still negotiating with the Council about the loyalty oath, and if you can give Cornelia a chance, things will go smoother."

After we said good-bye, I cogitated on Cornelia's situation. Perhaps she, like Nancy, was trying to do something with her talents, such as they were.

My pledge to give Cornelia a chance was tested later that night when I heard the low murmur of her and Oswald's voices and laughter as they came in the house. Their footsteps faded as they went down the hall toward the stairway and then up to bed.

twelve

half-baked and fully cooked

Oswald looked as innocent as a bunny the next morning. But while bunnies *appear* innocent, their reproduction patterns belie fluffy purity. He had already made coffee when I got up and went into the kitchen. He gave me a sideways glance and said, "Are you over your tantrum?"

"I don't have tantrums," I said. "I occasionally express outrage at injustice."

He had the nerve to smirk as he handed me my coffee. I went to the table and saw a book there. There was a photo of a wolf on the cover. "I was wrong," he said.

"I'm glad you're finally admitting it."

"That creature is not an Eastern timber wolf. It's a Mackenzie Valley wolf." He came to the table and flipped the book open to a bookmark.

There was a picture of a wolf that looked exactly like Pal.

"There is a vague resemblance," I admitted. "Something of a similarity around the muzzle perhaps."

"A vague resemblance?"

"A strongly vague resemblance. Which is nothing at all in the general scheme of the animal world. Dogs and wolves are practically the same genetically."

"Small alterations in genes can result in drastic differences in character and behavior."

"I'm aware of that. And your point is?"

He gave me a hard look.

"All right, all right," I said. "But he's been around all this time and nothing has happened." I moved closer to Oswald, running my hand over his yummy firm thigh. "Oswald . . ."

"Good morning!" Cornelia walked into the kitchen wearing a slinky black nightgown with a matching robe that wafted back as she walked. The word "negligee" came to mind.

Oswald took my hand, which was moving northward, and held it. "Morning, Cornelia. Sleep well?"

"Like the dead." She looked around the room, her eyes falling on the coffeepot as if it had personally disappointed her.

"I could fire up the espresso maker," Oswald said when he noticed her expression. "Or would you like orange juice?" He went to the fridge and took out a pitcher of blood orange juice.

"Juice only." She shook her head at the muffins I took from the cupboard.

"What's on the agenda today?" I asked.

She sipped her juice before answering. "We went over the plans and requirements with Ernesto last night. He has the arch and platform from Sam and Winnie's wedding in storage, and he'll give them a new coat of paint."

"Is there anything that I can do?" I asked.

"Of course!" Cornelia said. "You'll be sewing the traditional marriage costumes, the bride and groom's tunics."

I tried to catch Oswald's eye, but he was suddenly fascinated with the scenery outside the window. Turning to Cornelia, I said, "I don't sew. I can sew on a button, but that's about it." My few needle skills were learned from my *abuela,* who had shown me how to hem dishcloths and darn socks. My mother Regina always threw away anything that was imperfect in her eyes, yet another reason she had frequently forgotten to pick me up from the library.

Cornelia said, "They are such simple garments. A child could sew them."

"Oswald has excellent needle skills," I said. Sure, he usually worked with human flesh, but his technique was renowned. "Can't he sew his own tunic?"

Cornelia and Oswald exchanged a look with each other and laughed. "No, darling," she said. "The bride does this as a display of her love and wifely skills. The Council expects our tradition to be honored."

I sighed. "Cornelia, are you telling me that you're going to sew the wedding tunics when you get married?"

"Membership has its privileges. I shall hire someone to do it for me and we'll all pretend that I've done everything myself from shearing the sheep to weaving the cloth." She shrugged her narrow shoulders. "That is, if I ever decide to marry. Oswald, you should have seen the last fellow the registry matched me up with," she said. The vampires had a dating service that matched up members based on their fertility levels. "One of the Van Burens, I can't remember which because they all bore me to distraction."

"Now, Corny, don't be mean. The Van Burens aren't flashy, but they're good, honest men."

She started laughing. "If I ever fall into a coma, I'll be sure to look them up, dear."

Oswald glanced at his watch. "I've got to run. Are you two going to stay around here, or will I have to bail you out of jail this evening?"

"Ha ha and ha," I said. "Will you be back for dinner?"

"I'll call later."

He kissed me good-bye and then kissed Cornelia, too. It was only a kiss on the cheek, but I didn't think he needed to get quite so close to her.

When he'd gone, Cornelia said, "Come upstairs and I'll give you the drawings of the tunics."

I accompanied her to the guest room and she gave me a sketch of a dark red, hooded cloak, embroidered at the cuffs and hem with flowers and fruit, for Oswald, and a simpler red gown, for me. I asked, "How am I going to make these?"

"It will take a few hours, but isn't Oswald worth a little effort? Here is a detail of the needlework." She gave me another sketch with an illustration of intricate embroidery.

"Are these pomegranates?" I asked.

"Yes, and grapes, figs. You should use a heavyweight silk fabric and silk thread. Let's go into town and buy your supplies."

She seemed to accept that I would drive her car. I flicked on the stereo and was surprised to hear an intriguing modern tango. "This sounds familiar," I said. "I think my friend Mercedes had this band at her club in the City. Have you been there? It's called My Dive."

"Not yet, but I've heard of it."

"You should check out the schedule before you go. Her taste is very eclectic."

"Ian is so passionate about music, you know, and he's always introducing me to new things."

At an antique store in town, Cornelia bought a variety of tiny objects, including a china pillbox and silver hair combs. "Ilena will like these, don't you think?"

"They're pretty. I don't know much about her taste."

"Very chic, which is to be expected with *most* of Ian's women."

"I don't doubt it," I said, unable to resist adding, "But she did seem a little . . . bloodless."

"Not everyone can be a pretty, chubby little pickle like you." Cornelia laughed merrily.

"I can't believe Ian told you that," I said, even more embarrassed to feel my cheeks grow hot.

"Not Ian. Ilena told me. She couldn't believe that you and he . . . Well, it was unlikely."

"Yes, especially since Oswald, who is so handsome and smart and successful and a decent human being, is more my type."

"Then aren't you lucky to marry him!"

We stopped at a quilting and crafts shop, and the sales clerk sold me fabric and silk embroidery floss for the wedding tunics. I signed up for a beginners' sewing class that met twice a week.

Then we went to a small café on the outskirts of town. As I parked, I noticed that the *For Sale* sign was gone from the nursery next door. A wholesale grower's truck was parked in the drive, and a guy was unloading flats of bright annuals. This was the nursery I'd considered buying, but I'd been unwilling to deal with the chore of running a business.

And now I was stuck with remodeling a loft.

We were shown to a table on the back patio under the shade of old pear trees, their ripening fruit hanging pendent.

We shared small plates of food and a bottle of a light, fruity red wine. "Cornelia, is this your first job?"

"Hmm?" She was sorting through a fruit salad, picking out all the juicy blackberries, and popping them between her crimson lips. "I've always seen my life as my job. Ian thought I'd like it."

"Do you?"

"I don't know why I didn't think of it myself," she said.

Curiosity overcame caution and I asked, "What was Ian like as a child?"

"He was the same," she said, and then her expression softened. "After my parents died, I was sent to his family. He was just a boy, but he took my hand and said, 'Now you will be my sister and I will be your brother forever.' He took me up to the bedroom next to his. He'd brought in all his favorite things, books, toys, a globe, his old teddy bear. He stayed close to me, making sure I wasn't alone or scared. He liked to spin the globe and tell me about all the places in the world we'd visit when we grew up." She smiled. "He kept his promise and we have visited all those places."

I couldn't see her eyes behind her sunglasses, but I heard the catch in her voice as she said, "That's why I'm so happy that he's found someone who makes him happy."

"So you think she's the one, then?"

Cornelia smiled. "What I think isn't important. He believes she's the one. I hope to help coordinate my brother's wedding."

"Won't the Council object if Ian marries an outsider? Even if her family is associated with your people?"

"They'll be furious. But Ian doesn't let them dictate his life," she said. "Enough about my family. Let's talk about your wedding. Oswald will want to make improvements, naturally. What procedures have you planned?"

"I'm not having any procedures. Oswald loves me as I am."

"How sweet of him to say that! But Milagro, do be realistic. He is in the business of beauty."

"That's his business, which is not my life. I'm not going to be anyone's showroom exhibit."

"Don't be so touchy! I was obligated to ask in my capacity as the wedding adviser," she said soothingly. "How are your baking skills?"

"I can make cookies and brownies. Why?"

"You'll have to make the traditional bride's cake."

"Why does the bride have to make . . . ? Never mind. It's a display of her wifely skills, right?"

"You do catch on. You'll have to start immediately since the dried fruits must soak in the alcohol for two months, and the cake itself must be aged for an additional month so that its flavors ripen."

"Is this a fruitcake?" Like any sensible person, I hated fruitcake. "It *sounds* like fruitcake."

"You'll need to make enough for the wedding party." She reached into her handbag and took out a small binder. "Here are recipes that have been used in the last few generations."

The notebook held copies of recipes. Some were beautifully written, but others were typed and some were illegible scrawls. One had measurements with descriptions like "half the size of a peahen egg."

"Which is the best?"

"Choose any one you like. Sam and Winnie had a delicious spice-and-currant cake."

"I'll use that recipe, then."

"A pity that it's a family secret." She patted my hand. "Don't look so sad, pretty, chubby little pickle. Not every girl gets to marry a vampire."

"Cornelia, if you call me that one more time, I will drown you in a vat of holy water."

"Meow! Kitten with a whip."

I'd had enough of this tête-à-tête. "I think I'll pass on dessert. I'd like to go to the nursery next door."

"Wise decision. Skip desserts now and Oswald won't have to suck them out of your hips later."

"No one is ever going to cut me again, Cornelia."

"You mean besides Oswald. It *is* in your vows."

I tried to hide my surprise as I remembered the monogrammed penknife Oswald had given me. "I meant besides our recreational activities," I said.

We paid our tab and went to the nursery. The small, narrow building out front had been painted and there were new flower beds around the shrubs. The wonderful fragrances of greenery, compost, and mulch calmed me.

The inside of the shop hadn't been set up yet. Taped boxes were stacked on the floor by the bookshelves and display racks. I admired the jean-clad, taut rear end of the man bending over the counter by the register. I heard a sigh and saw that Cornelia was also appreciating the view.

"Hello," I said.

The man stood and turned and I recognized my blue-eyed piratical acquaintance from the botanical garden. He was as lustworthy as I remembered, in a Whitney Farms Organics T-shirt that stretched across his rangy shoulders, his long black hair tied back with a length of green gardener's twine. "Alfred Joseph!" I said. "What are you doing here?"

"Joseph Alfred," he corrected. "After you told me about this place, I checked it out and here I am. I needed to invest in something and get out of the City for a while."

I sensed movement next to me. Cornelia had shifted her slight weight to one leg and was wearing an "I vant to suck your everything" expression. "Cornelia, this is Joseph Alfred. We met in the City."

Joseph Alfred gave her a huge, unabashedly heterosexual grin. "A pleasure," he said.

"I'm sure it is," she murmured low enough to make him come closer.

I made a note to add that one to my catalog of flirting tricks.

"If you can hold on a sec, I'll show you around," he said.

"That would be marvelous, Mr. Alfred," Cornelia said.

"You can call me Joseph, sunshine," he said.

While Cornelia and I were waiting outside at the entrance to the lot, I said, "Are you suddenly interested in gardening?"

"You have the oddest ideas. He's got a unique quality, don't you think?"

"If you mean he's got a world-class butt, I am in complete concordance."

I heard someone cough behind me and turned to see Joseph Alfred standing there. I said, "Geez, you can sure sneak up on someone."

He looked amused. "Let's start with the deciduous shrubs and make our way around to the annuals."

Although the nursery wasn't finished, he'd already set out areas for different plant groups. He'd built a large arbor to cover the shade plants and even cleaned out the old pond for water plants. "I'll bring in the six-packs of petunias for Joe Average, but I'm going to specialize in rare and unusual fruit trees. I'll be getting in some improved varieties of heirloom pears that are resistant to fire blight."

"I'm going to be a regular customer."

"I'll give you the professional discount. In fact, if you've got any free time, I could use a part-time staffer."

Cornelia smiled and said, "She doesn't have any free time. She's getting ready for her wedding."

He could have had the decency to look disappointed, but instead he gazed at Cornelia. "I don't suppose you'd like a gardening job."

"You understand me so well already," she said.

He walked us to the drive, but he and Cornelia were so engrossed in each other that I wandered into the nursery again, jotting down descriptions of things I might want to buy later.

When I rejoined them, I saw a small critter scamper into the shrubs. "The animals have already discovered the new habitat," I said.

Joseph frowned. "I'm going to get some cats to keep vermin under control."

"Good luck," I said. "Our barn cats can barely keep up with all the field mice."

He walked us to the car and opened the driver's side door for Cornelia. "See you at seven, angel."

"Adieu, Joseph," she said.

When we were on our way back to the ranch, I said, "Did you make a date with him?"

"He made a date with me."

"I didn't think he was your type." I was hoping she wouldn't do something so terrible to him that I wouldn't be able to go back to the nursery.

"Gorgeous has always been my type, darling."

thirteen

the villainy of a fruitcake

When we got back home, Cornelia made appointments at the spa in town and dashed back out again. I spent the afternoon on my *fauxoir*, creating a fascinating meeting between *Don* Pedro and a wise witch woman in an Amazonian tribe. I put her in a parrot feather headdress, which added a nice visual, and she revealed her wisdom by repeating people's words, causing them to reflect on what they had said, the way psychiatrists do.

When I finished the scene, I looked at the fruitcake recipes. Oswald's grandmother had taught me a little about judging recipes, and my inexpert assessment was that these were stinkers. I called Edna and was happy when she answered her cell phone.

"Edna, how are you?"

"Good afternoon, Young Lady. What have you done now?"

"I deeply resent your implication that I only call you when I'm in trouble."

"Hmph."

"Where has Thomas taken you?"

Edna told me that while Thomas was shooting scenes in Montreal, she was visiting museums and enjoying all the amenities of their luxury hotel.

"Thank you for the highly edited, G-rated version of your stay with your sexy and addled young paramour," I said. "You'll never guess who has darkened our doorway. Cornelia Ducharme." I gave her a brief rundown of recent activities. "Now I have to make some horrible fruitcake. All the recipes look vile. Some call for suet. Isn't that something lardy that you put in bird feeders? Where is your recipe?"

"I don't recall," she said.

"But you keep all your recipes."

"I keep all the ones that work, Young Lady," she said rather quietly. "My cake was not a harbinger of a happy marriage."

Edna seldom spoke of her marriage. "How thoughtless of me to ask, Edna. I'll make do with one of these," I said. "You know, it's so quiet here without you that I find myself enjoying Cornelia's company. But it's like being friends with a rattler."

"Cornelia isn't terrible, Milagro. She developed a shell after her parents died, and Ian has always indulged her."

"He suggested she take this job, which is funny considering that he never seems to work."

"It is not becoming for a young lady to gossip."

"Please tell that to the other family members, who all seem to know everything about me."

"They are not young ladies and cannot be held to the same standards that you so woefully fail to meet."

"I miss you. When are you coming back?"

"In another week or so, I think. Thomas wants to talk to you."

I regressed momentarily and became excited that a Hollywood actor wanted to talk to me.

He came on the line and said, "Milagro?"

"Hi, Thomas. I hope you're treating Edna well."

"I treat her like the goddess she is. I need you to go to her cottage, get my black suit, and have it dry cleaned and sent to me."

"You're kidding, right?"

"That's the kind of attitude that makes Edna appreciate efficient room service. Overnight it."

Edna got back on the line and said cheerfully, "We're going out now, but I'm sure you'll do something distinctive with the cake."

"You're saying distinctive, but you mean inedible."

She chuckled. "I'll see you soon, Young Lady. Don't forget to send Thomas's suit."

I went to the Love Shack and found three different black suits in the closet. I took all of them to the dry cleaners in town and paid extra to have them delivered express to Thomas. When I returned home, I put together a tray of cheeses with crackers for cocktails.

Oswald and Cornelia came home within minutes of each other.

"Would love to chat, but I must get dressed," Cornelia said. Her glossy ebony bob was perfectly sleek, and she had a new shade of crimson polish on her nails.

Oswald and I sat out on the terrace and I told him about meeting Joseph Alfred at the nursery and his date with Cornelia. "I learned about the fruitcake wedding cake today. Vampire fruitcake wedding cake, it's one of those things you don't imagine."

"Nobody really likes it," he said. "The one at Sam and Winnie's wedding was tasty, though."

"Oswald, is there anything else you want to tell me about a bride's duties?"

He stared out at the fields. Ernie, accompanied by the dogs, was gathering up the horses for the evening. "There's the cake and the tunics. That's it, I think."

"Really? What about the bride's oath to allow her husband to take her blood?"

I was watching his face. The indirect, soft golden light made his gray eyes so clear and his pale coloring so lovely.

"It's in the vows, but I don't want you to do anything you don't want to do."

"But it's what you want, isn't it?"

"I'm a vampire." It was the first time he'd ever said it to me. "I'm a vampire and I'd like to make love to you the way we used to. And if you want to take my blood, too, I'd really like that. I thought you enjoyed the tastes you had."

"I did, Oz, I had that craving . . ." I liked to think I was sexually liberated, and I'd had his blood before, once accidentally when I was infected and the second time when I craved it during a state of delirium. "After Cornelia goes, we can try. We'll take it slowly, light some candles and get out the massage oils."

"Milagro, there's no way I can do that without having sex."

I leaned into him. I kissed his smooth neck and rubbed my breasts against him. "So, let's have sex."

"We made a promise."

"A promise to the damn Council. The longer we keep it, the

less sense it makes to me. We have no guarantee they won't come up with some other reason to exclude me."

"We'll try doing it this way, and if it doesn't work . . ."

"What then?"

"I don't know. Most of my life, I had nothing to do with them. Then I met you . . ." He smiled and reached out for my hand. "They blame me for bringing you into our lives, but how could I resist you?"

I squeezed his hand. "I *am* pretty irresistible. I don't know how that escaped Nixon's notice."

We sat and watched the sun setting, and soon Cornelia came back downstairs, dressed in a skintight black cocktail dress and sky-high heels. Sapphires glittered on her ears and on a necklace that dropped into her plunging neckline.

"You look stunning, Corny," Oswald said. "Enjoy yourself."

"Don't wait up."

Oswald and I had a quiet meal of leftovers. Afterward, he went to the barn to talk to Ernie about ranch business, and I went for a run. I did two circuits of the fields, and then I visited Daisy's grave. I talked to her while I waited to see if Pal would show up. "I miss you, Daisy, but I'm not so sad anymore. I think of all the fun we had together. I'm not replacing you with Pal. No one could replace you, but he's a nice dog. You'd like him."

I woke up when I heard Cornelia return at around 2 a.m. At least someone got lucky tonight.

Sometime later, I heard howling. I looked out the window and spotted the pale yellow moon behind the trees. Our dogs and the neighbors' dogs heard the howls and set up a ruckus. The animals were livelier than usual tonight. I saw the outlines of small creatures moving in the grasses, and a striped cat leaped off a fence post and toward the barn.

The cool breeze came in through the window and I wished that I, too, were a wild creature in the night.

Oswald left early, telling me not to hold dinner for him.

"Will your schedule let up soon?" I asked.

"Not unless I get a partner."

He'd mentioned it before, but there was always the complication that an outside doctor might figure out Oswald's condition. "It would be great if someone else could handle some of the responsibilities."

Cornelia was sleeping in, so I looked through the recipes again and selected the one that seemed least awful. Most of the ingredients were relatively common: currants, dates, dried plums, nuts, poppy seeds, pine nuts, and honey. The cake was flavored with cardamom, nutmeg, and other spices, and preserved with the horrible, potent booze that the vamps used in ceremonies. The recipes called it "green wine" but I thought of it as green death.

Dried pomegranate seeds were included in every version of the cake recipe. I brushed aside the coincidence of my discussion with Ian about Persephone and pomegranates. The vampires' genetic line had started with merchants on the Silk Road, and they had carried pomegranates with them, so it was reasonable that their descendants would use the fruit in traditional recipes.

I looked up the history of pomegranates in one of my gardening books. The shining clear crimson seeds symbolized fertility and had often been used in marriage ceremonies. Vampires needed all the help with fertility that they could get, and they loved the gorgeous red juice.

The local market wouldn't have half the things I needed, and neither did the high-end market near Oswald's offices. Several phone calls later, I found an Indian grocery in the City that sold dried pomegranate seeds and all the spices I needed.

I went upstairs to ask Cornelia if she wanted to go with me. She was lolling in bed, wearing some lacy confection of a bed jacket and talking on the phone. Her face, bereft of makeup, was surprisingly pretty and she looked much younger than she usually did.

I stood at her door while she made arcane arrangements to visit friends in Corsica or Kosovo or Cozumel. She mentioned all three, and I wouldn't have been surprised if she'd included the high-security prison at Corcoran.

When she finished the call, I told her, "I'll pick up the cake ingredients the next time I go to the City. I don't know where to get the 'green wine.'"

"Ernesto has some out at the barn," she said. It didn't strike her as odd that she knew the contents of the property better than I. "You shouldn't wait to get started on the cake. You should go to the City and buy those things today."

"Do you want to come along?"

"I've got far too many phone calls to make. Take my car if you like."

I was happy to, since her rental car had a working sound system. "Thanks, I will. Did you have a good time with Joseph last night?"

"He's got a lovely surliness. I almost want to see him again tonight," she said. "But I wouldn't want to give him the impression that I like him excessively."

"Heaven forbid. Oswald won't be back for dinner, but I should be back in the early evening."

"I shall keep myself entertained," she said.

I changed into jeans, a white cotton tank, and sandals. The City could easily be twenty degrees cooler, so I took along a light sweater.

Cornelia's car was a pleasure to drive. I settled onto the cushioned leather seat, adjusted the numerous features, turned on the music, a bruising jazz mix, and got on the two-lane highway out of town. The engine was so quiet and the car so insulated that I felt cocooned inside.

The car was much more responsive than my truck, and once I got on the mountain, it took the curves effortlessly. I put down the window because I loved the smell of the forest. At this time of day, midweek, there was very little traffic. I was looking forward to a few hours of shopping by myself.

The music suddenly stopped.

When I glanced at the dashboard I saw that the lights had all gone out. The quiet engine was completely silent. There was a sharp turn ahead. I turned the steering wheel but it didn't respond, and then I futilely jammed down on the brakes as the car flew off the side of the road.

The car crashed through branches and the air bags inflated, protecting me, but blocking my sight lines. I heard the shriek and tear of metal, and the car was bumped and battered roughly on its downward trajectory, bashing me from side to side.

After a few seconds, the car crashed into something and stopped, leaving me squeezed between the side and front air bags. The car seemed to be at a sharp angle, tilting forward. It felt as if it was shifting gently back and forth.

With my free right arm, I reached around my seat and felt for my tote. I pulled it close enough to fumble around inside until my fingers found the cool, hard surface of the penknife

Oswald had given to me. Opening it with one hand took a long time. My short gardener's fingernails kept slipping on the groove to open the blade, and I realized the genius of automatic switchblades.

When I finally succeeded, I slashed the air bag in front of me, which deflated with a prolonged hiss. Through the cracked windshield I saw the hood of the car dropping off into the air, which I sensed was not a good thing. I reached for my phone, but there was no signal here on the mountain. I shoved it in my cleavage for now.

I couldn't unbuckle my seat belt, so I sawed through the thick nylon webbing, making my movements small and careful.

I needed to get a better view of my position. The automatic locks had trapped me inside. As I shifted my body, slowly moving to the backseat, I heard an ominous creaking. I didn't wait for more. Bracing my back against one back door, I covered my face with my arms and kicked the side window across from me as hard as I could.

The safety glass shattered and when I uncovered my face, I saw a scatter of small pieces on the car seat. The car teetered, and I twisted around as quickly as I could and launched myself out the window, into the soft red dirt.

The car creaked again and then fell slowly over the precipice. Branches snapped loudly, metal crunched, and there was a loud bang and the rumble of rocks falling.

And then it was quiet.

I wormed forward on my stomach and peered over the hillside's edge. Far below me, the mangled wreckage of the car lay in a rocky creek bed. My phone, dislodged by my wriggling, slipped out and tumbled forward into the ravine.

I hoped that Cornelia had bought rental insurance.

Cornelia.

Cornelia had declined to come along. Cornelia had said that the cake ingredients must be bought today. Cornelia had told me to take her car.

That evil Eurotrash, spa-slut, vampire bitch had tried to kill me. She *was* after Oswald! I would wrap my fingers around her bony chicken neck and squeeze until breathing was just a memory to her. I would beat her with her own stilettos until she had more holes than a summer eyelet frock.

Furious, I squirmed backward to firmer ground, and then stood. I was shaking with rage and adrenaline. The remaining shards of glass on the window had slashed my arms and the tops of my feet. I had dozens of fine cuts on my collarbone.

The blood dripped along my skin even as the wounds quickly mended themselves. The seat belt had yanked harsh red welts across my torso, and my ribs and knees hurt as if someone had hammered them.

I looked up toward the road. All I could see was a steep incline and dense forest growth. I heard the faintest hum of a car every few minutes. I attempted to scale the slope, but the ground kept sliding beneath my smooth-soled sandals. I grabbed at shrubs to pull me up, and their shallow roots would give way, and I'd slide back down with a handful of branches.

I'd heard that it was always easiest to find victims who stayed close to the site of an accident. Perhaps someone had seen the accident. I called out, "Hellooo! Help!" until my throat was so hoarse I could only rasp.

While I waited to be rescued, I sat on a mossy stump and thought of terrible things I would do to Cornelia. When the pleasant coolness of the afternoon turned chilly, I lost patience with waiting.

I was about halfway over the mountain, so I turned back in the direction of the ranch and began struggling through the brush on a path roughly parallel to the road. I tried to remember James Fenimore Cooper's Deerslayer stories, in which broken branches were always relied upon for tracking. I snapped twigs as I walked, in order to leave a trail for rescuers. If I was in here long enough, I'd have to learn to weave clothes out of bark.

The straps on my sandals broke and I abandoned them. I'd start trying to make my way through one area, only to have my route blocked by impenetrable brambles or boulders. My clothing was ripped and filthy, covered with splotches of blood. My fingernails were broken, my feet hurt from the repeated cuts and healings.

When darkness came, the temperature plummeted. I still couldn't see any signs of civilization ahead, and I no longer heard any traffic in the distance. Thirsty, hungry, and severely cranky, I decided to sit for a few minutes and reassess my situation.

My biggest worry was that Oswald would get home before me and walk right into the clutches of diabolical Cornelia, who might tell him anything—that I'd stolen her car and run away from home to join a circus, or that I'd gone off with Pepper on a cross-country crime spree.

I had to admit, she'd come up with an effective little plan, one that wouldn't ruin her manicure. My mother Regina could have learned a thing or two from the vampiress.

The nighttime animals came out. Branches shuddered in the wind that kicked up every evening. As I sat there listening to the forest sounds, I heard a howl in the distance. I stayed motionless, wondering if it was a dog or a coyote. It came again, far off, but clear enough to cause all the other animals to fall silent.

I stood up, took as much air in my lungs as I could, and howled back.

The creature responded.

I forgot the murderous women in my life and walked toward the sound. The wolf howled and I responded. I stumbled and fell many times in my rush to find him.

Then there was a loud crashing through the bushes and the wolf ran toward me, his golden eyes shining even in this deep darkness.

"Pal!" I cried. I crouched down and put my arms around his big body, sank my face into the thick warm fur of his neck. When I released him, he danced around me happily.

Suddenly he raced off. I screamed, "Pal! Pal!" I tried to go after him, but he was much faster than I.

I began crying in sheer frustration. But if he could get here, then I could get out. I wiped my dirty, wet face with my dirty, grimy hands and began walking again.

As suddenly as Pal had disappeared he was back again. "Forget it," I told him. "You already ditched me. Fool me once . . ." I continued on my way, but he took the bottom of my shirt in his big, sharp teeth and held me to my place. I smacked his head. "Let go, you stupid dog."

He growled slightly.

"Same to you," I said, but he wouldn't let go. "Fine, have my damn shirt." I jerked forward and my shirt ripped.

The animal ran around me and blocked my way.

I stared him down, calculating my chances of winning a fight without suffering grievous injuries. I dashed to one side and the animal knocked me down. I grabbed for his snout, but he leapt out of my reach.

We began a dance then of feints and strikes as I tried to get away and he tried to stop my progress. He never bit me, but he did nip and I did swat. It was more like a physical version of bickering than a screaming argument.

I had picked up a rock and was about to throw it at the wolf when I heard an amplified voice: "Is anyone there?"

Dropping the rock, I shouted, "Hello! Hello! I'm here! Please help me!"

When I turned to Pal, he gave me one last look and then trotted off into the underbrush.

"Stay where you are!" came the voice. "We're coming down."

The rescue crew took half an hour to get safely down from the road. The brawny man who clambered down turned the beam of his flashlight on me, and I became aware of my torn shirt, dirt-covered tatas, and filthy, bloody clothes. "Jesus Christ!"

"Thank God you're here!" I said, and then remembered that I was engaged, so I crossed my arms over my chest with ladylike modesty.

"We're going to get you to a hospital right away. I'm going to do a quick check of—"

"I'm fine. I just want to go home. My car crashed."

"Where is it?"

"Somewhere down in the creek."

He looked astonished. "And you made it out?"

"It took a while."

"The blood . . . was there anyone else in the car?"

"Just me."

He didn't look convinced. "Did you hit your head?"

"No, yes, I don't think so, but I'm fine." I saw his flashlight playing over the blood on my clothes and skin. "I had a nose-bleed, but it stopped. Can you get me out of here?"

He radioed up that I wasn't hurt and then he tied a rope around my waist, and I was soon hauled up the steep slope. When I reached the roadside, there was a sheriff's car with flashing lights and an ambulance.

"I'm okay, I'm okay," I kept telling the paramedics, and I gave the sheriff my name and address. While the paramedics were trying to convince me to let them examine me, the sheriff walked out of hearing distance and began making phone calls.

Finally, the paramedics gave up and said, "She seems to be okay."

They wrapped me in a blanket and the sheriff came over and said, "You're lucky we got that call."

"What call?"

"Someone called a little while ago and gave us your location. He gave us the road marker and said there had been an accident. How'd he know that, when you said your car went off this afternoon?"

"Someone called you? Who?"

"You tell us," the sheriff said as he put me in the backseat of his car. "You live at Doc Oz's place, right?"

"Yes. I'm his fiancée."

"I just called there. He didn't answer."

"He's still at his office. He's not coming home until later."

"You sure he's at his office?"

"No, I staged a car accident to murder him and his body is at the bottom of the ravine," I said sarcastically. When the officer's eyes widened, I said, "Of course, he's at his office. He's *always* at his office." I gave him Oswald's cell phone number, but he didn't answer. Then I gave him Oswald's clinic number and no one was there either.

"You better hope that Dr. Grant shows up," the sheriff said. "You got an awful lot of blood on you for a person with no injuries. That must have been some nosebleed."

That's when it occurred to me that Oswald might be in trouble. Hell hath no fury like a vampire bitch scorned. What if Cornelia had planned the crash to keep me permanently out of the way so she could hurt Oswald?

"Hurry." I had to get home and make sure Oswald was all right.

"I'm going the limit. Or do you have a reason to hurry?"

"I'm the victim here, you jackass."

"You know, I've spent years dealing with victims, and you, little lady, don't strike me as one."

There are times when it is best to shut the hell up. I grew more and more anxious on the ride. My stomach cramped with nerves and I broke into a cold sweat. The sheriff had a look of satisfaction when he saw me clutching the blanket tightly. I wanted to smack the snide right off him, but he'd probably interpret that as a propensity for violence.

Oswald, Oswald, Oswald, I thought, please be okay.

fourteen

like a rat in a trap

We got to the gate of the ranch. I fumbled frantically with the car door until the sheriff said, "Let me unlock it first." I jumped out and quickly pressed the code that opened the gate.

I didn't wait to get back in the car. I ran down the drive to the house, not caring as I stepped on the sharp edges of gravel or the broken walnut shells from last season's crop. "Oswald!" I screamed. "Oswald!"

The sheriff's car followed closely and the dogs came forward in a pack, barking and jumping around me and the car. I ran around to the car park, but Oswald's car was not there. As I opened the back door to the house, I saw Ernesto coming from the barn at a fast walk.

"Oswald!" I called as I rushed into the kitchen. "Oswald!" I went through the dining room and into the empty living room.

I was calling as I went to the dark study and family room, growing more panicked with every second.

I dashed back to the staircase. Cornelia stood on the landing of the second floor, looking down at me, an expression of horror on her face.

"Young Lady?"

"You demon bitch!" I lunged toward the stairs, but arms grabbed me. The sheriff and Ernie pulled me away as I screamed, "Where is Oswald? What have you done with Oswald?" I may also have shrieked that I would kill her. I didn't want to hurt Ernie, but I could knock him out and then proceed to killing Cornelia.

I heard a sharp, quite distinct click and felt my arm wrenched back. Ernie and the sheriff released me and I jerked forward, stumbling hard onto the staircase. The sheriff smirked and stepped back as I twisted my hand, trying to free it from the handcuff that was attached to the wrought iron railing.

"Now calm the hell down," the sheriff said. He glanced up at Cornelia, who looked the very picture of country elegance in riding pants and a white blouse. He said to her, "This one's gone bat shit."

It was insult upon injury. I was screaming at him that she might have killed Oswald and clattering the handcuff on the banister, so we didn't hear the car arrive or hear the footsteps approaching.

"What is going on here?" Oswald stood in the doorway, alive and whole and fabulous.

He stared at the scene: me covered in dirt and dried blood, wearing a bra and jeans, and trying to tear the rail off the banister; Cornelia standing composed at the top of the stairs; the sheriff leaning against the wall; Ernie with his hands on his hips.

"Oswald!" I cried in relief. "You're alive!"

"Hey, Doc Oz," the sheriff said politely. "We rescued this *person* from the side of the mountain. She *claims* that her car went off the road into the ravine."

"Oswald, why didn't you answer your phone?" I asked. I thought he should crush me in his arms now, murmuring words of comfort and love, but he stood back.

"I was on my way home. You must have called when I was on the mountain. Are you all right?" Oswald didn't wait for my answer, but said to the sheriff. "Would you please release her?"

The sheriff looked disappointed and unlocked the handcuffs.

I glared up at Cornelia. "*She* loaned me her car and the engine totally went out. If it wasn't for the air bags, I'd be dead."

Cornelia faked a shocked expression. "Milagro! I had no idea . . ."

"Right," I shouted. "You want Oswald for yourself and thought you'd get rid of me!"

Oswald said, "Sheriff, thank you for bringing Milagro home. She's a little excited now. Let me see you out. Ernie, keep an eye on Milagro."

The sheriff said to me, "We'll be in touch."

I glared at him, just daring him to say anything else.

Oswald left the front door open as they walked out. I could hear him talking quietly to the sheriff. I stared up at Cornelia and then lifted my forefinger and made a slashing gesture across my neck.

"You're mad!" she hissed.

"*Cálmate,*" Ernie said. He looked concerned as he gazed earnestly at my blood-and-filth covered *chichis*.

I suddenly felt weak and I dropped down on the steps.

Oswald came back in the house, closed the front door, and said, "Thanks, Ernie. Would you bring some of the calf blood here?"

As Ernie left, Oswald said to Cornelia, "I'll be up to talk soon."

He took me by the elbow. "Let's get you washed up and in clean clothes."

I shot one last look at Cornelia before letting Oswald lead me back to the maid's bathroom.

He asked, "Can you stand for a shower, or do you want a bath?"

"Shower."

"How much blood did you lose?" The silver penknife fell out of the pocket of my jeans as he undressed me.

"I don't know. I'm tired."

He lifted my chin and looked in my eyes. "If you take some of mine, you'll feel better."

I stared at the knife on the white octagonal tile floor and thought about his smooth, lovely skin. I couldn't bear the idea of cutting him. "Your knife saved me. But no, I don't want to use it on you."

I saw the disappointment on his face.

I stepped into the shower and let the steaming water rinse away my filth. I washed my hair and lathered myself with the last of the fragrant almond-honey bath gel from an expensive spa. When I looked down at my body, my skin was as unblemished as on the day I'd been born. Too bad I couldn't wash my brain.

When I came out of the shower, Oswald dried me with a thick terry towel. He was looking at my body the way a doctor looks at it: dispassionately trying to assess its condition. Well, he *was* a doctor, but I wasn't used to him treating me like that.

"I was pretty cut up. I had to get out through the car's back window."

He held an old, plaid flannel robe for me. He must have taken it out of the closet that held all the stray clothes guests had left. I slipped my arms into it and pulled the belt tight.

I walked barefoot with him to the living room. Even though the temperature was pleasant, Ernie had laid a fire and set out a carafe of blood, water, and glasses near the fireplace. I was hungry, but I'd start with a drink.

"Tell me what happened," Oswald said.

I relayed my story and he listened calmly. When I finished he said, "Why did you assume that Cornelia was trying to kill you?"

"Don't you think it's suspicious that she got this wedding counselor job just as we announce our marriage? And then there's your former relationship with her."

"You're saying that Cornelia took the wedding planner job in order to come here, kill you in a faked automobile accident, kill me out of jealous rage, and set you up as my murderer?"

It did sound a little complicated. "You have to admit that weirder things have happened since I met you, and I just let them go innocently by, la-la-la, too convinced of the benevolence of all mankind to suspect foul play."

He looked down at his nice custom-made Swiss shoes. Finally he said, "There is a zone between paranoia and obliviousness. I've got to call Gabriel and Sam and tell them what happened. Because of your display with the sheriff, things will have to be smoothed out." He took my hand and squeezed. "I'm glad you're okay."

He made me his favorite comfort food, a bowl of oatmeal with raisins dried from our own grapevines, and put me to bed. "Can't I sleep with you tonight?" I asked.

"I'd rather keep you at a distance from Cornelia. You're going to have to apologize to her tomorrow."

"What if I'm right?"

"Good night, babe." He pulled the blanket over me, then turned out the light, closed the door, and left.

In bed, I wondered if I should have taken Oswald's blood, and I tried to fantasize about sex with a little bloodsucking. But I simply couldn't bring myself to eroticize cutting Oswald. My instinct was to protect him, not cause him pain.

My mind turned to the night when I'd been attacked, when Ian had given me his intoxicating blood and licked my skin, sticky with my own blood.

How easy it would be to press the blade of a knife into the skin on Ian's chest, putting my lips to the scarlet blood welling there and probing with my tongue until the skin closed. And to have Ian's dangerous white teeth break my skin and suck at my flesh.

It was because I didn't care about hurting Ian that I could even think this way. Because I associated him with things twisted and darkly carnal.

Why couldn't I crave Oswald's blood the same way I craved Ian's? Oswald's had been the gateway drug, the fruit-flavored wine of the vampire world, and I was like a junkie jonesing for the hard stuff. It was merely a chemical reaction, I told myself, a bride's jitters.

I steered my errant thoughts back where they belonged: to Oswald, his smooth, unmarked skin, the delicious curve of his lean hips, his facile mouth, those remarkably talented fingers, and all his other amazing manly parts.

I slept late and when I awoke, Sam and Gabriel had already arrived to deal with the situation. I found them in the study with Oswald and Cornelia.

Gabriel was looking through the Womyn's Sexual Health Collective catalog.

"Reading this is extremely educational," he said as he stood and gave me a hug and a kiss. "How does a girl fall off a mountain and still look fabulous?" he asked.

"Hey, guys," I said. The situation must have been serious to bring both the family counsel and the security dude here this early in the morning. I sat next to Gabriel and leaned against him. His redhead's pallor looked washed out and there were pale blue shadows under his green eyes.

Cornelia was lounging on the tufted leather chair in tight jeans and a formfitting tee. "Are you feeling less stark raving, darling?"

"Cornelia, just give me an excuse . . . ," I said.

Oswald shot a look at Sam, who was sitting at the desk.

Sam looked all business in a brown suit with a boxy traditional cut. He got up and came to me, saying, "How are you? Winnie's very concerned."

I hugged him. "Sam, good to see you. I'm fine *now.*"

"Good, good. Let's have a talk."

The vampires always behaved as if they were oh so civilized. "Sure, why not? Let's all pretend that we can talk about this attempted murder reasonably."

My loyal fiancé said to his cousins, "You see what I mean?"

Sam looked at me and said, "Milagro, we are taking this incident seriously, but let's not jump to conclusions. We have no reason to believe that Cornelia would do anything like this."

Cornelia looked bored and said, "If I wanted you dead, you'd be dead, Young Lady. I wouldn't use some rococo plot."

"That's a comfort," I said. "I, too, would kill you more directly. I'd be happy to demonstrate."

167

"Ladies!" Sam said. When we both sat back, he continued: "We've hired someone to investigate the crash scene. When he reports back, we'll reconvene. Oswald, have you talked to the sheriff?"

"Yes. He's suspicious about the blood that was on Milagro's clothes," Oswald said. "He thinks the accident was staged."

Gabriel took my hand and said, "Unless a body is found, he can't do a thing. We'll monitor their communications to make sure they don't get too interested in finding out why Milagro wasn't hurt. Oz, the sheriff is the head of the widows' and orphans' fund. I've told him you're making a contribution in gratitude for their good work rescuing Milagro."

I wondered how much money Oswald would have to spend to calm things down. "I'll reimburse you for that," I said. "Not that we should have to pay because of his misapprehension."

"I'll take care of it," Oswald said.

"I *said* I'd pay for it."

He gave me an irritated look. "You can't afford it."

Cornelia could barely keep from smiling. "If we're done, I must get ready for a lunch date. Oswald, may I borrow one of your cars?"

"Sure." He said he'd drive his Jeep today and gave her the keys to the sedan.

She stood and left the room, blowing a kiss to Sam and Gabriel on her way out.

In the late afternoon, Sam came to tell me that the investigator had found the car and was coming to give a report to all of us. Oswald would be home in a few minutes to join us.

I washed my face and dabbed on a little clear lip gloss. I considered putting it on my cheeks because I'd heard that it helped deflect punches in a fight. Not that I'd be fighting Cornelia, I thought as I pulled my hair into a low ponytail that would be hard to grab. And even if I did, I could snap her like a tortilla chip.

When I went to the living room, Oswald and Gabriel were already there, standing at the far end with a bulky man in a striped polo shirt and wrinkled cotton pants. The man had a receding hairline and crooked nose.

I went across the room and said hello.

"Milagro, this is Frank."

"Nice to meet you," the man said, and when he shook my hand, I felt the strength camouflaged by the layer of fat. I'd want him at my back in a fight.

"Nice to meet you, Frank."

"Nasty business you had." He gave me a long up-and-down look, which managed to appraise me both as a woman and as a car crash survivor. "Not a scratch on you."

"She's a tough little thing," Cornelia said as she walked into the room. "Cornelia Ducharme."

"Frank," he said.

"Is that your name, or your character?" she asked.

"Let's hope it's both," I snapped.

Oswald took my hand and pulled me to a love seat. He looked at Sam, who steered Cornelia to a pair of chairs on the other side of the sofa, putting some distance between us.

Gabriel and Frank remained standing. "We found the car, but it's totaled, not worth the cost of hauling up to the road," Frank said. "I sent one of my mechanics to take a look. This is what he found." Frank pulled my telephone and some wiring and a plastic baggie out of his pouchy pockets.

"What's that?" Sam asked.

"The phone still works," Frank said, tossing it to me. He showed the wires to Oswald. "Chewed up wiring."

"So it *was* sabotage," I said.

Frank said, "Not *cut* wires. *Chewed* wires with rodent hairs and droppings. The casing is stripped, too, which is typical. Some rat or squirrel got in under the hood and ate up the wiring. I could have them analyzed for you, but I don't want to waste your money. Most likely, the wiring was just barely connected and then couldn't hold any longer."

"Rats?" I said. I had had issues with rats, but this explanation was absurd. "Rats did that? Why would rats eat wires?"

"Rats' teeth never stop growing," Oswald said. "They'll chew on anything around and they crawl into cars because they're attracted to the warmth of an engine."

Gabriel said, "I've heard of that occuring in colder climates. What do you think, Oz?"

"It could have happened at the rental agency, but it's more likely it happened here," Oswald said. "The cats are always at the barn these days, not keeping up on things near the house."

I remembered Daisy crouching in the grass by my garden. "Daisy used to hunt anything that came near the house."

Cornelia gave me a bemused glance. "I do hope you won't accuse me of orchestrating a rat attack against you."

I felt deep in my gut that the accident was not an accident, but how could it be anything else?

Sam asked Frank who had called the sheriff's office.

The big man shook his head. "Don't know. The call came from one of the roadside emergency boxes, and when the sheriff got there fifteen minutes later, the caller was gone. Some guy, that's all they know."

I said, "Maybe someone heard me shouting for help. I wish he'd given his name so I could thank him."

Frank said, "He'd a left his name if he cared."

Gabriel thanked Frank for coming and we all said good-bye to him. Then the cousins walked him out of the house, leaving Cornelia, Oswald, and me.

I forced myself to turn to Cornelia and say, "I would like to apologize. I was wrong and I should not have made assumptions."

Cornelia enjoyed her little moment, making significant eye contact with Oswald and letting me stew for a minute before saying, "I accept your apology. It's only a bride's nerves."

I had been wrong, wrong, wrong, and she was being gracious. So why was I fuming?

Oswald said, "Ladies, this was an unfortunate accident. Now, can we put it behind us?"

I nodded, and Cornelia said, "It's already forgotten."

"Good." He stroked my head and said, "I'm going to the barn and see about moving one of those cats up here. Ernie and I will check the other cars to make sure they're okay." He loosened his tie and undid the top button of his shirt.

When the cousins reconvened, Gabriel advised Oswald to contact the sheriff with a copy of Frank's report about the cause of the accident. He said that he and Sam would update the Council on the situation.

"What does the Council have to do with this?" I asked.

"We have to make a report every time local authorities get involved with our activities," Sam said. "It's a precaution."

"I shan't file a complaint against you, Young Lady," Cornelia said with a wave of her manicured hand. "I'm ever so parched."

That's why Cornelia was so ready to forgive me: I was now in her debt.

"I'll make the drinks," I said.

fifteen

wherein our heroine's sanity is questioned

Sam couldn't stay for cocktails, so I walked him outside to his car. "Check it for rat damage," I said.

"I'm sure it's okay," Sam answered, but he popped the hood and peered inside. "Looks fine," he said and closed the hood. "May I say something?"

"Sam, you can always say whatever you want to me."

"We all realize that your past experiences may have made you *cautious.*"

" 'Cautious' being a euphemism for 'paranoid.' "

"No, not paranoid," he said quickly. "But overly suspicious. We're all *cautious,* Young Lady, but—"

"But I shouldn't accuse someone of trying to kill me on pure speculation?"

"Yes, that's right."

"Sam, I admire your calmness and rationality, but I hope that you can understand that an extreme situation inspires an extreme reaction."

He gave me a slow smile. "It's in those extreme situations that calmness and reason are most important."

"We'd have to be more specific about the extreme situation before I'd agree." I admired Sam, but he lacked a flair for the dramatic. "Sam, have you heard back from the Council about the loyalty oath?"

"They haven't gotten back to me." He looked off for a moment and then said, "This incident won't help."

"They're not going to blame me?" I asked, stunned.

Instead of answering, he gave me a hug and said, "Come visit us soon."

Cornelia was on her second martini and in such a good mood that my concerns that she would exploit the situation began to dissipate. Gabriel's presence always cheered us, and I was disappointed when he left.

Cornelia came into the kitchen while I was making dinner, ostensibly in search of cocktail olives. I handed her a bottle and she said, "Joseph told me that Oswald should grow olive trees here."

"I've thought of that," I said. "Even an acre could give us a nice crop in some years."

"Really?"

Well, that's all it took. As I chopped and sautéed vegetables, I started talking about an olive grove and other possible gardening ideas. Somehow I was soon describing the differences between annuals and perennials, and deciduous versus evergreen plants. I discussed the value of botanical names.

"Common names can be colorful, like kiss-me-over-the-garden-gate, but they're not precise. If someone mentions mock-orange, he could be talking about a variety of *Philadelphus* or about *Pittosporum undulatum,* which is also called Victorian box." This was one of my favorite shrubs, and the heady scent always made me think of being in love. I'd planted one beside the house, where I hoped it would survive the winter cold.

She said, "Ian finds your fanaticism amusing, but that's more than I ever cared to know."

Since Oswald wasn't around, I asked, "How is your brother? And Ilena?"

"Wildly happy together. He called last night and I told him about your accident. He'll be relieved to learn that you were only a victim of rats." She laughed, and when I didn't join in, she said, "Try and see the positive side. A girl in trouble is irresistible to Oswald. He wants to have some troubled female leaning on his strong and capable shoulders."

After our meal, we settled into the family room with blood spritzers and watched a Dutch film about a young artist who goes mad when her lover abandons her. I found it quite tragic and blinked back tears. Cornelia seemed to think it was a comedy.

When I gave her a look, she said, "Oh, Americans always take love so seriously."

"Cornelia, what *is* your nationality, anyway?"

"I'm a citizen of the world, darling."

It was the same answer her brother had once given me. I thought they probably had a stash of various passports and identification documents.

I took a few dog biscuits outside and wandered into the fields calling for Pal. He probably didn't even know he had a name.

I went through the garden, inhaling the scent of mock-orange, and remembered a poem I'd read somewhere about the scent of the blossoms. I'd look it up tomorrow.

As I washed up before going to bed, I kept looking at my engagement ring glittering in a china dish on the vanity. Beside it was the silver penknife.

The next day, I decided that I was done with being passive and patient. The first thing I was going to do was get behind the wheel again. I told Cornelia I was running a few errands and would be back soon.

"If you don't return, shall I alert a pest control company?"

I could have come back with several snappy rejoinders about Cornelia and vermin. But now I owed her. "Can I pick up anything for you in town?"

"A case of the palest rosé you can find," she said. "That little spa has a nail polish called Bruised that I like. And please bring back the latest issues of the magazines, including both French and Italian *Vogue*."

"Sorry, but the store only carries the domestic edition."

"What good is that? Oh, bring it anyway."

I took my keys and went to my little green truck. Before leaving, I looked in the engine. It stank of the mothballs Ernie had put in there to deter rodents, but nothing was obviously amiss.

On the way down the drive, I hit the brakes and played with the steering. Everything was fine. There was nothing to worry about.

Although the town was small, the local market had a fine selection of wines from local wineries. I found a suitably uncommited rosé and bought a case, along with magazines and groceries. The cozy spa was out of Bruised but recommended a similar red-black shade called Gangrene.

I kept the truck's windows down, not just because my air-conditioning was broken but so I could better listen to the engine. My confidence in the vehicle was restored by the time I pulled into the parking lot at the nursery. A new sign with *Lupine Fields Nursery* on it had been raised above the front door. Joseph came out front as I got out of the truck.

"Hey, muffin!" He gave me a huge hug, lifting me off the ground for a few seconds.

"Hi to you, too!" I said. It was always so delightful when people were happy to see me. And by people, I meant handsome, hunky guys.

When he put me down, he asked, "How are you?" and it sounded like an actual question, instead of just a cordial remark.

"Good. I'll be better after a little retail therapy here." He kept looking at me, and I realized he'd probably heard about the accident. In a small town, word got around fast. "My car went off the road on the mountain, though."

"I heard about that. What happened?"

Recalling Cornelia's jokes about the rats, I said, "Mechanical failure. Faulty computer thingy. Totally a fluke."

"That road is a menace."

"It is. Cars go off it all the time, especially in the winter," I said. "That's why they have those emergency roadside call boxes. But usually the drivers just ram into some trees and their alcohol level keeps them from feeling any pain."

"You were so worried about my car swipe, and here you are acting nonchalant about flying off a mountain road."

"Like you, I'd rather not think about it right now. Let's enjoy the day. I love the name of your nursery."

"You mentioned the lupine blooming in the spring and it seemed like a good enough name."

"Just wait till you see it. The hills turn the most marvelous shade of blue-purple. What's new in your stock?"

"Let me show you."

As we were walking back to the nursery, Joseph sniffed and looked around. "What's that smell?"

I shrugged. "Mothballs. These clothes were in storage."

I bought a flat of thyme, several lavenders, rosemary, and annuals that would bloom in autumn. When Joseph said that he'd like to see my garden sometime, I realized that he probably hadn't met many people here yet.

"Come to dinner tonight," I said. "Cornelia will be happy to see you, and you can meet my guy."

He grinned. "Cornelia's something, isn't she?"

Some "thing" was an accurate assessment. "Yes, she is."

"I like that hard edge with the femininity. I hate clingy, needy women, and Cornelia's not that."

"So you *do* understand Cornelia," I said with surprise.

"Oh, yeah, I get her. Just like I get you. Under all the sexiness and friendliness, you're a complicated chick, aren't you? I'm only here because I had to get away from my ex. Who are you hiding from?"

I laughed, but it was a little forced, since I'd first come here to hide. "You accuse me of complexity to flatter my ego. I'm sure that works with some girls."

"Nah, usually they just check out my butt and that works."

I laughed as I loaded the last of the plants in the truck. "So can you make it to dinner, or not?"

He said he'd come after work, and I gave him directions. As I said good-bye, he gave me a terrific hug.

At the ranch, I called Oswald's offices and left a message that Joseph was coming to dinner. Then I called his grandmother. "Hi, Edna. Do you know that I nearly died the other day?"

"Hello, Young Lady. Sam told me the news. He said that you accused Cornelia of trying to murder you."

"The murder claim might have been premature, but I did really nearly die."

She paused. "Of course, I'm happy you're all right. You have more lives than a cat."

"So it seems, but I still got freaked out. It didn't feel like an accident. It felt intentional."

"I can see how you would think that, but Sam said the investigator didn't have any doubts that it was accidental."

"I know. That's what perplexes me. I'm extremely perplexed. I'm beyond perplexed. Superplexed even. Überperplexed. Come home."

"Since you're fine, there's no need to curtail my holiday."

"Holiday from what?"

"From your field of chaos and drama."

We snipped back and forth before moving on to other chatter. I told her about Joseph Alfred, the new nursery, and my quasi pet, Pal. Finally, I asked a question that had been on my mind. "Edna, do you think Oswald is attracted to women who are in a state of crisis? Do you think he was attracted to me because I was in a state of crisis?"

"What peculiar questions."

"That's not an answer."

"Young Lady, you make your attractions evident enough to any breathing heterosexual male."

"Yes, and some adventurous nonheterosexual males as well, but that is another nonanswer."

"Are you bickering with me?"

"I'm really trying to, but it's more fun doing it in person when I can see you sneering at me."

"Good-bye, Young Lady."

"Good-bye, Edna."

I found Cornelia in the pool compound, floating in the blue water, her narrow butt sunk in the middle of an inner tube. The day's bright, clear light was filtered through the translucent roof, keeping her safe from the sun's rays. The vampires lived longer and healthier lives, but I was frequently struck by pity for them.

"Corny . . ."

"Don't call me that."

"Cornelia, Joseph is coming for dinner."

She sat up so quickly that the inner tube rolled over and dumped her in the water. She splashed to the surface, sputtering, her hair plastered to her head. It was the first time I'd ever seen Cornelia lose her poise, and I wished I had a camera.

She swam to the edge of the pool and pulled herself up. I tossed her a towel. She sniffed and said, "What is that—"

"Mothballs. Dinner's at seven."

She dried herself, saying, "I suppose I could help you with something."

"You're kidding, right?"

"No, I could, mmm." She thought for a moment. "I could arrange the flowers."

When she had dressed and put on her enormous straw hat, we went out to the garden. I didn't entirely trust her with my precious Felco pruners. I thought she'd either snip off her fingers or kill one of my plants, but I showed her how to cut the stems of fragrant old roses. "This one is '*Rêve D'or*,'" I said.

"Dream of gold," she translated.

She gathered lacecap hydrangeas and pretty spirea branches.

I saw how she selected the flowers and sought out things that balanced their color and texture. "You have an eye for gardening," I said.

"I used to garden with my mother. My first mother. She was a wonderful homemaker."

"Was it hard going to live with Ian's family?"

She thought before saying, "Quite different. His parents, *our* parents, were in their adult world and we were in ours. Ian took care of me." She turned to me and said, "I would do *anything* for him."

I got the distinct feeling that "anything" included everything from picking up his mail when he was out of town to slaughtering his enemies. "Were you raised in the children's quarters?"

She pulled her hand back sharply from a bush. A drop of red blood appeared on the tip of her finger. She eyed it lovingly, then put it to her mouth, sucking for a moment. When it had stopped bleeding, she said, "Didn't Oswald tell you?"

"We don't talk about Ian or his family."

"Would you like to know the family shame?"

"You don't have to share anything you don't want to."

"Our parents are addicts," she said bluntly.

"But how? If they're like Ian," I said—and thought, like me, too—"they wouldn't really feel the effects of alcohol or drugs."

"They don't have his level of resistance to drugs, but that's not their problem. They're addicted to blood."

"But it's just a craving." A strong, sometimes overpowering craving.

"They were always looking for the most exotic taste, traveling everywhere, drinking from heroin addicts, the terminally ill, virgins, whores, monks." She watched my face and I didn't bother to hide my horror. "You know where the most exquisite blood was, don't you, Young Lady? In their son's small body."

I wanted to tell her to stop talking, but I didn't.

"They used to call him to their room every night. They told him he was sick and they needed to check his blood, just take a small vial. Then they'd lock themselves up and we wouldn't see them until the next afternoon."

So that's what Mrs. Smith was alluding to when she mentioned his difficult youth. "They're monsters," I said.

"Don't be so squeamish, darling. They were only human, *our* type of human, and otherwise they're very loving and thoughtful. Ian put a stop to it when he was old enough to realize what was happening, and he's never let anyone else taste his blood since then." She smiled and said, "Except you. But you're always the exception, aren't you?"

All my life, all I'd ever wanted to be was an ordinary human *chica,* to be part of a larger whole, to be normal. "Yes, I am always the exception."

She sighed and said, "I shouldn't have shared that with you, but secrets can be such a burden."

Poor Ian, I thought. Poor Cornelia. "Don't worry. I won't tell anyone about this."

"I'm relying upon you, darling. Now where are your vases?"

sixteen

to kill a mock-orange

I had time to shower and change into clothes that didn't reek of pesticides. The scoop-neck blouse I wore revealed lots of interesting pulse points to attract Oswald's attention. I wasn't sure of many things, but I was sure of this: life was too precarious to give up lovemaking with a fabulous man in the hopes that blood-drinking bureaucrats would give you vacation time-shares.

Oswald came home carrying his suit jacket. I was in the dining room, setting the table. "Hi, babe," he said and then stopped and took a longer look.

I lifted my chin to lengthen my neck. I would learn to relax and satisfy my future husband's needs. After all, I'd done it before. "Hello, Oz."

He gave me a kiss, but pulled away when I tried to prolong it. "Why did you invite this guy to dinner?"

"Cornelia really likes him and I like him, too."

"Cornelia likes a lot of men. So do you. He must be good looking."

"You know me—I'm happy to talk to anyone about horticulture. It doesn't hurt that he has a totally rocking body."

"I'm glad that's cleared up." Oswald kissed me again, and then his lips traveled just below my ear. I shifted my body toward his, pressing against his hips. I closed my eyes and enjoyed his warmth, his delectable Oswaldy smell, his beautiful lean body.

The dogs began barking as a truck approached the front drive. I nipped Oswald's pink earlobe. Ears were full of blood, and normal people pierced ears every day. Later tonight, I'd give cutting his lobe the old F.U. try and prove that I was capable of being everything he desired in a wife.

The buzzer for the front gate sounded.

Oswald took his arms from around me and looked down at the front of his trousers. "Why are you getting me all revved up?"

"It's in my job description. You save that, uhm, revving for later, and I'll get the gate."

I took one last look around the house. Everything seemed in order. The crystal wineglasses gleamed and the silver had a lovely warm sheen. I'd even ironed the napkins. Well, not ironed in the technical sense of the word, but I had thrown them in the dryer until they weren't wrinkled anymore.

I walked up the drive and opened the gate for the truck with the Lupine Fields Nursery sign on the side and waved Joseph in, closing the gate after the truck. He waited a few yards on, and I hopped into the passenger seat and said hi. He was looking particularly spiffy in a blue polo with an organic compost company logo and olive green pants. His dark hair was loose and smelled marvelous, like pine-scented shampoo.

I directed him to the car park, and when we got out of the truck, the dogs surged toward us. Just as quickly, they backed down, slinking away. "That's odd," I said. "They're usually delirious to meet a guest."

Joseph shrugged his rangy shoulders and said, "Dogs always keep their distance from me."

"Me, too, lately. They've decided they belong to the ranch hand, Ernesto." I slipped my arm through his. "Let's have dinner first and then I'll show you around."

He looked around at the magnificent oaks and walnut trees, the vistas out to the mountains, the small vineyard, and the barn and pool compound. "This is all yours?"

"Not hardly," I said and laughed. "The ranch is Oswald's. I own some of the plants in the garden. That's about the sum total of my worldly belongings."

"This will be yours when you get married." Even though I'd worn the low-cut blouse for Oswald, Joseph was not oblivious to my charms. "You look real pretty, cookie."

"Thank you. So do you. That shirt makes your eyes look as blue as bachelor's buttons."

The wind was really blowing this evening and the trees rustled loudly and my skirt blew up around my hips. I laughed and pulled it back down. "We're having cocktails inside tonight," I said.

My friend suddenly started and looked around. "What was that?"

I listened, but the only thing I heard beyond the wind was a creature chittering in one of the trees, probably a squirrel. "Nothing, just the wind," I said, leading him inside. I closed the door against the dust and leaves swirling on the ground.

Oswald was already in the living room, and I introduced the

two men. I could tell from Oswald's expression that he was surprised at Cornelia's current beau. I filled glasses with ice, poured in pomegranate syrup, tequila, and grapefruit juice, and garnished the drinks with a slice of lime.

"What's this?" Oswald asked.

"I just made it up. It's like a Tequila Sunrise, but with pomegranate syrup and grapefruit juice. What should I call it? A Tequila Moonrise? But it has red streaks. Maybe a Blood Moon."

"Blood Moon is another name for Xquic," said Joseph. "I learned about her because there's a corn hybrid named for her."

I made him repeat the word and spell it. He added, "She was a Mayan deity, a maiden of the underworld. She had to gather corn to prove that she was a virgin even though she was pregnant. She had twins who defeated the death gods."

"What is it with goddesses of the underworld and seeds, or seeded fruit?" I asked. "I've never heard of that myth, although I know a little folklore. I'm using some of it for a writing project now."

Joseph said, "Does this have to do with that nut *Don* Pedro?"

I couldn't tell him that he was right. "I've always been interested in folklore. I use it as inspiration for some of my stories."

"Milagro writes fiction, you know," Oswald said. He mentioned rather proudly that I had a degree from F.U.

I was thinking of how I'd like to write a story that connected the myths of Xquic and Persephone. I'd modernize it, and perhaps the underworld would be represented by the scary new sovereign wealth funds and the maiden would represent—

"Good evening, darlings!" Cornelia glided into the room so smoothly it was as if she was on rails. She was in one of her fantastic outfits: a narrow black skirt, an ivory blouse with a froth of ruffles at the cuffs and neckline, and elegant sandals with high heels. Her lipstick was as deep red as the ruby earrings that dangled from her lobes.

And damn if Joseph and Cornelia didn't look smitten with each other. Oswald and I exchanged amused glances as they kissed hello and gazed into each other's eyes.

We learned a little more about Joseph. After getting his degrees in plant botany and genetics, he'd worked for a large lab.

"Did you leave because you objected to creating Frankenfoods?"

He looked amused. "Nah, doodlebug, I just hated being inside all day long. It makes me wound up."

"You're an outdoors type," I said. "Oswald gets stuck in his offices for ages."

"But I like what I do," Oswald said. "I've got my weekends to stretch my muscles here. Joseph, if you like to ride, you're welcome to use one of my horses and ride with Cornelia. She's a wonderful horsewoman."

"I bet she is, but horses and I don't get along."

"What animal *does* like you?" I asked.

"Human animals," Cornelia said playfully.

We began a long discussion on animal psychology, and pack versus herd mentality. Joseph seemed to know as much as Oswald about animal behavior and physiology, but when Cornelia looked bored, he started asking her questions about her travels.

Our conversation was comfortable, but Oswald was exhausted. I saw it in his gray eyes and the distracted way he'd stare off. Joseph asked Oswald about his job.

Oswald said, "I talked to someone today about joining my practice. It would give me more time for other things."

My heart jumped a little at the idea of Oswald spending more time with me.

"Such as expanding?" Cornelia said.

"It's too soon to say," Oswald answered.

"You can't mean it!" I said. "Why do you need to expand? I thought a partner would let you cut back on the time you spend . . ."

Oswald gave me a tight smile. "We can talk about this another time."

I hated that. I hated when people treated me as if I shouldn't bring up an important subject, or make an observation. For a moment, I longed for the freedom of my haphazard single life, when I'd said whatever came into my head without worrying that I was violating someone's sense of propriety.

"Let's talk about it after dinner," I said and returned my fiancé's tight smile.

Joseph saw that I was upset and said, "Any chance I can see your garden before it's too dark?"

I took him outside and we strolled down the paths that led between the planting beds. The breeze had settled a bit and only a few birds called now, turning over the evening to the chirping of crickets.

Joseph recognized most of my plants but asked about a few of the older rose varieties. He stopped in front of the mock-orange shrub and said, "Isn't it too cold here for this?"

"Probably. I thought it would be protected against the frost here by the wall, and I'll mulch and insulate it if we get a really bad spell."

"I thought you didn't believe in trying to impose your will upon nature."

"I'm just imposing my will on this one shrub," I said. "I'm not trying to do any DNA splicing with an iceberg. I'm just trying to help it survive."

"Things are always best in climates that suit their nature. You can keep something alive, but you can't force it to thrive."

"Are you talking about life, not just plants?"

"Is there a difference? I hope your mock-orange makes it through the freezes, kitten." He put his arm around me and we went back inside.

As I closed the door behind us, I thought I saw something, *someone,* among the trees. But the image vanished immediately. What the hell was going on with my eyes? I kept peering and finally spotted something very small, perhaps a squirrel, shifting through the shadows and leaves above.

We had coffee and a plum tart for dessert, and afterward Oswald and I left the other couple and went to the family room. "Are we going to have an argument?" he asked as he sat in an armchair.

"Yes, but first I want to ask you something. Something's going on with my eyes."

"Let me guess. Now you have X-ray vision. Can you see through my clothes?"

"I wish. But, no, it's as sharp as before." I could barely remember what it was like not to have perfect vision. "You know how I see outlines of living things at night? There've been a few times lately when I see something, but when I focus, it's something else."

"Like what?"

"Like just now I thought I saw a person in one of the trees, but it was only a squirrel or something. I mean, they're not even close to the same size or shape." I realized I was nervous when I began arranging the pillows on the long sofa.

"It's happened before?"

"Yes, once, in the City. I thought I saw a person, but it was just a dog. Again, there's the disparity of size and shape. Is it my eyes, or do you think . . ."

He stood and came to me, taking a pillow out of my hand and putting his arms around me. "I think you're the craziest girl I know, but I don't think you're *going* crazy. I'll call our ophthalmologist and see about an appointment for you." He sat me down. "There are lots of causes, but the most likely one is stress, babe."

I'd been under stress before and nothing like this had happened. "Is my vision changing again maybe?"

"It sounds more like a momentary visual distortion. We all have them—our brains misinterpret visual information until we focus. We'll get it checked out. I want you to be able to enjoy our honeymoon."

"All five days of it." I leaned in to his body. "Don't expand your business, Oz. Don't you have enough to do already?"

"Businesses are like sharks, babe. They gotta keep moving forward." He rubbed my back. "I'm hoping I can get us set up comfortably and retire early. How does that sound?"

"It sounds like it's too many decades away." I looked into his eyes and saw the worry there. "I know you love what you do, and I don't want to take that away from you, but what about our life together?"

"If you had more to do, you wouldn't need me around all the time."

"You knew who I was, what I was, that I was a writer, when we met. I haven't asked anything of you but *you*. I don't need to be rich or have *things*."

"We need financial security, Milagro. Our kind needs to be self-sufficient. I want to be able to provide for my family, our children if we have them."

I dropped onto the sofa. "We're back to this again. We never resolve this. We just keep going around in circles."

"It's been a tough week. Let's go to bed."

I looked up at him hopefully.

"Our own beds," he added.

"Oswald, if I'd died in that accident, what good would any of the Council's benefits be?"

"But you didn't die."

"You don't want me anymore, Oswald."

He laughed. "It's official. You *are* crazy, and I'm burnt out. Go to bed."

I went outside first to look for Pal. Wandering through the field I turned back to stare at the house. The lights glowed from the living room windows where we'd left Cornelia and Joseph. It was a beautiful house, but it would always be Oswald's house.

Pal had abandoned me yet again. I wondered if his owners were keeping him in at night now.

I went to my room, placed my wedding ring on the marble vanity, and washed up. I turned out the lights and went to the window to smell the fragrance of mock-orange before going to sleep.

The next morning, as I was getting dressed, I looked for my ring. It was gone.

seventeen

delusions, seductions, and evictions

I searched on the floor and on the bedroom dresser. I examined the sink, but the drain would have blocked a ring from being washed away. I crawled on the floor in the bedroom and bathroom, and even pulled all the sheets and blankets off the bed. Then I repeated my search. The ring was gone, baby, gone.

My bedroom door was closed. I had not heard anyone come in during the night. I tried to be calm as I went upstairs to our room. Oswald was sitting on the bed putting his shoes on.

"My ring is gone," I said. "Did you take it for any reason?"

"Why would I take your ring?"

I told him that I'd put the ring on the vanity last night and that it was missing. "I looked everywhere."

"I'll help you look again."

"Maybe . . . ," I began.

"I know what you're thinking, and you're wrong. Cornelia

191

went to her room a few minutes after you went to bed. Unless you think Joseph snuck into your room while you slept."

"I'm not saying that!"

We went downstairs and looked for the ring in the bathroom and my bedroom. I found a quarter under a chair cushion, my favorite pen, two rubber bands, and a mini tin of breath mints. "I didn't put it in any of these places," I said. "It was on the vanity."

The sheer curtains at the window fluttered in the slight breeze. "The window," I said.

Oswald went to the window and tried to raise it further, but it still stuck at about six inches. "Even if someone got past the dogs, no one could fit through that." He glanced at the clock. "I've got to run. Don't make any wild accusations until I get back tonight."

I had no idea what Oswald had paid for that hunk of shiny rock. "I'm sorry if I lost the ring," I said, even though I didn't believe I had lost it. But how could it disappear? "We'll find it."

"I'm sure we will, babe. Remember what I said about stress." He kissed my cheek. "I'm the one who should apologize for not really understanding what you went through with your accident."

"Why won't you trust me on this?"

"You said yourself that your vision is playing tricks on you. Besides, I've seen you take off that ring and leave it everywhere. Another guy might think you didn't even like it."

"Of course I like it! Do you think that I 'lost' it on purpose?"

"You're overreacting. It's insured, so if we can't find it, we'll replace it. In the meantime, try to decompress," he said and left.

I knew that something was wrong. Even though I'd seen the

chewed wiring from the car, the accident hadn't felt like an accident. Even though, yes, I often left my ring around, I knew I hadn't misplaced it this time. I also knew that I would have awoken if someone had come into my room.

I drank my coffee and stared out the window. Ernie's truck pulled up beside the house. He got out and picked a cardboard box out of the bed of the truck. He saw me at the window and waved for me to come outside.

"*Buenos dias,* Ernesto. What's up?"

He lifted the box toward me. "I got your rat catchers here." He placed the box on the ground and opened the top. Two young black cats leaped out and ran into the garden. "One male and one female, both fixed," he said as we followed them. They slunk through the flowers, smelling things and twitching their tails and ears.

"Are they house cats?"

"Nah, they're a little wild. Leave some food and water out for them and they'll settle in here."

I was trying to approach the cats when they spotted an open access door that led under the house. In a second they'd slipped inside.

"See, they're mouse hunting already," Ernie said. "I hope they won't get eaten up by that wolf of yours."

"He hasn't been around lately. But he's no trouble. You haven't heard of any problems with him?"

Ernie shook his head. "A wolf's a wolf, mama."

I don't know why I thought of Ian. I said, "He's someone's pet." Ernie handed me a bag of cat food and a dark green bottle. I asked, "What's this?"

"It's that special liquor. Cornelia said you needed to cook something. This stuff's so strong, you could strip paint with it."

"Thanks. I wish they'd let me use tequila instead."

I put out bowls of kitty chow for the cats. I hoped they wouldn't kill any of the birds.

When I went back into the kitchen, Cornelia was standing in front of the coffee machine, looking at it expectantly. She wore sleek cream trousers and a thin white knit top. "Just a cup of coffee, Young Lady," she said. "Joseph is coming soon and driving me to the airport."

I didn't know why she couldn't pour her own coffee. I sloshed some into a mug and held it out to her. "I thought you were staying to help me prepare for the wedding."

"But I have! I've given you the recipe and the sewing directions. You begin making the cake and work on Oswald's tunic, and I'll be back in ten days."

"Where are you going?"

She told me she was going to her friend's *finca* in Andalucia. "Her divorce has been finalized and she's having a long celebration. It's just the right time to leave Joseph," she said with a smile. "Before he gets too confident."

"You like playing games with men, don't you?"

"It is my favorite sport, darling, and obviously something you enjoy as well."

"I try to be sincere with them," I said as seriously and sincerely as I could.

"But you don't try very hard, do you? Now promise that you won't drag Joseph into the night to smell the flowers while I'm gone or waggle your generous wares at him."

"My engagement ring is missing, Cornelia. Have you seen it?"

"Of course I have." She looked at me and said, "Americans like garish stones, but you can have it reset. I'll give you the name of my jeweler, who will do wonders with all the gifts from your lovers. Although I know Ian's taste is impeccable."

"What an appalling thing to say! I don't have lovers!"

"Oh, darling, I don't judge you. You're young and all alone out here, bored and desperate for attention, what with Oswald working those long hours with gorgeous women who are devoted to perfecting their beauty."

I silently counted to five before I said, "Cornelia, do you know what happened to my engagement ring?"

"No. It's difficult enough to keep track of my own baubles." She gave me a look of mock shock, hand to tidy booby. "Unless you're accusing me of *stealing* your ring!"

"Not at all. I was only asking if you'd seen it." I sat at the table and looked into her dark eyes. "I would like to like you, but I don't quite trust you."

She sipped her coffee before speaking. "You trust the wrong people and mistrust me who has always told you exactly what I think, just because I'm not ashamed of being a vampire."

"I've done the best I can given the information I've had. But, Cornelia, if you try to hurt me or interfere with my wedding plans, I will retaliate."

"Now you're speaking like a vampire," she said with a smile. "Milagro, I promise you that I intend to stand at your wedding with the deepest joy as you give your vows."

I must have been out of my mind, because I almost believed her.

After she had gone, I loaded the plants I'd bought at the nursery and some compost in my truck and drove across the field to Daisy's grave. I planted the tallest lavenders at the center of the plot and a low variety of rosemary around it, and finished with the thyme. I hauled water from the pond with a bucket.

When I had finished, I stepped back and said, "There you go, girl. Now you'll always have flowers. There's rosemary for remembrance."

When I returned to the house, I made another attempt to befriend the black cats. They moved away when I approached and began exploring the perimeter of the house. At least I wouldn't have to worry about rodents while they were here.

Don Pedro called that afternoon and said, "How is my pretty little bat?"

It was easier to ignore the nickname than argue about it. "I've gotten through the story and now I'm going through the text again." I talked about the story as a joyous journey of discovery, evolution, and knowledge, and how I would show his initial skepticism, then trepidation, followed by acceptance, and finally celebration of his transformation.

I began telling him how I'd been inspired by the *Odyssey,* especially Odysseus's great cunning, and the trickster gods of the American West, but he didn't seem interested in the fact that I was using the Alexandrian structure of twenty-four chapters.

"As the great Lao-tzu said, 'God is in the details.'"

"Are you sure it was Lao-tzu, because—"

"I am concerned, my Miracle," he said.

"Don't be. I'll have everything done by your deadline."

"I knew I could entrust you with my life! However, you have been in my visions again. The twilight is a dangerous time, little bat, when you swoop out of your cave and others are waiting to pluck you out of the sky and taste your tender, sweet flesh."

I didn't always have the right instincts when it came to proper employee deportment, but I knew enough not to ask *Don* Pedro, "How high are you?" Instead I said, "Thank you for your concern. Talk to you soon!"

When Oswald arrived home in the evening, I was still working. He gave me a kiss and said, "How's your eyesight?"

"It's been fine all day."

"I scheduled an appointment with our best ophthalmologist, but he can't come out for a few weeks."

"That's okay. I'm on a streak and I want to finish this project. After that I can deal with vision issues, fruitcakes, and wedding clothes."

"You'll tell me if you see anything else weird, won't you?"

"Of course I will. Hope you don't mind if we just have leftovers tonight."

"That's fine. Did you find your ring?"

How had I forgotten about it? "No, not yet. I'll keep looking." But I didn't, because I was on a writing streak and went back to my *fauxoir* after dinner. Generally I avoided using humor in stories, because it inevitably undermined the gravity of my literary work, but I would include some here for *Don Pedro's* character.

I took a few minutes to update my other project, Nancy's Theory of Style, and then I put it away. I thought about Oswald sleeping upstairs alone. I suddenly felt very loving toward him. I changed into a red satin camisole and tap pants, wrapped myself in a matching robe, and went upstairs to our room. Oswald was sleeping on his back, sprawled diagonally across the bed, the sheet down around his waist.

I sat on the bed and began kissing his smooth shoulders, his marvelous chest. My hands slid under the sheet and his eyes opened.

"Don't . . . ," he mumbled.

"Stop?" I asked. "Don't stop?"

He gave a sleepy laugh. "Milagro, what are you doing?"

"Guess." I reached over him and pulled open the drawer of the bedside table. There, rolling around with pens and an emergency flashlight, was the scalpel he used to use on me. I took it out and removed the hard plastic cap covering the razor-sharp tip.

Oswald's eyes widened and he took a deep breath. I handed him the scalpel and pressed my body on top of his. He pulled me down beside him, then rolled on top of me, kissing my neck and breasts, before rising onto his knees.

I was looking into his eyes. "Don't stop," I said.

He bent over me, kissing me, his tongue sliding into my mouth, his free hand tugging at the tie of my robe. It opened and slid off my shoulders.

"I love you," he said as he brought the scalpel toward me.

I loved him, too. Which is why I was so bewildered when my hand shot out and gripped his wrist, and I pushed upward, flipping him off me and flat on the floor. The scalpel clattered across the room. I was standing directly above him, so I saw his expression change from astonishment to pain.

"I'm sorry! I'm sorry!" I was crouching down beside him. "Are you all right? I don't know why . . . I'm so sorry, Oz. I didn't mean to . . ."

He shook me off and stood up, still rubbing the back of his head. "Stop apologizing. I believe you."

"I can't stop apologizing. Are you okay?"

"It's just a bump."

I stood up too, and tried to take his hand, but he pulled it away and continued to rub his head. "Do you forgive me?"

"There's nothing to forgive. You just reacted."

I moved close to him, pressing against him, but instead of putting his arms around me, he pushed me away.

"Milagro," he said softly, "why don't you go to bed?"

When I tried to kiss him good night, he turned his face, and my lips landed on his cheek. So I went to bed, feeling awful and guilty. He missed what we'd had, and even though he'd said he didn't mind the bruises and red marks I'd left on his body when we made love, I hated hurting him.

In the morning, Oswald came to my room and said, "You're going to have to move out until we get married."

"Why?"

"Because you're not respecting our agreement. You knew I couldn't resist an offer like that."

My many objections were all nullified by the fact that I'd thrown him on the floor in the middle of the night. I pleaded with him to let me stay, but he was adamant. Two hours later, my truck was loaded with the green zebra-print suitcase, blankets, pillows, the fruitcake recipe, my writing gear, Cornelia's case of rosé, and several books. I tossed a few plastic packets of calf blood in a small cooler.

Oswald followed me around the house, telling me how this was for the best, but when he wasn't looking, I hid all the remote controls and disconnected electronic devices. As I was doing this, I came across the Womyn's Sexual Health Collective catalog that my friend had sent me. I shoved it in my jeans pocket because I thought it could prove useful.

"Will you be at Mercedes's or at Nancy's place?" Oswald asked as I got in the truck and slammed the door. He knocked on the window until I rolled it down.

"Maybe, or maybe I'll go to that stupid loft."

He reached through the window and turned my face to him. "You know I don't want you to go, but I don't know any other way to get through this period."

"The other way is to tell the Council to go to hell and to let me back in your bed. We can go slower. I can concentrate and not . . . not react like that. I'll be careful, I promise."

"Don't you think I want to do that? The only reason I don't is because I care about you and your future."

I saw the concern on his face and I began to cry. "I love you, Oswald Grant, but that doesn't mean you get to make these decisions about my life."

"I love you, too, which is why I've got no other choice." He leaned in and kissed me. "Drive safely. Call me when you get to the City."

I nodded. "Water the plants on Daisy's grave," I said and I drove away from Casa Dracula.

I watched him in the rearview mirror, standing in the drive, watching me leave. My emotions were wild enough to propel me to the edge of the mountain. Then I saw the tall trees that marked the initial rise uphill. I drove into the shadowed coolness and my heart began pounding. I slowed my breath and watched the speedometer. The brakes and steering worked perfectly as I rounded the curves.

A broken tree trunk marked the place where Cornelia's car had flown off the road. I wondered again who had called the sheriff for me.

Only when I reached the sunshine where the slope descended into the vineyards below did I relax my grip on the steering wheel. I'd beat the traffic and I arrived in the City before I knew it.

After picking up a latte and muffin at a café, I parked in the loft's garage and hauled my things upstairs. It looked even more depressing with my sad blankets and pillow set on the floor and a cardboard box serving as my desk.

I checked my phone a few times to make sure it was working, since Oswald would be calling soon, begging me to return. I would forgive him and then we would reunite for a passionate session of lovemaking and tender promises not to fight again except when we wanted to have incredible make-up sex.

But while I was here, I might as well make the most of my time. I called Nancy and invited her over to talk about the wedding, and I called Mercedes and told her I'd be stopping by the club.

My last call was to my friend and gardening client Gigi Barton. I'd met the extravagant socialite and heiress ("It's not worth sneezing at if it's not Barton's Tissues!") when I'd gone to Nancy's wedding with Ian. Gigi's assistant told me that she was out of town, but that I was welcome to come by any time to see the garden.

Nancy arrived a few hours later, carrying an oversized leather tote and a pressboard folder. She looked around the loft and asked, "Are you staying here?"

"Oswald and I had a fight. He thinks we should hold off on sex until we get married."

When she finished laughing, she said, "That isn't a bad idea, actually. It might make sex after marriage less *pfft*."

"I thought you and Todd were . . . very compatible," I ventured.

"We were, until his interest turned to producing little Todds—*Todditos,* your people would call them—who would get a generous trust fund from Daddy. You have no idea how lucky you are to be poor."

"Yes, I'm grateful for that every day," I said. "But for the record, I don't consider myself poor."

"I love that about you. Did you mail the invites?"

"Didn't you get yours?"

"Yes, but I thought that maybe you'd just mailed one to me to trick me into thinking you'd sent them all. I still think you should have more bridesmaids. It seems rather stingy to only have Mercedes as maid of honor." She sighed dramatically. "I'll try to pass it off as restrained, and people will understand that I'm not a bridesmaid because of my official duties."

I was glad that Nancy had managed to rationalize her absence from my wedding party, when I had been excluded from hers. "We can go shopping for a dress while I'm here."

"You should have done that months ago. But I have solved your problem." She sat cross-legged on the folded blankets and opened the folder. "Do you remember my cousin Sissy?"

"The costume designer?"

"Yes, but she's bored with those grungy actors, so she's branching out into fashion. Here's her design for your dress."

She handed me the folder and I saw a pen-and-watercolor sketch of myself wearing a version of the old movie star dress I'd said I liked. The style of the dress had been altered to floor length and looked like a wedding gown, and it was shaded in the palest violet. A sample of gorgeous heavy satin was pinned to the drawing.

"It's so beautiful," I said.

"It will be cut on the bias so that it flows," Nancy said. "You don't need a veil, just a flower in your hair and pink pearls, I think. I'll loan them to you and they'll be your 'something borrowed.' You have to see Sissy ASAP for a fitting."

Nancy bothered me with a lot of details about things I had to do and handed me wedding magazines with marked pages and notes. But I kept going back to the sketch of the dress. It was just right. "Nancy, you done good."

My friend grinned. "I told you I would. It's so easy to deal with someone who doesn't care. You have no idea what it's like arguing with women who think they know what they're doing."

"I care! Really, I do, but I realize that Oswald wants the type of wedding that I couldn't put together by myself."

Nancy tilted her head. "It's your wedding, too. If you *really* cared, you'd be calling me up twenty times a day with ideas and suggestions. Where's your ring?"

"I misplaced it."

"If you don't like it, you can have it reset. I marched Todd right back to the jeweler to buy a better stone. There's so much more to judging a diamond than cut, clarity, carats, and color."

"Nancy, promise me that you will always use your genius for frivolity, not for evil."

"I make no promises." She packed up her things and stood. "I have some furniture in storage. Do you want to use it here until you remodel?"

"Oswald will be begging me to come home any second, but it would be nice to have a place to sit when I drop by."

She said she'd have it delivered and we arranged to meet later in the week at what she called her cousin Sissy's atelier. I didn't think I'd get any writing done, so I wrapped myself in a blanket and went to sleep during the day on my native soil, like a vampire.

eighteen

exile on vein street

I awoke to the sound of ringing. I picked up my phone automatically, and it took me a moment to realize that the ringing was the doorbell. I pushed the intercom button and a man said, "Delivery for Ms. Los Dos Knockers."

"Come in."

In a few minutes, two scrawny guys were at my front door with a pink velvet sofa in the hallway. The older guy leered at me and said, "You must be Ms. Los Dos Knockers."

"It's De Los Santos."

He looked down at a clipboard. "I got Los Dos Knockers here clear as, uh . . ." His gaze became fixated on my own *dos* knockers, and his companion hid his grin behind his hand.

"Yes, whatever," I said. "Bring in the sofa."

It wasn't just the sofa. There were chairs, rugs, delicate side tables, a desk, and drapes. The guys hauled in a disassembled queen-sized bed and several unmarked boxes. The prevailing theme was pink and froofy. The boxes held dishes, towels, linens, an entire apartment's worth of things. Oswald had given me a toolbox for my truck, and I fetched it and found a screwdriver. I put together the bed and hung the drapes with tacks.

The overall effect was *house:* crackhouse, whorehouse, madhouse, all of the above. I felt strangely pleased, especially by the desk set up by the window. I called Oswald's office, and the office manager told me that he'd gone out to dinner with an associate.

"He mentioned that he was thinking about expanding," I said. "I didn't know he was already interviewing partners."

"This doc wandered right in here today," she said. "Said she's heard about him and was looking to invest."

"Really? What's she like?"

She laughed. "Nowhere as pretty as you, hon. Nice, but a little, I dunno, twitchy, I guess. Sharp little features. Little bitty hands. That's good for surgery, you know."

"Is it normal for someone to just walk in and ask about a job as a plastic surgeon?"

"It's not normal—it's lucky if she's half as good as she seems. She said she was here on vacation and fell in love with the place. Dr. Oswald is checking her references and credentials."

I said good-bye and then left a message on Oswald's cell phone telling him I was thrilled I was staying in the City and adding, "No need to call back tonight. I've got a million things to do and I'll be going to the club."

And I did. I showered, noting that I needed to buy a shower curtain the next time I was out, and then I had a refreshing blood spritzer. I went through the Womyn's Sexual Health Collective catalog until I found the fuzzy pink handcuffs that Oswald had noticed. I ordered them and a few other interesting products to be delivered to the ranch. The next time I decided to let Oswald taste my blood, I'd make sure I couldn't hurt him.

Feeling more hopeful, I decided to go out. I found a corner café and ate a rare roast beef sandwich while skimming through the magazines Nancy had left.

I turned a page and saw a radiant bride in an exquisite mermaid dress with rows of silk scallops edged in silver. The model was Ilena, whose blond hair floated around her glowing face. I was fascinated and disturbed by the sight of her as a bride. Not that she was really a bride, just a skinny, apathetic model. A skinny, apathetic model who looked astonishing and was also a financial brainiac.

Since it was just after 5 P.M., I drove to Mercedes's club, arriving before all the parking spots were filled by the evening crowd. A tall transvestite sashayed down the street in leather pants and boots, and a few drunken homeless guys rallied up the energy to whistle.

I was parking my truck up the street when I thought I saw Ian Ducharme's dark curly head in my rearview mirror. When I turned around, he had already disappeared around the end of the block. I hurried down the street, and when I got around the corner I saw only a cluster of dark-haired Mexican men in front of a small bar. Which reminded me of my appointment with the eye doctor.

The club wouldn't be open for hours, and the doorman, Lenny, was hanging out in the box office.

"Hey, sugar, good to see you. How's life in the sticks?"

"Not fast enough for you, Lenny. Is the boss around?"

"She's in her office. I'll let you in."

My friend was sorting through receipts, her dreads bobbing a little each time she turned her head.

"Hola, mujer."

"Milagro!" If I hadn't known her better, I might have thought she looked as if she wasn't absolutely overjoyed to see me. "What are you doing here?"

"I thought this was my home away from home," I said and dropped into a chair. "I'm having Issues with this whole vampire thing and the wedding."

"I thought you wanted to join them and be a part of everything."

"I did, but I didn't think their Council would come into my house, drink all my booze, flood the toilet, and try to screw me."

"Don't get me caught up in your *arroz con mango*. Is this going to take long?"

"Yes, it's going to take long, and what does that mean anyway, rice and mango? It sounds delicious, but is it a dessert, or a side dish, like plantains?"

She leaned back against her desk. "It means a sticky mess. You're always getting in these situations."

"*I* am just trying to live my simple little life, writing and gardening. The *Council* is causing all the problems. I have to sew wedding clothes and make a fruitcake and suffer sexual deprivation! And Oswald is going along with them."

She just looked at me with her big brown eyes.

"What?" I asked.

"You're going to tell me some crazy story, aren't you?"

Just for that, I made sure to relay my recent travails in excruciating detail. When I stopped talking she said, "Why the hell didn't you tell me about the car accident?"

"I don't know. I'd feel stupid calling you and saying that rats ate my car wiring."

"You still should have called!"

"I always feel like I'm bothering you with all my drama."

"I grew up with a Cuban mother—I can deal with drama," she said. "If you don't want to join them, don't. Oswald's trying to do the best he can for you, and if you ever had to deal with a mortgage, you'd appreciate what the Council is offering you."

"Did I tell you that Oswald gave me a loft to remodel and sell?"

"I'm not going to get into your relationship, but that man loves you." She stood up and said, "I've got to get the house ready."

"How's business?"

She brightened. "Good. We're selling out about half our shows. Oh, your friend Frankie called. I might hire him."

"Really? That's great, and it will get his mom out here to do shows more often."

"If you can be happy for me doing well, I think you can show a little enthusiasm for Oswald expanding his business."

"It's not the same," I stammered. "He works crazy hours, and he's already got so much money—"

"It *is* the same. Go help the bartender prep for the night. Don't eat all the cherries."

"I never eat all the cherries," I said. I usually ate all the orange slices and munched on peanuts, but she didn't need to know that.

The show that night was fantastic. It was just an indie rock band, but the lyrics, what I could understand of them, were really evocative. I joined the crowd on the dance floor, and if there was a really pretty young guy dancing right next to me for most of the night, well, I hadn't invited him to stand there. And if he bought a few drinks for me, and I treated him to a drink or two, that was just cordiality.

And if I let him put his slim arms around me and ask me to go with him to a party, that was just nostalgia for my old life, remembering what it was like to run off into the night with a boy who smelled of clean boy sweat and excitement and rash decisions. I held up my hand to display my engagement ring— and remembered that it was missing.

"I'm engaged," I said.

"You're breakin' my heart," he said, dropping his head and looking up at me through his long eyelashes. "You sure?"

"I'm sure."

Soon he moved on to another girl, and I said good night to Mercedes and her staff and went back to my funky loft.

Oswald called just as I walked in the door. "Hi, babe," he said as if nothing was wrong. Maybe nothing *was* wrong.

"Oswald," I said. "How was your dinner?"

"How did you . . . never mind. It was good. This woman's amazing. She's a perfect fit for my office, specializing in eyes and noses, but she does good neck work."

When your fiancé is a vampire and admires someone else's neck work, it's time to become concerned. "You're getting in awfully late from a business dinner."

"I knew you were at My Dive, probably flirting with some helpless innocent."

"He wasn't helpless or innocent," I said, laughing. "How come you're not jealous?"

"Who says I'm not?"

"What about you going on a date with another woman?"

"Yeah, I was getting all turned on when we were discussing billing methods."

"So what's her name? Is she sexy?"

"Her name is Vidalia Littner, and no."

209

"Vidalia? She's named after the onions? I find this very difficult to believe. Are you lying to me?"

"A little, because she's got a high-strung sexiness."

When I didn't say anything, he asked, "Are you still there?"

"Yes, but I'm waiting for you to beg me to come back."

I heard him sigh. "I don't mean to be patronizing, babe, but I put you in this situation. I'm responsible for you."

It was an old discussion. He felt guilty that he'd first infected me, but it wasn't as if we could go back and undo what had been done. "Oswald, I'll go along with this on one condition, that you'll agree to get over your guilt."

"It's not that easy," he said. "Do you mind being away so much?"

"It's not that bad," I admitted. "I can get a lot done here, and I can work with Nancy on the wedding. But I miss you, Oz."

"I miss you, too. I also miss the remote control for the television. Where did you hide it?"

"You don't need it because I'm going to entertain you right now. Get comfortable and let me tell you what I'd do if I was there." I settled into a fuzzy fuchsia armchair, switched off the light, and began to elaborate. I said to him, "I'm wearing a skimpy exam gown and I'm on the exam table. You come in wearing your white coat and tell me that you're a doctor, I should trust you . . ."

I treated our separation like a vacation and the days flew by. I went to the Indian market, found dried pomegranate seeds, and bought the other dried fruit for the cake. I dumped them in several wide-mouth glass jars and poured the nasty green vampire alcohol over them. Then I put them in a cupboard and forgot about them.

I found a group called Stitching & Bitching that met every

afternoon in a bar and worked on crafts while talking about politics, culture, and relationships. The chicks in the group hauled in portable sewing machines, and they helped me with the tunics, even taking over the embroidery when they saw my clumsy stitches. In a city filled with eccentrics, my project was never questioned.

Another level of needlecraft was being done by Nancy's cousin. Sissy was all business as she fitted a muslin model of the wedding gown on me and explained boning in undergarments and the importance of trying out shoes, hair, and the gown together. She had a bolt of the pale violet satin on a shelf with other fabrics. It shimmered softly, and when I touched it, the satin felt cool and smooth.

Oswald and I kept up our phone calls and I became more comfortable with incorporating his fantasies about our lovemaking. I still hesitated, however, when I described how I would take out a knife and cut him. How could I hurt someone as wonderful as Oswald?

One day I looked at my *fauxoir* and knew it was complete. It was 350 pages of fabrication, hyperbole, purple prose, and specious nonsense. In other words, it was perfect. I called *Don* Pedro to arrange delivering the document and collecting the rest of my payment.

I was surprised when he told me to meet him at an expensive restaurant on the water. It was an unusually balmy day, and the hostess led me to a table outside. The breeze carried the fresh saltwater smell, and sailboats dotted the bay.

Don Pedro was sipping iced tea and wearing a white guayabera, neat tan slacks, a bolo tie, and a panama hat. His worn leather satchel was on a chair beside him.

"Milagro! It is done, then?"

"I've got it right here. Both a printed copy and the file."

He signaled to the waitress and I ordered a cranberry juice and a salad.

It was then that I noticed a big man in a dark shirt, jeans, and brown leather sandals standing off to the side of the patio. He was watching me, but not in a lascivious way. *Don* Pedro slathered butter on a piece of bread and talked about the seagulls and how he had once spent a day as a seagull eating sardines in Monterey Bay.

I placed the thick manuscript on the table in front of him and told him what I had written. He read a few pages, careful to hold them at the edges to keep them neat, and he smiled broadly, showing his neat rows of teeth. "Perfect! Perfect! You have captured me exactly, as I knew you would."

His smile and praise made me sit taller. "I'm glad you like it. I think it's—I'm very proud of it." I explained the themes I'd worked into the story, and suggested that he search for a legitimate printer to turn out the *fauxoir*.

"There are so many scam vanity publishers out there, *Don* Pedro. Please be careful not to go to anyone who overcharges or makes promises he won't keep." I didn't want to see the silly little man cheated, and I'd even looked up honest businesses that specialized in self-published memoirs. I handed him the list and said, "You'll probably want to get a few estimates and compare them. All of these companies have good records."

He patted my hand with his neat, small one and I saw that his nails were neatly trimmed and buffed. *"Muchas gracias* for looking out for me. I will take your advice." The waitress brought over our bill and he said, "Now it is time for me to pay you, Milagro." He handed me a check for the balance of his payment.

I looked to make sure everything was right and said, "It was a pleasure doing business with you, *Don* Pedro. I hope your family and friends enjoy your memoir." I thought about asking him to send me a copy of his book, but he'd probably be printing up a few dozen copies at most, making each one an expensive present.

"I'm sure it will be a huge success! It is our secret though, yes?"

"A promise is a promise." I glanced over and the big man was still standing there. "*Don* Pedro, I don't mean to alarm you, but a rather large fellow seems to be watching us."

My companion smiled and said, "He is my associate. He is a great follower of my teachings and he thinks I am too naive to be safe in the big city!" He laughed. "I asked him to join us, but he is trying to learn to shape-shift to a snake and so he eats infrequently."

"Well, good luck on that." I had nothing against snakes; they ate rodents, which made me hope that the new cats were working out at the ranch.

We bid each other good-bye and the little man said, "Fly in joy, magical bat!" Looking into my eyes he said, "You will conquer your enemies, and we shall meet again in this world or another."

"I look forward to it."

I was smiling as I watched *Don* Pedro and his hulking friend walk toward the parking lot. I knew I'd probably never see him again, and I was more than a little sad to know that my story would soon be forgotten.

Edna finally returned from her long sojourn. She came through the City on her way home and visited me at the loft. I kissed her soft cheek as she came inside.

"You look tan and rested, except for the tan part," I said.

She was wearing a chic wraparound print dress. Her silver hair had been cut short recently, showing off her neck and shoulders. My mother Regina would have said Edna had perfect posture. Edna looked around my new domicile and blinked. "It looks like an explosion at the Pepto-Bismol factory."

"I'm glad you like it. Nancy gave me the furnishings."

"This is the same young woman who is planning your wedding? Oswald's mother will be overjoyed."

"Nancy has lulled Oswald's mother into quiescence by sending her daily updates and dropping names. May I offer you some tea?"

Edna went to the window and said, "At least one can enjoy the view *out* of the room."

I filled a saucepan with water and put it on the stove. "I'm getting to like this place, and I'm getting a lot done here for the wedding." I went to the closet and took out the wedding costumes.

She tilted her head and looked at the groom's robe. Some seams were a little crooked, but they wouldn't be too visible at night, when the ceremony would take place. The embroidery by my fellow Stitching Bitches was of a better quality.

Edna started laughing at the garments, and I said, "I think they look pretty good!"

"I'm sure you do."

I found my tin of tea and spooned some directly into the saucepan of water. Edna rolled her eyes, so I said, "I'm making do, okay? How was your trip?"

"Marvelous, if only because I missed your contretemps with Cornelia."

"So she wasn't trying to kill me. But I'm sure she's up to something. She's inexplicably crazy about the guy at the local nursery."

"Is he good-looking?"

"Very, and he's got this really manly vibe and he's kind of surly."

"Then what is inexplicable?"

"One, he is not rich. Two, he is not a vampire, and she's a snob about that, isn't she?" The tea came to a boil and I turned off the heat. "You may remember that Cornelia once called me a common Mexican girl."

"How can I forget, since you bring it up every time Cornelia is mentioned?"

"Well, I'm just saying . . ." The tea seemed reasonably dark, so I poured it into two mugs that I'd picked up at the Dollar Store. I handed one to Edna.

She stared at the design on the mug—a koala surrounded by pink hearts—and then she sat on the watermelon pink velvet sofa. "Mugs like this make the world a worse place to live," she said. "Cornelia felt that you'd slighted Ian."

"I couldn't keep going out with him after he offered me a thrall as a treat," I said. "But that was then. Now he has a new girlfriend. She's a nuclear physicist and Miss Universe, or something."

"You mean Ilena?"

"I met her in New York. She insulted me." Edna raised her brow inquisitively and I added, "I'd rather not go into it. Suffice it to say that it was a very unkind remark about my appearance." My will broke under Edna's penetrating gaze and I said, "She called me a chubby pickle!"

Edna burst into laughter, and I huffed, "Well, that's the last time I expect any understanding from you!"

"I understand very well, Young Lady. How is your cake progressing?"

I showed her the lurid concoction that was steeping in the cupboard. The green liquor had tinted the fruits a horrible slime green.

"That looks as bad as this tea tastes. Let me take you to a proper tea."

We went to one of her favorite department stores to have afternoon tea under a stained-glass cupola. She looked around with a satisfied expression and said, "It's good to see you again, Young Lady, even though I enjoyed my time away."

I grinned at her. "Someday you will reveal the details of your tawdry relationship with your addled young lover."

"I do not have a lover," she said coolly. Then she gave me a sly grin. "And if I did, I would never tell."

An hour passed quickly and we said good-bye. She promised to look for my engagement ring, visit Daisy's grave, and alert me when Cornelia reappeared.

I walked back to the condo in the cool of the evening. Buses jammed the streets, and the sidewalks were crowded with people going home, going out, living their busy lives. I missed Oswald and my garden and even elusive Pal, but it was easy to fill my days here.

I wrote the outline for a story about a young woman who is lured to the underworld, a metaphor for the dark powers of consumerism. I went to the library frequently, happy to sit in the company of other readers among the thousands of books.

The vampire ophthalmologist came to the City and examined my eyes. He gave me a clean bill of health, and I forgot about my earlier visual distortions as quickly as most people forget a cold.

Nancy and I met frequently, and I continued to transcribe her declarations on style, planning to give her the composition book as a gift after the wedding. I convinced her to use wild-flower seeds as party favors, but I lost my battle to hire a rock band at the reception when Nancy joined forces with Oswald. He wanted a cover band that would play his parents' favorite standards, and since he was writing the checks, I gave in.

Once while we were at Sissy's, waiting for the designer to finish a phone call, Nancy asked if my father would be giving me away.

"My father gave me away to my grandmother when I was a baby. He doesn't need to do it again." I was wearing my gown and holding my arms straight out so I wouldn't be pricked by the pins Sissy had just placed for alterations.

"Don't be Milacious. It won't look right if you just walk down the aisle on your own."

"We shouldn't count on him. It's likely my parents won't even show up."

"Of course they'll show up. Your mother Regina will want to meet Orestes because he's a plastic surgeon."

"Oswald. Do you know that Cornelia, Ian's sister, was visiting and she asked what 'procedures' I was going to have done before the wedding? The nerve."

Nancy shrugged. "If I was marrying him, I'd have the works—except for my nose, which is perfect, and my boobies, which are wonderfully perky, don't you think?"

I agreed that they were perky.

"Then there's maintenance, not letting everything slide downward, and then your husband is off with one of his *associates* for business meetings and comes home looking too satisfied with himself."

"Oswald might be expanding his firm. There's a woman doctor who wants to join. Her name is Vidalia."

"Like the onions?" Nancy blew her bangs out of her eyes. "I would be careful if I were you."

"According to him, she wants to meet me. We're having dinner as soon as I get all this stuff done here."

"They *always* want to meet the wife or girlfriend. They like to suss out the competition and figure out their angle of attack."

"Nancy, is everything okay with you and Todd?"

"Of course. Don't forget I have a pre-nup guaranteeing my eternal bliss—in one form or another. What about you? Have you met with a lawyer yet?"

"I don't own anything but your old pink sofa, Nancy."

"You have the loft. You have your health and youth and you've allowed him exclusive access to your bodacious tatas and your fleshtastic booty. You've supported him in his career. I'll give you the name of my attorney. You'll totally heart her. She's a barracuda in Armani."

"Thanks, but no thanks."

"I'll give you her name anyway."

"Nancy, I hope that Todd realizes how talented you are at this event-planning thing."

"Toad doesn't care what I do, which is fine by me."

"*I* care what you do, and you're doing a fabulous job."

She was doing such a fabulous job that all I really had to worry about was the RSVPs, which Oswald was sending to me, and the hotel arrangements at the coastal resort town. We'd reserved a block of rooms and booked a restaurant for the Friday evening rehearsal dinner and Sunday brunch. When the hotel's wedding coordinator called me, I hoped it wasn't bad news and asked, "Is anything wrong with our reservations?"

"Everything is fine!" she said. "I was calling to offer you a complimentary night here to tour the rooms and finalize arrangements."

"Really? That would be wonderful!"

I immediately called Oswald.

"That's awfully generous of them, but I can't get away," he said. "Yes, book the reservation for seven-thirty."

"What do you mean, you can't go, *and* book the reservation?"

"Sorry, I was talking to someone else. I'm having dinner with Vidalia tonight to talk business."

"*Another* dinner with her? I thought most business is conducted at lunch meetings."

"Yes, another dinner. It will be a very erotic encounter. We're going for Chinese and meeting with Sam and her attorney."

"Have you gotten that far already?"

"I know it's happening fast, but she wants to start soon, and the more I think about it, the more I know it's the right thing to do for my business. And for us."

I had the disturbing sensation that I was living in the bizarro version of Dr. Jekyll and Mr. Hyde. I'd hooked up with wild Mr. Hyde, and now career-driven, well-mannered Dr. Jekyll was taking over his body more and more often. But if I could be happy for Mercedes, I could be happy for Oswald. "That's great, Oz. I really hope it works out."

"Thanks, babe. You go and have fun. The hotel's a little more comfortable than your loft, and there are a lot of good restaurants and boutiques around. Buy yourself a few new outfits on me. Why don't you take one of your girlfriends and have a girls' vacation?"

nineteen

one-way ticket to hell, please

Nancy and Mercedes couldn't come and even my slacker pals were unavailable on such short notice. The next morning, I packed the green zebra case, including the wedding tunics so I could work on the embroidery on my solitary evening, and drove south.

I passed the congested urban areas, then the generic sprawl of surburbia, and finally drove along a highway that ran parallel to the scrub bushes and grasses of the coast. The drive took me in and out of warm weather and ocean coolness.

I'd called the winery where our wedding would be held, and the owners invited me to come for lunch, so now I navigated a circuitous route down into the valley of a beautiful mountain range. The west side of the range was close enough to the ocean for pines, redwoods, and firs, but madrones and chaparral grew on the warmer, protected eastern slopes.

A narrow road led through a valley of vineyards. Real operations for the winery had been moved to a new facility, and I reached the old stucco building that was now rented out for events. I got out of my truck, inhaling the scent of ripening fruit and the yeasty, fecund smell of old fermentation. Oswald and I had discovered this place when we'd had time for road trips.

The friendly owners gave me a private tasting and helped me to select wines that would complement the dinner. They told me it was too bad the fog was covering the local village where my guests would be staying. "But that's how it is most of the time and your guests won't even get the daytime sun here, since your wedding's in the evening."

"My guests won't mind. They're always going on about the damaging rays of the sun," I assured them, holding up a glass of a smoky, fruity pinot to catch the light.

I backtracked to the coastal village and drove through the picturesque streets to the elegant hillside resort where most of our guests would stay. I introduced myself to the unctuous concierge, who escorted me to the complimentary room. "It isn't as large as the honeymoon suite, but I hope it will be satisfactory."

Then the event planner and I met and she gave me a tour of the rooms and amenities. We went over the necessities for each suite (which included cranberry juice, tomato juice, sunscreen, and canvas hats and visors).

As evening came on, I took a walk through town, which was all of four blocks long. I looked at all the expensive little shops filled with useless items and over-indulgent services. The streaked blond store clerks gave me that "Are you worth our time?" look, and decided that I wasn't. I looked too much like the busboys in their fancy restaurants. Perhaps, too, my anti-pathy for the cliché landscape paintings and outrageously priced resort wear was evident.

I turned away from the shops and went down to the beach, taking off my shoes so I could walk along the shore. An after-noon party was winding down on the terrace of a waterfront restaurant. I listened to the bright laughter and talk and watched as people began to leave the paved terrace and walk to-ward the street. They were the sort of people who bought resort wear. The women's pastel dresses billowed in the ocean breeze and they clutched sun hats to their blond heads.

"Milagro! Milagro!" a voice called out. I looked through the group until I spotted my friend and gardening client Gigi Bar-ton. A former model, the socialite was a marvelous stretch of a woman, clad now in nautically inspired navy and white, with a red scarf tying back her golden mane. She must have been wear-ing ten pearl necklaces, from chokers to long ropes. She was as famous for her fake jewelry as for her real wealth.

I waved to her and went to join her, brushing the sand off my feet near the restaurant's deck and putting my shoes back on. She came forward and gave me a hug and two air kisses with her bright red lips. "Thank God you made it!"

I hadn't been invited, but Gigi always made the endearing assumption that I was part of her crowd. "Gigi, how've you been? This is amazing—I just called you, because I wanted to do a checkup of your garden."

"When you know everybody, you always see them every-where. It's so convenient, because you're never a stranger any-where." By everywhere, she meant wealthy enclaves, and by everybody, she meant the rich who inhabited them. By this thinking, one was able to ignore inconsequential people who populated those vast wastelands without boutiques and Michelin-starred restaurants.

"How have you been? Is Bernie here?" Bernie, the tabloid stringer, dated Gigi.

"Oh, he's out in the desert again. He said he doesn't have time to read with all my activities. I'd almost believe he loves his first editions more than me. Where is your handsome fiancé?"

"Oswald's working. I'm here finalizing a few things for the wedding."

"Of course, Bernie and I will be there, and I know Nancy will do a wonderful job planning things, but you can always ask me, too! I think my fourth wedding was the most elegant, but my first was the wildest. I'm showing my age, but that's when trashing hotel rooms was de rigueur." She turned and called, "Lord Ian, which was my best wedding?"

The crowd of people behind her shifted, and then I saw Ian Ducharme. He came forward, more casually dressed than I'd ever seen him, in a dark blue sweater over a pale blue shirt, jeans, and a panama hat tilted at a jaunty angle, casting his eyes in shadow. He saw me and his eyes widened a little, but otherwise his demeanor remained the same as he said, "I was only at the second, Gigi, and it was splendid. You were a dazzling bride."

Gigi laughed and gripped his arm affectionately. "Oh, that was my famous white-bikini beach wedding! Milagro, we'll see you at dinner and after," she said as her friends began to drag her away. In another minute everyone else was gone; only Ian and I remained.

Panic rose in me, and I considered running into the ocean and swimming out far enough where all I had to worry about was the sharks. But what did I have to be nervous about? I smiled politely and said, "Hello, Ian. I meet you on one coast and then the other."

"Another coincidence?" he said dryly.

"Do you think I'm stalking you now? The hotel invited me to visit and I'm finalizing arrangements for the wedding." I was silently cursing Oswald for not joining me here. "And you? Where is Ilena?"

"She has other obligations."

I didn't ask if he meant that she had other obligations at the moment, or if she wasn't here at all.

"I'm sorry we ended things on unpleasant terms," I said. "I do hope we can continue to be friends."

I didn't expect him to burst into laughter, but he did, and I snapped, "What is so damn funny?"

When he finally stopped laughing, he looked more relaxed and said, "You and your attempts to be polite."

"You think I'm incapable of fitting in with your swanky society pals?"

He stepped forward and took my hand. At his touch, a hot fizz went through my body. He looked into my eyes and asked softly, "Why are you so eager to be like everyone else when you're Milagro De Los Santos?"

I wanted to step closer, close enough to smell his cologne, feel his warm breath on my face. I wanted to reach out to confirm that his sweater was cashmere, and then press myself along his body, extending the low electric buzz wherever flesh touched flesh. But I yanked my hand free and said, "I don't want to be the miracle of the saints. I never applied for the job, I don't like the hours, and I sure as hell don't like the company. Damn vampire councils, creepy rituals, and people kidnapping and trying to kill me. Your people treat me either like a carnival freak or as a container of high-grade recreational substances." I stopped because I remembered that Ian's own parents had treated him like their personal drugstore.

"Now you sound more like my own girl," he said.

" 'Your own girl' is five-feet, eleven-inches of taciturn attitude dressed in designer rags."

He looked satisfied, as if he had won some point. "I must be on my way. I'm confident you'll be able to stave off any attacks by wharf rats."

"I *already* apologized to your sister! It's not as if she hasn't been vile to me in the past. You told me yourself that she and Oswald—"

"She's moved on and is quite infatuated with her friend Joseph."

Was he assuring me that he had moved on, too? "Yes, we've all moved on, and I'm very glad of it."

"I'm so very glad you're very glad," he said smoothly, making me want to scream. "Perhaps I'll see you at dinner. Good-bye, Milagro." He turned and began walking in the opposite direction of town.

I watched him go, feeling an unwelcome pang. "No one invited me to any dinner," I muttered into the wind.

But when I returned to the hotel, the desk clerk handed me a note scrawled on one of Gigi's hot pink note cards. It said, "8 p.m., Hayden's," with a surfeit of *x*'s and *o*'s in lieu of a signature. The clerk told me that Hayden's was a restaurant and gave me directions.

I went upstairs to my room and called Oswald's office, but he'd already gone off for his meeting with Sam and Vidalia. I left a message for him that I'd run into Gigi and was joining her group for dinner. "You know Gigi. I won't be back until late so let's talk tomorrow."

I took a bath and luxuriated through my important girly grooming steps. I was a fabulous *chica* and I would look fabulous tonight. I poured myself into a red silk dress, applied too much eye makeup, and dabbed on the hotel's complimentary eau de toilette sample.

I put on a lightweight coat and walked in my silver high-heeled sandals to Hayden's. I stood at the entrance of the dark-paneled restaurant. The room was filled with laughing, chattering people, but my eyes went right to Ian, who was with a small group at the bar. He turned and looked at me as I took off my coat and checked it. He nodded in greeting, and I gave a little wave in his direction.

I said hello to Gigi and got involved with a group of her friends who were talking about one of the hot new memoirs. They all knew the author and claimed he was a habitual liar. The conversation was most illuminating, but I was always aware of the vampire on the other side of the room.

Hayden's was a seafood restaurant, and our group was served huge quantities of prawns, crab, scallops, and oysters, and the white wine flowed. Ian was sitting at Gigi's table, and I could hear her peals of laughter over other voices.

As we finished our meal with after-dinner drinks and desserts, Gigi came by each table and handed out a list. "Two-hour time limit, everyone!"

"What is that?" I asked the man next to me.

"It's for the scavenger hunt. Each table is a team. Can you run in those shoes?"

"Like the wind."

Ninety minutes later, my dress was hiked up to my hips as I balanced on his shoulders and pried off a nautical street sign (*Anemone Way*, for 125 points). When I spotted the flashing red light of the police car, I shouted, "Cheese it! It's the cops!" to my team. My partner nearly dropped me, but another teammate caught me. I made it safely to the ground, handed one of the guys the sign, and we scattered in all directions.

The emergency plan was to meet back at Hayden's. I was the first from my group to return. My stomach cramped with a craving for something red, and I went to the bar. "What red wines do you have by the glass?" I asked the bartender.

I felt someone standing close behind me. I looked into the mirror above the bar. "Hello, Ian."

"Hello, Young Lady."

The bartender handed me a drinks menu and I turned to Ian and asked, "Where's your group?"

"They're on their way back with our haul. I believe they had to collect one last lawn gnome."

"One hundred and ten points," I said. "That might give you the win. Although we did get a photo with twins, which is worth two hundred points. They're fraternal, not identical, twins, but it still counts."

"It will be a close contest." His smile showed only in his eyes, and they crinkled at the corners.

I looked down at the menu and said, "I need something red to drink, or maybe I'll get a burger."

"I know a place," he said.

"You always do."

We said good-bye to those members of Gigi's party who were straggling in, dragging traffic cones, cases of Spam, and Dalmatians, and walked down the main road through town.

We commented on the charm of the town, the quaint architecture, the sound of the water, safe topics.

Ian led me down a dark side street and to a small but lovely stone building, with wild California grape scaling the walls and covering them in red-hued leaves. Light glowed through the amber windows. *Bar None* was painted in delicate black script on an unobtrusive driftwood sign.

Instead of going to the front entrance, Ian said, "This way," and we went in the small alley between buildings. He knocked on a side door.

"Your life is full of back alleys and side doors," I said. "Is anyone going to answer? Is this even a restaurant?"

"It's just the sort of restaurant you need."

The door opened a few inches, a gaunt man dressed in a gray shirt and black slacks peered out, and then he opened the door fully. "Welcome, sir!" he said. We stepped into a hallway with plastered walls and a dark plank floor.

"Hello, Nelson. This is my friend Milagro."

"Pleased to meet you, Miss Milagro." Nelson walked toward the end of the hall, saying, "We're quiet this evening, but I hope we can offer something to please you."

We followed him upstairs to a large landing with a rough-hewn wooden door. Nelson opened it and we walked into a cozy room that looked more like a living room than a restaurant. Oxblood leather armchairs were grouped with sofas in conversational areas. Seascapes hung on the pale blue walls, and seashells and nautical ephemera decorated tables and walls.

A few attractive middle-aged couples sat here and there, sipping what looked like red wine. They looked at us as we walked in and smiled in recognition at Ian. Nelson showed us to two

228

chairs in a corner. "Your server will be with you shortly, and if there's anything else you want . . ."

"Thank you, Nelson," Ian said, and the man left us.

"I don't see any food. I don't see any food because this is a vampire bar," I said. I had been to a vampire bar once before. It had been filled with young vamps and their thralls, all black leather and PVC. This was a different scene. "This town is a vampire hangout, so I should have expected a vampire bar, right?"

"It's one of the town's attractions. I assumed you knew about it."

"Oswald tries to protect me from things he thinks will shock or offend me."

"He has gentlemanly instincts," Ian said. "Although you don't seem to be pleased about his efforts."

"I like to make those choices myself. I'm not a hothouse flower."

"I've never mistaken you for one."

An attractive waitress came to our table, wearing the same black and gray combination as Nelson. "Good evening. May I tell you our specials?"

"Sure," I said, waiting for her to describe some local sheep breed, or maybe even fish blood.

She signaled to other staff, who came forward. "We have Helen, who is a lactovegetarian and B positive," she said, and a young woman smiled pleasantly, all whole-grain goodness.

The waitress smiled toward a buff young man. "We have an excellent O positive, Bob, a personal trainer, who is on a high-vitamin and antioxidant regimen." Bob nodded his head toward us, then stepped back.

"We've also got something very rare—Sandra," she said as

another woman came forward. "She's been completely organic for twenty years and is AB negative."

"You're talking about these people," I said quietly.

"We draw the blood and serve it at body temperature," the waitress assured me. "You can witness the draw if you like. We guarantee the quality and source."

Ian sighed and said, "Bring us a bottle of your freshest animal."

"But . . . ," she began before realizing he was serious. "We have a refreshing wild otter, caught and released after harvest just this morning."

"That will be fine," Ian said.

As she went to get our drinks, I slumped back against the chair. "Why, why, why."

"Because we are vampires."

"Go ahead, then. Have a glass of Sandra or Bob."

"My taste for human blood has been somewhat spoiled by something finer," he said lightly.

We sat silently until the waitress came back and poured the otter blood in wineglasses for us. She topped them with a salty Italian mineral water, added dashes of Worcestershire sauce and Tabasco, and a squeeze of lime. I tasted mine. It was pleasantly briny and the citrus set off the depth of the otter. "Very nice. Thank you."

The blood went zinging into my system, reviving me. I looked up to see Ian watching me. Other things started zinging in my body. I listened to the music, a romantic old Van Morrison song. "Cornelia told me that you taught her to like all kinds of music."

"She gives me too much credit. She's always loved music."

Like a tumbler in a lock clicking into place, I realized something. "You're Mercedes's investor." He nodded. "Why didn't she say anything to me?"

"Mercedes thought it was a good idea to keep friendship and money separate, and I agreed."

"Oh, so I wouldn't feel compelled to be nice to you on her behalf."

The corner of his mouth twitched upward. "No, she didn't want you to feel guilty on her behalf the next time you and I had some conflict. She seemed to think it was bound to happen."

"Mercedes is one smart *galleta.*"

"Without a doubt."

"When are we going to argue next?"

"Soon, I imagine," he said.

"You're probably right." I realized we'd both shifted in our seats to mirror each other's positions. I remembered seeing him for the first time and how he'd made me think sex, sex, sex.

I said, "It seems like a long time since we first met. I was so clueless about your kind, stuck out there at the ranch with Winnie hating me and Edna treating me like some two-bit skank."

"You were holding your own, Young Lady."

"I thought you were flirting with me just because I was there."

"Not so. I'd gone there especially to meet you. Cornelia insisted on coming along, complicating matters as she does. From all reports, I expected you to be a rather obvious fortune-hunter."

"The Council still tries to buy me with money."

"When it's affection that you value. I would have had better luck with you if I'd offered you a kitten," he said and smiled. "I thought you'd be impressed with me, because—"

"Because you're an impressive man. Women want you and men want to *be* you."

"You're mocking me now," he said.

"A little. But it's still true." We sat quietly and finally I put my hand on his, and that simple contact made the warmth rush through me. I trembled with the sensation. "You feel that, too, don't you? Something different than with others."

"It's always been different with you, Milagro. Every time you're near . . ." He stopped speaking and I looked into his dark brown eyes and I felt us breathing in time with each other.

In a matter of moments, he had paid and we were out the door, in the alley. My thoughts were a filthy mess of selfish justifications. I thought of Nancy's trifecta, and I thought of my true love for Oswald, and I thought of having one last night of wanton sluttery, and I thought that sex with Ian would stop my recurring fantasies of him. But more than anything, I thought, I want him, I want him, and all my morals and ethics were nothing compared to the way my blood recognized and desired his, moving in me like the ocean to the pull of the moon.

Ian shoved me against the rough stone wall and kissed me, his mouth tasting the way I remembered, but more delicious in its familiarity. His leg parted my thighs as his lips went to my neck.

My hands were running down his back, pulling him to me. His scent aroused me, too, and the feel of the muscles under his clothes. We made our way, grabbing and kissing, to a modern house on a hillside street.

As soon as we were inside, I began yanking off his jacket and his shirt. We undressed as we moved to the master bedroom. I shrugged out of my coat, and he pulled off my dress, leaving me only in panties, bra, and heels. He went to the fireplace, lighting a match under the kindling, and in seconds flames flickered yellow and blue.

It was as if my every capillary came alive and the entire surface of my skin was erogenous. My blood rushed up to meet his touch, and I had to feel all of him. I rushed to unbuckle his belt and pull down his slacks while he was trying to take off his shoes and socks. We would have fallen over, but he held me around the waist and soon we were naked, clutching each other.

I spread my fingers out on his chest and his muscular shoulders, thinking him beautiful, loving the look of him.

He pushed me back and lifted me atop the dresser. I wrapped my legs around his waist, and I began nipping his skin. His smooth self-control was gone, and he shuddered as I stroked him.

Out of the corner of my eye I saw the gleam of the gold penknife. I grabbed it and pulled away far enough from Ian to open it. "Ian."

"Yes," he said, and I did something I'd never done before. I didn't hesitate, but quickly drew the blade across his shoulder, deep enough to break the skin. I pressed my mouth to the blood that welled there. Pleasure, exquisite and crimson, engulfed me in the seconds before the skin smoothed over the wound. I cut him again on his chest, this time using my tongue to pry the cut open for additional seconds of pleasure.

My body opened to him instinctively and my blood called out so insistently that I handed Ian the knife and said, "Hurry."

He scored an arc on the upper curve of my breast, but instead of pain, it was an amazing release. His body shook as he drank my blood and we moved against each other. Handing the knife back and forth. Once holding our palms together against the blade, then smearing the blended blood on each other.

We licked and bit each other like animals. No, like vampires.

When we were done, I kept my legs and arms around him and he carried me over to the bed, where we collapsed panting.

"You're intoxicating," I said and used the tip of the knife to prick his neck. I sucked at the thick drop of blood and moaned.

"You're the only one I've ever let take my blood."

I knew it wasn't true, but I wasn't going to bring up his parents' abuse now.

"My own girl," he said, using his endearment for me.

"Do you call Ilena that?"

"Only you," he said, and I wanted to believe it.

We spent the night in a mad tumble across every surface of the room, and all through the hours we savored each other's blood. I felt liberated from caution and able to use my strength without fear of hurting him.

I wanted the night to last forever, but dawn came as we were in the shower, exhausted but sliding our soapy hands over each other, still kissing and biting.

When we came out of the bathroom, wrapped in towels, the sight of the bedsheets flecked with drying blood did not bother me.

I leaned against Ian and said, "I'll have to go soon."

"Why?"

"This was my last hurrah. I've got to get home."

He stepped away from me suddenly. "Aren't you staying?"

"I've already stayed too long. Now we both move on. You to Ilena, and me to my marriage."

He looked astounded, then angry. "How long do I have to wait for you to get over your childish infatuation with Grant?"

"I love Oswald."

"If you love him, why are you here with me?"

"I don't know . . ." I said and I didn't. "Because every time you're around, you make my life more confused. Things with Oswald were fabulous until you gave me your blood."

"If I hadn't, you would have died."

"If I hadn't been with you, I wouldn't have been hurt."

"*You* asked me to accompany you that night," he said. "You continue to act as if all of this is merely accidental, that *we* are merely accidental."

"It is, and we are. I didn't intend this. I don't want to want you."

Ian stared at me a moment and then he said, "Get out. Get out of my life." He turned and left the room.

I don't know where he went, but he wasn't in the living room when I collected my clothes and dressed.

I'd been wrong: I had been able to hurt Ian.

I had acted without regard for Oswald, but now I felt a wracking guilt for treating Ian as if he was disposable. And that misplaced emotion left me wondering exactly what kind of heartless, twisted bitch I'd become.

I walked outside and didn't recognize the neighborhood. I teetered on my heels down the hill and toward the water. I found my hotel, got my things together, and headed north. It was time to straighten out my relationship and my life.

I knew one thing for certain now: I knew I was capable of doing the things that would make me a proper vampire bride for Oswald.

twenty

seriously on the rocks with a twist

Oswald was in the study and there were neat piles of folders on his desk, and coffee mugs here and there.

"I'm home, honey," I said, hoping that my voice didn't sound too flagrantly whorish. I went to kiss him, suddenly paranoid that he would smell Ian on me. Which was impossible. I'd showered again at the hotel, and the only thing on my clothes was the faint stench of mothballs from the ride.

"Hi, Mil," he said, looking confused. "What are you doing here?"

I dropped onto the sofa. "I live here and I'm going to stay here. I didn't see your grandmother's car out there."

"She's staying with Winnie and Sam this week."

"She never seems to be home anymore," I said, both bothered that Edna was gone again and relieved that I wouldn't have to hide anything from her sharp eyes. I pulled a business card out of my pocket and picked up the phone. I punched in a long series of numbers.

"Who are you calling?"

I smiled at him, and when the woman on the other end of the line answered, "Hello," I said, "Mrs. Smith, this is Milagro De Los Santos. I'd like to speak to Mr. Nixon."

Oswald had abruptly stood up and was mouthing "Stop! Stop!"

I turned away from him and said, "Yes, well tell Mr. Nixon that I've changed my mind about all of our agreements. The Council is stuck with me and I'm stuck with them, and I strongly recommend that they get over themselves."

Oswald was now standing in front of me, trying to grab the phone from my hand. I hunched over it and covered the mouthpiece, saying, "She put me on hold. What is it?"

"What the hell are you doing?"

"I'm declaring my independence," I said.

Mrs. Smith got back on the line and said, "Mr. Nixon will be coming to meet with you and Dr. Grant in two days."

"Fine," I told her. "I'll give him a tour of the countryside. If he's not afraid of heights, I'll take him to a winery that has a funicular. Everyone loves a funicular. Adios."

I hung up and said to Oswald, "Nixon's coming to visit in two days."

He ran his hands through his hair and said, "I can't believe you just did that."

"Believe it, because it's done. I'm starving. Do you want some lunch?"

He didn't want lunch. He wanted to argue with me. He was

shouting that I should call back and apologize, while I made a pot of coffee and whipped up an omelet. "But I'm not sorry. I should have done this from the beginning."

"What is wrong with you? Why are you throwing all our work away?"

"You've been going along with the Council for my sake, and I've been going along with them for your sake, and neither of us is happy. The fact is that even if I do everything they want, they'll never fully accept me, and I'm done with trying to alter who I am for others. I'm done with selling out."

"Ensuring your security is not selling out."

"Then why do I feel so compromised, Oswald?"

I ate while he glared at me, and then I took the scraps out to the cats. Oswald followed me outside and watched me looking for them.

"Where are the cats?"

"Under the house. Unless your wolf ate them."

"Ha ha and ha," I said, even though it was possible. I left the food out for them. "Has Pal been around?"

"Not since you left. Don't you want to ask me how I've been?"

I looked at the man in front of me. Even tired and rumpled, he was fabulous. "Besides being angry with me, how are you?"

"The deal with Vidalia is going through. She's going to cover things so we can take a real honeymoon for a month. Anywhere you want to go."

"Really?"

"Really."

I threw my arms around him and kissed him, wishing I didn't feel so tainted. "Thank you, Oswald. You are wonderful and good and I love you."

He pushed me back so he could look at me, and I saw that

he was still upset with me. "When I come back, we're expanding the business. Since you're declaring your independence, I'm going to declare mine, too. I'd like to work as much as I need to, without getting grief from you."

Be careful what you wish for . . . "All right, but can we do something—make a fresh start? Let's not have any more surprises. Let's not try to change each other, okay?"

"Okay."

"Oswald, I went to Bar None yesterday."

He looked uncomfortable. "I was going to tell you about it."

"It's fine, but you've got to realize that I'm more creeped out by the family secrets than by—well, I'm still creeped out by a bar with people on the menu, but you've got to stop trying to protect me. It just puts me in the position of looking stupid."

"It's difficult not to keep secrets after a lifetime of hiding who you are."

"Oswald, there's nothing you could do or say that would make me love you less," I said. "Now when am I going to meet Vidalia?"

"Soon. You'll like her even though she's serious. She's got killer recommendations and incredible empathy for those who want to transform themselves."

For some reason I thought of *Don* Pedro's dream of me as a pretty bat and I smiled. "I think the desire to transform oneself is universal. Ask Vidalia when she can make it to dinner."

He brushed my hair back from my face. "I'm going to run to the clinic for a few consults. I can reschedule them if you like."

"Do what you have to do."

"I'll be home later. Love you."

"Me, too."

239

I did love him. He was a kind man, a good man, a man who deserved someone better than me.

We'd get married and I'd adjust to his career drive and he'd adjust to my more meandering writing efforts. We'd be happy here with Edna in the cottage and Sam and Winnie visiting. His parents and I would establish a truce, and I'd find another literary agent and prove to Oswald that writing was a legitimate vocation. If Pal came back, I'd adopt him officially, get a license and shots for him, and have him neutered.

I would be faithful to Oswald for as long as I lived. I would be worthy of his love.

After Oswald left, I still felt amped up. I went through my mail and found the shipment from the Womyn's Sexual Health Collective. I left the fuzzy pink handcuffs on Oswald's desk in his study and hid the other items for our wedding night.

Then I changed into my jeans and drove to the nursery. Joseph was busy helping a few customers, so I explored the row of annuals and waited. When he came out, he said, "So, peaches, where've you been?"

"Went to the City to finish a few projects. How's business?"

"I could still use some help. Any chance you'd be interested in a few hours for the next week?"

"We've got a guest coming, but if you don't mind me working around that, I can help out."

He didn't, and I started my duties by arranging a display of plants to tantalize customers. I enjoyed arranging the plants as an example of ways to use foliage for texture and color and how flowers could be used to accent structure.

While I worked I wondered if I should have thrown myself at Oswald's feet, confessed, and begged for forgiveness. Something was wrong with me, however, and though I knew that I had done something wrong, wrong, wrong, I didn't regret my night with Ian. I told myself that Oswald would benefit from my indiscretion when I gave him what he most wanted, my blood.

When I finished the displays, I went into the small office at one side of the retail shop and made a mock-up of the descriptive placards that could be used to help customers. I'd turned on the radio and was listening to salsa when Joseph came into the office.

"I just closed up," he said. "What have you got there?"

"It's a sample of a sign that you can use for lesser known varieties. I'll add in growing requirements and suggestions so people will know how to use them in their garden. The right plant for the right place and all that. People buy more if they have information and a photo of the mature plant."

"Good idea," he said. He watched me as I stapled the label to a stake and then put the stake in a one-gallon tricolor abelia. "I wish I knew how to dance."

"Interesting non sequitur," I said. "Everyone can dance."

"I mean partner dance. I want to take the princess out when she comes back, but I don't know how to dance to this."

I put down the plant and said, "I'll teach you and I won't even charge for it."

I cranked up the volume and we went to the shop, where there was a clear area in front of the counter. I taught him to dance the way that Mercedes had taught me. First we listened to the music until Joseph was able to hear the two-measure phrases and clap on the beat, and then I guided him in the basic moves. He stepped on my feet a few times, but otherwise he moved well for a big guy. "You're not half bad," I said.

"That's what all the girls say."

"I bet they say more than that. Stop bopping your head to the music. It isn't suave. Half of salsa is looking as if you want to ravish your partner on the dance floor."

He turned his blue eyes to mine and pulled me closer. "Like this?"

I felt my temperature rising. "You're a natural."

Thirty minutes later, Joseph was able to move comfortably across the floor and turn me without hurling me into the rack of seed packets.

He tried to dip me, and I was bent backward laughing when we heard a loud crack and a windowpane shattered. My city instincts took over, and I twisted and pulled Joseph down to the floor with me.

"What was that?" he said, trying to stand.

I yanked him down again. "Stay here."

He looked at me like I was crazy. We waited a long minute before getting up to inspect the broken window. A small rock lay with the shattered glass.

"I thought it might be a gunshot," I said.

He unlocked the front door and went outside, with me right behind. "Probably some kid." He looked around, but we were the only ones on the street. Then he gazed at me. "You're real strong for someone your size, pookie."

"I eat my vegetables."

"I mean, *real* strong. I saw you moving around those trees in fifteen-gallons. You lifted them like nothing."

"I'm kind of a freak that way."

He looked amused. "That's okay. I'm kind of a freak, too. I mean, not in a sexual way, although I am willing to—"

"No need to explain!" I said, not wanting to know the details of his relationship with Cornelia. "Sorry that this happened. This town is usually so safe. I hope it's not because you're new."

"Kids are kids," he said looking upward.

I followed his gaze to the branches of an old pine. The branches rustled slightly in the light breeze. The lowest branches of the tree were easily fifteen feet up. "No one climbed that. Come on, I'll help you clean up."

I swept up the glass while he broke apart a pallet so he could board up the window. A glass sliver sliced my finger and I hid it behind my back so Joseph wouldn't see the skin heal itself. He was noticing too much already.

As I left, Joseph hugged me good-bye and said, "Be careful."

It seemed an odd way of saying good night. "The town really is very safe. You've got nothing to worry about here."

"So says the girl with the locked gate at the drive to her ranch."

"It's not my ranch, and the gate's locked so no one opens it and lets the horses loose. I feel so safe I sleep with my window open every night." I didn't mention that no one could get in the jammed window.

I picked up a sandwich at the deli—eggplant and red pepper on focaccia—and mentioned to the owner that someone had broken the nursery window. She hadn't heard of any similar incidents, but word would get out. People would be watching for a rock-throwing miscreant.

Back at the ranch, I ate my sandwich outside on the terrace with a chicken blood spritzer. This was usually the time we'd all sit here and watch the sunset, but everyone was gone. I sipped the drink and realized the chicken blood had gone off. I set it down and gazed at the fields and the mountains beyond.

I wished I had someone I could confide in. I had done

something awful, so why didn't I feel awful? It was the blood. The blood had changed me. If I kept going this way, I'd soon feel comfortable slashing people right and left, taking on a bevy of thralls. Possibly hot, buff thralls who slavishly fulfilled my every sick vampire whim.

When you're faced with evidence of life's perversity or your own, sometimes it's best to just go to bed.

The next day I was up early and already out in the garden, pulling up all the little weeds that had rooted in my absence. Oswald came by on his way to his car, looking more cheerful than he'd been yesterday. "Thanks for the present," he said with a grin. "Although pink isn't my color."

"They're for our wedding night—if you want to wait that long."

"I'd like to keep my agreement with the Council, and who knows, maybe the situation can still be salvaged."

"Your hope springs eternal."

"I've got another thing that springs, too," he said.

We were laughing and I was reaching under the branches of a hydrangea when I noticed an odd little mound of dirt. "I hope these cats aren't using my garden as a litter box," I said. I used my trowel to inspect the mound.

"They're cats. Kiss me good-bye, but don't get me muddy."

Something glinted in the dirt. I picked it up and shook off the dirt. It was my engagement ring.

I glanced up at Oswald.

"I told you you'd misplaced it," he said.

"I didn't! I'd never leave it lying in the dirt! I left it on my bathroom counter."

"Milagro."

"Oswald."

"How else would it get there? It's right outside your window."

"Do you think I just tossed it out one night?"

"I don't know anymore," he said. "It doesn't matter. Put it somewhere safe, or if you don't want it, I can exchange it for something you like."

Of course he was skeptical; I wondered myself if I'd absent-mindedly dropped it, if I'd unconsciously been trying to get rid of it.

After he left, I washed off the ring and put it on. It still looked strange on my hand. Maybe I should exchange it for something else, but I couldn't imagine another diamond ring I'd like better. Nancy would know, so I'd ask for her opinion.

Out by the pond, the plants on Daisy's grave were growing nicely, especially the thyme, which had filled in the crevices between the rocks. I was watering the plants and feeling all too aware of how isolated I was here, without Edna, Sam, Winnie, the baby, Gabriel, the relatives who'd been ever-present when I first lived here. I thought they'd always be here, but they'd moved on with their lives.

And I'd misjudged Oswald, thinking that he was an easy-going slacker. But easygoing slackers didn't finish med school and specialty training and then set up a private practice.

I'd hardly had time to wallow in loneliness when a car honked outside the ranch gate. It was Cornelia, in a new rental car. She parked and I tensely carried her bags to her guest room, afraid that Ian might have told her what had happened, or that she would sense it herself. But she nattered on about her trip, not needing conversation so much as an audience.

We went back downstairs, when she remembered why she was here. "Have you finished the wedding garments?"

"I've got them in my room," I said and she followed me there. "How is Joseph?"

"Good. I'm teaching him to dance so he can ask you out."

"You see, he's smitten," she said with a laugh. "Mr. Nixon called and told me that you are utterly out of control. He insisted I get here as soon as possible."

"Do I look out of control?" I took the red silk tunics out of the closet. "I've just got to finish the hem of Oswald's."

Cornelia's gaze went to my hand. "You've found your ring! Not quite your style, but it is beautiful." She took the gowns from me and said, "I'll take these up to my room and compare them against the sketches to make sure the embroidery is accurate. Mr. Nixon was trying to fault me for your behavior, but I explained that's just your Latin passion."

"Gee, thanks for perpetuating the stereotype," I said. "Can we talk about my wedding now?"

"We *are* talking about your wedding. How is your fruitcake?"

"The dried fruit is still soaking in that evil booze at my place in the City. I'll pick it up the next time I go there."

"No! You've got to stir the mixture every week so everything marinates evenly! You'll just have to start all over again and hope the cake has time to age properly before the wedding."

"I'm going to talk to Nixon tomorrow about this nutty cake."

"How tragic if you should be the one to break this beloved tradition after all these centuries. Oswald may understand. He is so very understanding!"

"I didn't say I *wouldn't* make the cake. I'll make the damn cake, okay?"

I stewed over stewed fruit for the rest of the day. When the phone rang, I answered with an annoyed "Hello?"

"Keep away from my man," hissed a woman. It sounded as if she was speaking through a cloth and I had to struggle to decipher her words.

Glancing around first to make sure Cornelia was nowhere near, I said quietly, "Who is this? Ilena?"

"You can't keep off him, whore, slut. But he's mine. Let him go, or you'll regret it." Then the line clicked off.

Ilena could have gotten our phone number from one of the Smith women, but *was* it Ilena? The voice had been so indistinct that I couldn't say for certain, but who else could it be? She hadn't said my name. Perhaps it was a wrong number.

The utter foolishness of what I'd done finally hit me. I thought of all I'd risked—my home, my relationship, my friends—for a few hours of sex, and self-loathing gripped me like a riptide.

The phone was ringing again. I snatched it up hoping it was the woman so I could put a stop to this nonsense now, before it escalated. "Hello."

"Milagro, this is Jason."

Jason had been my literary agent, and I thought I'd never hear from him again. "Hey, Jason! What's up?"

"You heard the news about that big Latino book sale, right?"

"I've been out of the loop for a few days. What sale?"

"A memoir. Fierce bidding war, and it sold for seven figures. I thought of you because it seemed kinda your thing, an ethnic story with folklore and paranormal elements. If you've got anything like that, nonfiction, the market is hot now and I might be able to make a sale."

A Latino memoir with folklore and paranormal elements. "Who's the author?"

"*Don* Pedro Nascimento," Jason said. "Charismatic little shit with a cult following. He's lived with aboriginal tribes all around the world and claims to be a shape-shifter. Talk is, the memoir is flat-out brilliant."

It was at this point that I began cussing. I started in English, went on to Spanish, and repeated myself several times. When I finished, I said, "I wrote that memoir! That's *my* story. That lying, thieving, trifling son of a bitch!"

Jason paused before saying, "Milagro, maybe we can talk some other time. I've got another call coming in. I'll get back to you."

I stormed to my bedroom and slammed the door shut. When I calmed down sufficiently, I called Sam and told him what had happened.

"I'll look into copyright law and we can discuss it tomorrow. I'll be there for the meeting with Mr. Nixon."

"He's talked to you already?"

"Oswald asked me to come. He's worried."

"I know. Will you please bring Edna back with you? I miss her."

The rest of the day wasn't any better. Cornelia stayed in her room calling friends for hours. When Oswald came home, I told him about *Don* Pedro's knavery. Instead of being outraged, he looked at me with a bewildered expression and said, "How do you attract these oddballs to you?"

"You tell me. You're one of them!"

Cornelia chattered away at dinner, while Oswald and I sat edgily across from each other, thinking about the visit from Mr. Nixon. After our meal, she insisted that we try on our wedding tunics. Oswald took his to his room to change, and I went to my room.

The gown had been made to fit close to my body, but when

I tried to put it on, it stuck at my bustline. I tugged and wiggled until I got it on. Looking in the mirror, I saw confirmation that it was far too tight. It pulled across my body and threatened to tear at the seams. I looked like a giant shiny crimson larva.

How could this have happened? It had fit fine before. But I hadn't been doing my usual running while I was away. Could I have gained weight that quickly? It seemed odd, because my metabolism had sped up with the infection—but maybe that had been a short-term effect.

Cornelia knocked on the door and called, "Time for your runway walk!"

"The dress needs some work," I said through the door.

"Don't be shy! Oswald's dying to see his beautiful bride! I need to give you information about the ceremony, too."

Reluctantly I went out to the living room. Oswald was by the fireplace. The tunic flowed from his shoulders to the floor, and he looked as if he was from a different time and place. Even my clumsy embroidery was transformed when seen in the soft evening light.

Cornelia held a manila folder at her side as she admired Oswald, saying, "You look so gallant!" Then she turned to me and began laughing.

Oswald's expression was one of mingled dismay and amusement.

My face grew hot. "I don't know what happened. I'll let it out."

"You can't let silk out, Young Lady," Cornelia said. "You'll have to start over again, or lose your puppy fat. Oswald can vacuum it out of you."

"It does look a little snug," Oswald said.

Et tu, Oswald? "I'll work it off with some extra running."

Cornelia gave me a pitying look and held out the folder. "Here's the wedding ritual. The officiant, that new fellow, will call in a few days and we'll do a rehearsal on the phone. I wrote it out phonetically, because his pronunciation is rather poor."

As I reached for the folder, I felt the fabric straining at my shoulder. I excused myself and went to take off the constraining gown. A seam ripped as I yanked it off. I was so upset by the gown disaster that I didn't even look at the folder and set it aside on my desk.

I put on a pair of sweats and went outside. My elusive friend, Pal, appeared and joined me for the first few of my many circuits around the fields. A creature howled somewhere off in a stand of trees, and Pal stopped to listen before taking off into the night.

When my legs were shaky and I was drenched in sweat, I finally quit. Getting married shouldn't be so complicated, I thought as I crawled into bed. All I'd wanted was a simple ceremony with the man I loved. How had it all come to this? My thoughts flitted from my own infidelity to the angry woman to *Don* Pedro's duplicity to the vampire Council to the gown that made me look like a giant worm, and I didn't sleep the entire night.

twenty-one

put a fork in her, she's done

The next morning, we were all in a mood. Oswald was irritated because he'd had to rearrange his appointments and was also worried that I'd do something that would further antagonize Nixon, who was expected that afternoon. I was staying close to the house phone so I could grab it first if the angry woman called again.

I was happy that Sam and Edna came early, bringing a box of warm croissants, but then Sam pulled me aside and told me that *Don* Pedro's apparently simple confidentiality agreement was actually a very tidy, waterproof document.

I was reaching for a croissant when Cornelia sauntered into the kitchen and shook her head. She was dressed in skintight toffee-colored jeans and a thin tank that showed every vertebra of her skinny spine. I left the pastries and had a shot of chicken blood, followed by a mug of black coffee.

251

Edna, sleek in a mauve blouse and chocolate slacks, was tearing a *pain au chocolat* into bite-size pieces. "I haven't seen Nixon in years," she said.

"He seemed like a jackass."

Sam, who was walking back and forth across the floor, said, "He follows protocol quite strictly. He's very traditional."

"That's what I said—he seemed like a jackass. Sam, will you stop pacing? It's making me crazy."

"I don't know what Nixon's going to say. The Council believes you've disrespected them," he said. He took a seat and started jittering his foot.

"So is it like in a gang, where dissing starts a war?" I said. "Because I haven't had a chance to come up with my gang colors and signs."

"There are better times to be flippant, Young Lady," Edna said. "I know you're frustrated, but take the time to listen to what Nixon has to say. For your sake."

"That's exactly what we've been trying to tell her, Grandmama," Sam said.

"Although Milagro is right," Edna said. "Nixon *is* a jackass."

"I give up," Oswald said. "I'll be in my study."

I followed Edna back to her cottage and told her about my tunic problem. "Edna, do I look as if I gained weight?"

She looked me up and down. "It's hard to say. You've always had a few extra pounds."

"That's my decorative fat," I said defensively. "I like my curves. I don't want to be a scrawny bone creature like Cornelia and Ilena."

"No one expects you to look like them, Young Lady."

"If that isn't bad enough, I just got ripped off for a writing project, my *fauxoir*."

"So Sam told me. Who can we trust if we can't trust eccentrics who hire ghostwriters for their shape-shifting memoirs?"

"I'm glad you find this so amusing."

"You do attract them."

"That's what Oswald said, but maybe it's the writing business that attracts crazies."

"That's also true. Why ever did you sign away your rights?"

"How was I supposed to know he'd sell it for a fortune? His notes were preposterous. I was the one who made up all the stories and gave the memoir a theme, structure, and meaning." We were standing outside her cottage and I was absentmindedly picking the dead leaves off a climbing rose. "Sam says I have no case against *Don* Pedro. It's infuriating."

"It does say something about your writing, however."

"Yes, it says that a crazy little freak is more credible with the literary world than I am."

"Would you prefer it if your *fauxoir*, as you call it, was really just for *Don* Pedro and his friends, ignored and forgotten?"

"There is also the money factor. He paid me a pittance because he said it was just for family, thereby misrepresenting the situation. He got paid a fortune."

"Young Lady, if you were really so concerned with money, you might be more agreeable to the Council."

"It's very different to earn money through one's craft than to be given money for complying with unreasonable demands."

"No one could ever accuse you of the latter."

I leaned against the cottage. "I don't know, Edna. I did try, especially with the wedding, to do what Oswald wants, because, well, because all I want is to be married to him and be a real part of your family."

"You'll always be a real part of our family, Young Lady."

And that was enough to make me cry. She put her arms around me and let me sob on her pretty blouse. After a few minutes, I struggled to control myself, and she said, "Is everything all right?"

I sniffled and wiped my eyes. "I guess I've got wedding jitters. Once it's over, and we all settle here and things go back to normal . . ." Her expression made me stop. "What is it?"

"I'm going to be moving," she said. "Thomas wants me close by and I think you and Oswald need your privacy. I need my own place, too. Don't look at me like that. You must have imagined that this would happen eventually. I've given enough indications."

"I thought you were just talking! I didn't think you'd really . . . Thomas isn't right for you, and I'll miss you."

"Thomas is right for now," she said dryly. "I'll miss you, too. I bet you never thought you'd hear me say that when we first met. Now go wash your face and make yourself presentable."

I was in my room doing as she ordered when I heard the buzzer sound for the gate. A delivery truck was there and I signed for a package from Nancy's cousin, Sissy.

Inside the large cardboard box were layers and layers of crisp white tissue, and when I opened them I saw luscious folds of pale violet satin.

I took the dress out and held it before me in the mirror. It looked as if it would fit me perfectly. It was so pretty that I couldn't bear to put it away in the closet. I hung the hanger on a hook near the window, so that the slight breezes would air it out.

As I walked through the house I heard Cornelia's voice upstairs, so I went to her room. Sam was sitting on her bed as she reached into one of her bags and said, "Here it is," as she brought out a gorgeous gift-wrapped box. "It's the next size up so the baby can wear it next winter."

"Hi," I said and stood in the doorway, thinking of the kitschy tourist T-shirts I'd bought for Sam's toddler. Now that I knew how to sew, I could make something more personal for her. "Cornelia, my wedding dress just arrived. Would you like to see it?"

"Of course! I'll be right down," she said.

But when I went to my bedroom, the wedding dress was not on the hanger.

I checked the closet even though I knew I hadn't put it there. I turned around, knowing that things don't just vanish. A flash of color caught my attention. I looked out the window and saw my dress.

Cornelia and Sam had come downstairs and were in the kitchen as I stormed through. They followed me outside to the garden. My beautiful, beautiful dress was tangled in a freshly watered bed of roses and smeared with mud.

"How could this happen! Who did this?" I was shouting and trying to extricate the dress from the thorny branches but the softly sheened satin was snagging and catching.

Sam looked confused, and Cornelia's expression was intrigued. She even said, "Isn't that interesting?"

When I freed the dress from the rosebush, I held it aloft and shouted at Cornelia, "Did you have anything to do with this?"

Sam looked at me as if I was crazy. "She's been with me for the last hour."

Oswald, attracted by the shouting, came outside. "What's going on?" Oswald asked as he took in the scene.

"Someone took my dress from my room and threw it in the mud."

Cornelia said, "It was not I. I have a witness. I'm completely innocent."

"Not guilty is *not* the same as innocent," I snapped.

Everyone began talking over one another at this point. Cornelia noted that I'd also lost my ring. Sam thought no one should jump to conclusions. Oswald wondered if there could be a rational explanation.

I ranted about a conspiracy and people being out to get me and added, "What about the car crash?"

Sam said, "We've already settled that it was an accident. The evidence was conclusive."

"There are no accidents," I said, which was contrary to my belief that life was indeed a series of haphazard occurrences.

Oswald drew me aside and said, "Babe, you need to calm down."

"I don't want to calm down!"

"You went through a crisis recently. Have you noticed any 'lost time'?"

Though he spoke soothingly, I was not soothed. "Lost time? Are you implying that I did this myself?"

"It's a symptom of disassociative fugue states. Think about it—the vision distortions, the ring, this dress. They all happened after your accident."

I grabbed his arm and pulled him farther away from the others. "They also happened after Cornelia came," I hissed. I was also thinking about my first visual distortion in the City and the woman who'd threatened me on the phone. But Ilena couldn't have done these things.

"Sam was with Cornelia upstairs. How would she know how to sabotage the car wiring to look as if it had been damaged by rats? It isn't possible."

256

"How do I know what's possible with *you people*?" I regretted it the moment I said it.

"You are crazy," Oswald said.

I remembered an old movie called *Gaslight* where the husband tries to convince his wife that she's crazy by moving things around the house. "Someone's trying to make me think I am. These aren't just coincidences. They weren't precipitated by the accident—the accident was part of it."

Edna had heard the commotion and came from her cottage, and now everyone was watching us argue. Oswald failed to convince me that I was being paranoid, and I wondered just who was out to get me.

We were so caught up in our discussion that we didn't notice Sam leaving our group to open the gate for the car that had arrived. The black Mercedes rolled almost silently into the car park.

Ian and Ilena got out. She was wearing an expensive wisp of cloth that barely covered her hoo-ha, and her long legs looked even longer, her hair more blond, and her features more striking. My anger drained from me, and all I could do was hope, hope, hope that Oswald wouldn't suspect anything.

Ian barely glanced my way to say hello, and that hurt me more than it should. He said to Oswald, "Nixon asked that I join the meeting today, and Ilena wanted to see Cornelia."

Ilena gave me a cool greeting, but she had been that way when I'd met her before. Cornelia fell on the model with many kisses, flips of hair, and exclamations.

You'd think that a guy like Oswald, who looked at nekkid women as part of his job, would be jaded about what passed for beauty in the fashion world, but he was as dazzled as the others.

I did a quick State of the *Chica* summary: Some invisible

person had buried my ring and trashed my dress. Vermin had eaten the wiring in the car, nearly killing me. The man I'd last had sex with was here with his girlfriend, who'd called me a chubby pickle and possibly threatened me. My fiancé thought I was sabotaging myself while in a fugue state. A small loony man had sold my fiction as his own memoir for seven figures. My beautiful dog was still dead, and Edna was moving away. I'd have to make my wedding tunic again and start the stupid fruit-cake again. And Mr. Nixon was on his way here.

The only way I could have felt more miserable was if some-one had cracked a hive of yellow jackets over my *cabeza*. At least then I'd have an excuse to run away screaming. Now I smiled politely before slipping into the house and laying the damaged dress across my bed.

Edna helped me put together platters of sliced meats, cheese, bread, and fruit for lunch. She said, "I'm glad to see that you've composed yourself, Young Lady."

"Only outwardly. Inside I'm a boiling cauldron of rage," I said as I arranged grapes in a semicircle over a wedge of Camem-bert and fanned out crackers on a platter. "Oswald thinks I've been doing destructive things without being conscious of them. It is a rational explanation, but it isn't the correct explanation."

"What do you think is the correct explanation?"

"Someone is out to get me, which seems to have become an occupational hazard of being me. How else can you explain what happened to my wedding dress?"

Just then, one of the black cats that had been living under the house came slinking into the kitchen from the open back door. I bent to give it a slice of cheese and it dashed outside again.

Edna looked at the door and looked at me. "Cats can be very mischievous."

It would have been a reasonable explanation if it hadn't been for the threatening phone call. But I couldn't tell Edna about that because then I'd have to tell her about Ian.

Things were so bad that I was actually relieved when Mr. Nixon arrived after lunch. He looked more approachable in a light-colored suit, and he enthusiastically befriended the dogs who had come in search of leftovers and attention.

His affection for the animals made me feel kindly toward him. I was happy to step away from the guys glomming onto Ilena, so I went to Nixon and said, "The dogs have a great life out there, running in the fields and living in a pack."

"I have a boxer," he said. "She was supposed to be my wife's, but she decided that she owns me."

"My dog was like that. She adopted me."

He looked down at the four dogs surrounding him. "Which is yours?"

I pointed off toward the pond. "She died a few months back. She's buried by the pond, but I visit her every night after I finish my run."

He seemed interested in our conversation, but Gabriel arrived and it was time for our meeting.

Oswald managed to tear himself away from Ilena and said, "Good luck with Nixon."

"Won't you be there?"

"Gabriel and I are not invited," he said. "Milagro, please listen to Nixon before—please listen to what he has to say and think about the long-term benefits for us."

I nodded and then Sam called me to the study and closed the door. Ian sat in an armchair, his face impassive, gazing out the window, and Mr. Nixon was at the desk. He seemed friendlier since we'd connected on the topic of dogs. I joined Sam on the sofa and he gave me an encouraging, hopeful smile.

"So here we are again," I said.

Ian looked at Nixon and said, "The sooner we can conclude this matter, the better."

Nixon told him, "We do appreciate your time. It shouldn't take long." He opened a folder on the desk. "Miss De Los Santos has only to sign our loyalty agreement and I will be on my way. I'll just get a pen . . ."

He opened the desk drawer and I spotted a bit of pink fuzz. Nixon had, too, and he gave me a look of complicity before picking up a pen and then shutting the drawer. "Sam has explained that you have been going through a stressful time since your accident. The Rules Committee is therefore willing to allow you to reconsider your decision. Sign your name and our business is done."

I didn't even look at the document. "Thanks, but no thanks. I don't want to be a member of any club that relies upon fear and secrecy to operate."

Nixon took my decision calmly. "I see that you're resolute. You understand that you'll be forfeiting our protections?"

"Yes, I know."

Nixon turned to Ian and asked, "Ducharme, do you have anything to say to her?"

Ian stood. "No. If you have any other business with me, I'll be visiting Mrs. Grant at her cottage." He walked by me without a word and left the study.

I stared after him, feeling his coldness like a blow, and then I realized that both Sam and Nixon were watching me.

Nixon leaned back in his chair and said, "I'll need a word alone with Sam and then I'll take your decision back to the Council. Best wishes on your upcoming marriage."

There had been no discussion, no arguments, no threats. "You won't interfere with my marriage to Oswald?"

"Is there anything I could say to change your mind?"

"No."

He shrugged his narrow shoulders and smiled. "Then what can I do? I hoped to convince you, but since I haven't, the Rules Committee will accept the inevitable. It is your loss, however, Miss De Los Santos."

I got up and went to the door and said, "There's just one more thing. Oswald, Sam, and Gabriel all tried their best to get me to agree to your terms."

"Our relations with the Grant family will continue as before. They are valued members of our community."

Nixon departed shortly after. The rest of the afternoon was a bittersweet reminder of what I'd loved best about being at the ranch: the company of friends and family. If others noticed the distance between Ian and me, they probably attributed it to Oswald's jealousy.

As the sun set, we sat on the terrace, drinking martinis, noshing on olives and bread, and talking over one another. Our mood warmed and softened, *espíritu de los cocteles*. I breathed the clean country air and I was glad that at least one of my issues was resolved.

Edna and Cornelia left with Ian and his consort to meet Joseph in town for dinner. Ian and Ilena would not be coming back. And that resolved another issue.

While Sam and Gabriel were chatting in the dining room, I caught Oswald by himself and said, "No more celibacy requirement."

He didn't look as happy as he should have. "I'm worried about you."

"I know I wasn't in a fugue state, Oz. Your grandmother thinks that maybe one of the cats—and they've been sneaking inside—dragged my wedding dress outside. Nancy will know how to clean it."

"I'm not just talking about the dress."

"We've got the wedding jitters. We're stressed out. We'll relieve that stress tonight and everything will be better." I believed that as I kissed him.

I left Oswald and his cousins. I changed into my running clothes and went out to stretch my legs, burn calories, and clear my thoughts. This was the first night that felt like summer, the heat of the day hanging on.

On my second lap, as I approached the pond, I saw someone standing near Daisy's grave. I stopped running and walked slowly until I recognized Mr. Nixon.

"Hi," I said. "What are you doing out here?"

He smiled and said, "I was bored at the hotel, so I decided to accept Dr. Grant's invitation to come back and relax."

I hadn't heard Oswald inviting Nixon back, but there was so much talk, I might have missed it. "It's lovely here at night."

He was looking up at the sky. "I've never seen so many stars. Do you see Romulus and Remus?"

I was struck by his suddenly whimsical nature. "Which are they?"

He stepped close and pointed up, saying, "There, the bright ones are Castor and Pollux."

I was staring into the sky when he pulled the gun from his pocket and pointed it at my head.

twenty-two

chain of fools

If he'd been aiming at another body part I'd have taken the chance of running. He kept facing me and took one step backward, just out of my kicking range. From his left pocket he pulled out the fuzzy pink handcuffs. "Put these on."

"And if I say no?"

"You have remarkable healing abilities, Miss De Los Santos, but even you can't recover from a bullet through your brain. Put them on."

I considered flinging them at his face, but he would still have a clear shot at me. "So it was you all along," I said. "You're the one who set up the car crash."

"Don't be ridiculous," he sneered. "That *was* an accident, but it would have solved all our problems. Now the bereaved misfit girl is going to drown herself close to the grave of her pet."

"No one will believe that."

"They will after your recent paranoid rantings. Of course, I wouldn't have to go through this messiness if Ducharme had eliminated you as he was supposed to do when you were first turned. A pity that I won't get to sample any of your blood."

"Ian and Oswald say it's the most incredible thing they've ever tasted," I said. "Wouldn't you like a drink before I go?"

He chuckled. "I'm not as easy to seduce as Ducharme. Not that he's interested in you anymore. No more stalling, Miss De Los Santos. Off you go." He pointed the gun toward my head.

"Won't the handcuffs be evidence of wrongdoing?"

"On the contrary! They'll be evidence of perversion and a disturbed mind. All the more reason for the Grant family to hush up your very timely demise."

"Go to hell."

"Ladies first." He waved the gun.

I took one step toward the pond, looking for a rock to grab. That's when we heard the short sharp bark.

Nixon kept the gun pointed at me, and I glanced toward the sound. Pal was loping toward me, but something was odd about the way he looked and moved. In a second I realized that the snarling animal was not Pal, but another wolf, smaller, a female. She leapt at me, jaws open, white teeth gleaming in the darkness.

I twisted my body and blocked her with my shoulder. She fell and came at me again. I kneed her chest, and she went back with a yelp. I tried to wrest my hands from the pink handcuffs, but they were stronger than they looked.

The wolf was crouching now, more cautious, as she circled me. I turned, too, and kept facing her, my arms as wide as they could be in their constraints.

When she went for my throat, I looped my arms around her and rotated her body so her back was toward me, and then I threw myself atop the writing creature. Her neck arched back, her jaws snapped in fury.

I could have killed her then, but she was such a beautiful animal. "For God's sake, Nixon, get help!"

He was watching in rapt fascination, the gun wavering in his hand as he tried to keep aim on me. He fired, and one foot from me the dirt kicked up. He fired again, and this time the bullet hit the wolf on her back leg.

The animal howled in pain and howled again. It was an unearthly sound and I felt the cry go through her body and reverberate in my own. Then her fur vanished between my fingers and her body lengthened and she was screaming in agony.

And I knew I really was suffering from mental problems because I was no longer holding a wolf, but a naked, shrieking, wounded woman.

I was trying to release her, but I couldn't lift my bound wrists over her head because she was flailing her arms, and then everyone was running across the field calling out my name.

I head-butted the woman and when she stopped waving her arms, I lifted mine over her shoulders and head. Nixon had dropped the gun and was running toward the road. I tackled him, yelling, "Give me the key! Give me the key!"

Gabriel and Sam pried me off him and pulled me up.

"Milagro tried to kill me!" Nixon said. "She's crazy. She just shot that woman back there."

I looked for Oswald and he was crouching by the woman, putting his shirt over her naked body, and saying, "Are you okay? Did she hurt you?"

"I'm the victim here!" I said. "That thing attacked me."

The tiny dark-haired woman was shivering and whimpering, looking up at Oswald with teary moo-cow eyes.

"Vidalia," Oswald said softly to her. "It's a flesh wound. I can take care of it inside." She was so small that he lifted her easily in his arms. He took one look at me and I saw something then that I'd never seen before in his eyes: fear and revulsion. Then Oswald carried the wounded creature quickly across the field to the house.

Gabriel had found the gun and said to Nixon, "We're going to deal with this now."

Nixon looked at me and said in astonishment, "So you saw it too?"

"I saw it."

"Saw *what*?" Sam asked.

"Oswald's new partner is a werewolf," I said. It was telling that Sam looked shocked, but Gabriel merely looked surprised. "Now will someone please take these handcuffs off me?"

Gabriel found the key in Nixon's pocket and threw it to Sam, who unlocked the cuffs. I tossed the fuzzy pink bands to Nixon and said, "Your turn."

Once Nixon was cuffed, Sam and Gabriel began marching him toward the house. I took a deep breath and looked back up at the starry sky.

Laughter, low, rich, and deeply amused, came from a stand of pines on the other side of the pond. I followed the sound to see Ian leaning against a tree trunk.

"Were you there the whole time?" I asked.

"I knew Nixon wouldn't be so easily appeased."

"Why the hell didn't you help me?"

He stepped close to me and said softly, "Because you don't need anyone's help. You're the heroine, Milagro."

"Ian . . . ," I began, but then I heard the cousins calling me, "Young Lady, are you coming? Young Lady!"

I turned toward them and shouted, "In a minute!"

When I turned back, Ian was walking away through the trees toward the road that passed along the ranch's northern boundary.

Gabriel was waiting in the kitchen. He poured a blood cocktail for me and I drank it in a few greedy gulps.

"Where's everyone else?" I asked.

"Oswald is stitching up Vidalia in the study, and Sam is questioning Nixon in the family room. He's trussed like a pig and not going anywhere. Do you want to tell me what happened?"

I relayed my story to him and his eyes widened when I told him about Vidalia's transformation. "Have you ever heard anything like that?"

"Nothing I ever believed."

Then I said, "I want to talk to her."

When we went to the study, Vidalia was on the sofa, looking like a child in Oswald's pajamas. Her pink polished toenails peeked out beneath the rolled-up pajama legs and she was clutching a box of Kleenex to her frail chest.

At the sight of me, her tears began flowing, but I wasn't feeling particularly sympathetic.

"Why did you try to kill me?" I asked.

"Milagro!" Oswald said sharply.

I looked at him and saw that awful expression again. "I don't know what she told you, but she attacked me in wolf form and went for my throat."

"What was I supposed to do?" she cried. "You stole him from me and we were supposed to be together forever!"

"Oswald?" I asked, looking at him. "You told me it was just business."

"Not Oswald!" Vidalia cried. "Joseph Alfred. He was mine

267

and you brought him up here and I watched how you stole him—with gardening and dancing and your big stupid boobs!"

"How did you see that . . . ?" And then I noticed her tiny little hands with her sharp little nails, her little sniffy nose, and I said, "You were watching from the trees."

"I was his snickerdoodle! But he wasn't going to get away that easily, especially to be with some low-class slut!"

Oswald had been watching this exchange in confusion and now he said, "What the hell are you two talking about?"

I thought he could have shown me a little more sympathy after what I'd just been through, but he remained standing close to Vidalia. I said, "Your new partner was the one who chewed the wiring in the car. She was the one who stole and buried my ring and ruined my wedding dress."

"I've had about enough of your insane stories for one night." Oswald spoke so coldly that I was stunned into silence.

Vidalia saw that she had scored a major point and she looked gratefully at Oswald and said, "Where's your beautiful fiancée?"

"Milagro *is* my fiancée," he answered flatly, swinging out an arm in my direction.

"I meant the chic woman . . . who sleeps upstairs with you, not your housemaid."

That's when I began laughing and laughing. I laughed until I was gasping for breath. When I could speak, I said, "This little rodent has been trying to kill the wrong woman."

It took us a while to sort out the story and we had to call Joseph to the house so that he could give us his version of things. He brought Cornelia and Edna back with him.

Vidalia sobbed so much that Oswald gave her Valium, and now she was curled in the corner of the sofa in the study, the rest of us crowding the room.

Cornelia looked at the petite shape-shifter as if Vidalia was something stuck on the bottom of her pointy-toed Italian boots.

"Vidalia's always been obsessed with transformation of the human body," Joseph told us. "She followed *Don* Pedro's teachings and realized that he was full of crap. But she still thought there was truth in shape-shifting myths and that drugs opened the door to those abilities. She hired me to do research on botanical agents that could induce trance states."

He'd gene-sliced peyote with other psychotropic plants, including hallucinogenic mushrooms that had traditionally been used by aboriginal peoples. "We experimented on ourselves," he said. "I discovered I had a real talent for shape-shifting."

"You're my Pal," I said, stunned.

"Always will be, sweetpea," he said and winked one blue eye. "Vidalia learned to transform, but mostly she was stuck to rodents and other small animals."

"I was a wolf finally today," she said proudly. "I couldn't maintain, though."

I looked at Joseph and said, "You called the sheriff when I had my accident."

"Yeah, there I was, buck naked on the highway," he said with a laugh. "I had a hell of a time keeping you in one place long enough for help to come. How'd you manage to survive that crash?"

"Air bags and I always wear my seat belt," I said.

"Yeah, right. Anyway, Vidalia got it into her head that we were mated for life." He cast a pitying look in her direction and said, "Honey, even in Disney movies, wolves don't mate for life with moles."

"I can't help what I feel," she whined.

"After she sideswiped me, I came up here to get away from her," he said. "Vidalia, how'd you find me?"

She stared blankly at him. "I saw you and this slut at the botanical gardens. I followed you here and saw that you'd come to be with her, the maid."

"I'm not the maid," I said.

She said, "You sleep in the maid's room and you do the cooking, errands, and gardening and you drive others around. That sounds like a maid to me."

Edna had turned her face to the wall, but I could tell that she was laughing by the way her head bobbed.

"Milagro's a writer," Gabriel said. "Please go on, Vidalia."

She said, "If I was going to stay here with Joseph, I needed a job. When I found out that Oswald was a plastic surgeon, too . . ." She turned to my fiancé and gave him a gentle smile. "It seemed only natural to work with him."

"Vidalia, what are the mechanics of shape-shifting?" Oswald asked.

Vidalia didn't respond since she was staring at Cornelia, who was resting her red-nailed pale hand on Joseph's thigh.

Joseph said, "The best I can explain is that it's got three factors. We shifters can loosen our cartilage and manipulate superficial color and texture changes. At the same time, we're releasing a compound that stimulates a chemical receptor in the olfactory bulb of others so they see what we're projecting," he said.

"I don't believe that," Oswald said.

"You're being pretty skeptical for a guy who has a store of animal blood in his barn," Joseph said, and the vampires looked around at one another. "Okay, the alternate explanation is that we really are harnessing some spiritual energy to transform into animals."

Oswald frowned and asked Gabriel and Sam, "What do we do with her now? What do we do with Nixon?"

Nixon was easier to dispatch. Phone calls were made to the Council; Gabriel would deliver him to the airport and hand him off to the vampire security detail. After Gabriel put Nixon in his truck, he found me in my maid's room, where I'd been washing my face. He handed the fuzzy pink handcuffs to me and said, "Nixon's got nowhere to go but back to the Council."

"How do we know they didn't send him to kill me? He told me that they sent Ian to kill me when I was first infected."

Gabriel was smiling but serious as he said, "Now you know why they call him the Dark Lord. I've never discovered what Ian does for the Council. Some things I don't want to know—you get me, *chica*? But Nixon could have just been talking to freak you out."

I brushed back his red-gold hair and kissed his cheek. "I miss having you here."

The rest of us talked late into the night about what to do with Vidalia. She had tried to kill me, but Joseph claimed that it was her animal self that had made her act so viciously. "If you can keep her from transforming, she'll be okay," he said. "She can't shift without the chemical help, and she should be running low on those meds."

Edna said, "I'll let you young people figure this out. Young Lady, walk me to my cottage."

As we went across the field, she took my arm in hers. "Once again you have escaped death. What do you think is just punishment for Nixon and Vidalia?"

"I'd like to slap them silly, yell at them, and have them apologize and admit the error of their ways. At least I've been vindicated. I wasn't being paranoid."

"No, you weren't. There were people out to get you."

I gave her a hug good night and walked back to the house, fighting off a fear that had nothing to do with physical danger. At the car park I met Sam, Joseph, and Cornelia, who were taking Vidalia to her rented house so they could destroy her stash of shape-shifting drugs.

Oswald and I were by ourselves.

He looked at me and I looked at him and I said, "Things have changed, haven't they?"

twenty-three

things that rhyme with bride: tried, lied, cried, sighed

It was a perfect day for the wedding, overcast and gray at the seaside town, with gentle, ocean-scented breezes. The hotel was filled with the vampire and Normal guests, gussying themselves up in all their finery.

When it was dark, everyone drove to the small winery, which looked magical. It was just as I'd imagined it would be. Dahlias in rich plum, crimson, and violet decorated every table, and purple grapes dangled heavily on the trellis over the patio. Festive strings of lights hung across the dance floor.

Then the music started, and the groom took his place beneath the trellis. He was handsome in a black suit and snow white shirt.

Everyone waited excitedly for the bride's procession. When Cornelia came up the aisle on her father's arm, she looked more beautiful than I'd ever seen her, wearing a floor-length ivory sheath. A sparkling diamond tiara held an antique lace veil on her dark hair.

Her father was a distinguished-looking man with iron gray curly hair, wearing tails, with a banner across his chest and medals and ribbons. He moved to stand beside his wife, an attractive woman in an elegant robin's-egg blue suit dress.

I wasn't going to come, but Cornelia had called several times, insisting that I attend since I had introduced her to Joseph. I'd arrived just in time to check in at the oceanside hotel and drive here. I'd taken a seat in the back row. I hadn't been sure about what to wear to a wedding that was supposed to be my own. So I decided to follow Mrs. Nice's advice and choose something classic: my white plastic miniskirt and a black-and-white print blouse.

Now I looked for friends and I saw them everywhere. Edna and Thomas were at the front, as were Sam and his beautiful family. In the row behind them were Gabriel and his guy, and my heart ached as I spotted Oswald with Vidalia. I saw Pepper's hulking frame, and off to one side was Gigi Barton with her beau, my friend Bernie. Nancy was at the back, directing things and looking fantastically efficient with a clipboard and a headset.

It wasn't until the tall man in front of me moved that I saw Ian's curly head and Ilena's platinum fall of hair.

The wedding couple was so happy and in love that their mood cheered the whole party. Tomorrow there would be another ceremony, the private vampire ritual. The Council had lost too much credibility to object to Cornelia's marriage to Joseph, since they'd been flummoxed by the very existence of werewolves. Among themselves, they dropped Joseph's name—

which happened to be Joseph Alfred Joseph—as if he were a celebrity.

The couple was pronounced husband and wife, and as they walked back down the aisle, I found myself tearing up. I told myself that it was because I was so happy for them, but my feelings were still tender, and I wished that I hadn't promised Cornelia that I would come.

I was trying to slip away unobtrusively when a familiar voice cried, "Milagro!" and Gigi Barton descended on me, the dramatic butterfly sleeves of her fluid dress making her look like an exotic bird.

"I'm having my next wedding here if I can convince Bernie to tie the knot," she said excitedly. Bernie was behind her, shaking his head at me, as she pulled me away. "Wasn't it lovely? Come help me find a real drink."

"It was lovely," I said.

"And I thought it was going to be you." She leaned close to my ear. "Don't be sad, honey. Your time will come. We both need a good belt of scotch."

She took my hand in her beringed one and tugged me toward a good-looking young waiter. And despite my efforts to get away, I was somehow lured into mingling with Cornelia's various relatives and fast-living friends and stylists.

I saw an opening in Joseph and Cornelia's circle and went to them. "Congratulations," I said and kissed the gorgeous groom. I hugged Cornelia, happy for her happiness. "Cornelia, you look radiant."

"Young Lady, you made it!" she said. "I'd like you to meet my parents."

Before I could make an excuse, Lala and Augustin Ducharme were in front of me and Cornelia was introducing us. I didn't know how to behave with people who had abused their own child because of an addiction. But Ian's father said, "A pleasure! A pleasure!" and Lala embraced me and said, "You introduced my little girl to Joseph! You're just as pretty as I thought you'd be."

They seemed so warm and friendly. Even knowing what I did, it was difficult to dislike them. I said, "I know you must be happy today." I glanced around, looking for someone to rescue me. Our biker buddy Pepper was just off to my left and I said, "If you'll excuse me, I must say hello to an old friend."

Pepper had crammed himself into a suit, and after he gave me a bear hug, the band began playing. "Come on, I can dance fancy. Did you check out the open bar? Nothing but the good stuff. Cornelia's a class act."

I followed Pepper's steps, surprised that he actually did know how to waltz.

"How you doing, hon?" he asked.

"I've had better days."

"You're gonna be okay. You need something to smooth out the edges?"

"I'll be fine. I'm always fine."

"Yeah, well, I took something myself and the edges are kinda melting." As I was laughing, he whirled me back against someone.

And I found myself looking up into Oswald's face, and suddenly I couldn't breathe.

"Hello, Milagro. You look like you're having fun."

"Oswald." My throat tightened just gazing into his gray eyes. He looked even paler than usual, and gaunt. His cheekbones stood out sharply, and his charcoal gray suit hung loosely from his shoulders. But he was still fabulous. "How are you?"

"Busy. We're opening another clinic for outpatient derma clients. Vidalia's throwing herself into her pro bono work." Vidalia was working off her misdeeds to me by spending every weekend providing medical services for the needy.

"That's great."

"How about you? My grandmother says your loft makes her eyes hurt."

"She's convinced that I'm keeping the pink furniture as a personal affront to her." I tried to smile, but there seemed to be a disconnect between my brain and my body. "I'm still writing and doing the gardening thing."

"Well," he said, glancing across the way to see Vidalia watching us. "I brought her because Joseph and Cornelia invited her. We're not dating or anything."

"You're a free man, Oz."

"My work takes up all my time. So, are you here by yourself?"

"Yes . . . I'm not . . ." I struggled to find words. "It's so good to see all our friends."

He nodded and then let out a heavy breath and said, "I better keep an eye on her to make sure she doesn't go off the rails."

"Good to see you, Oswald K. Grant."

He nodded and touched my hair. I leaned toward him instinctively, as I had from the moment I first met him, and I smelled his herb-scented sunblock. He smiled sadly and said, "I remember the day you bought that skirt." I nodded, waiting for him to say more. But then he turned and walked away.

He had been my world: the alpha and omega of my heart's wishes. I dropped my head to hide my face, my tears, my sorrow, and rushed away.

To get to the parking lot, I had to pass right by Ian and Ilena. I couldn't stop myself from glancing Ian's way. His eyes caught mine and I saw something there—was it regret, pity? I didn't wait to find out. I got in my truck and drove straight back to the hotel.

I threw my things in my green zebra case and dragged it to the lobby. "I'd like to check out of my room," I told the clerk and slid my key across to him.

"So soon?" he said.

"Yes."

He looked at his computer screen and said, "Yes, Ms. Ducharme's taken care of everything again. Have a pleasant evening and come back soon."

I was about to thank him when I realized what he'd said. "What did you mean, 'Ms. Ducharme's taken care of everything *again*'?"

He looked puzzled, but said, "I was referring to your last stay with us. It was put on Cornelia Ducharme's account."

"Of course. She's so generous. Thank you." Cornelia had set me up for failure by hoping that I would discover either her brother or Bar None. If Cornelia had made reservations here without my knowing it, she could easily have canceled Oswald's reservations as well, which would have explained the hotel problem on my trip east.

I went back to the City and continued trying to mend myself.

The Council, so willing to punish enemies without proof, was much more lenient with their own. Nixon "resigned" his position on the Rules Committee and gave me a settlement that was sufficient for me to pay Oswald for the loft. He refused to take the money so I just deposited it in one of his accounts.

As some genius philosopher once said, breaking up is hard to do. I'd heard there was a mathematical relationship between the length of time you were together and the time required for recovery, but I'd forgotten if the ratio was one month needed for every year together, or one month for every six months together.

I asked Nancy and she said, "Oh, I'm so over Todd already and I was with him since frosh year." She'd separated from her husband and was living in her apartment, trying to start a business as an event planner.

I'd given her the composition book filled with her style edicts, and after one of her sorority sisters had included part of it in a fashion column, Nancy was in demand as a style pundit, spouting insightful truisms such as "Leopard print is a timeless classic."

Don Pedro's *fauxoir* was rushed into publication, typos, grammatical errors, and all. I spotted it in a bookstore window downtown. The cover was a cheesy drawing of a man morphing into animals, including the inscrutable platypus. I bought a copy and pasted my name over *Don* Pedro's on the cover. I propped the book atop my desk, beside a bulletin board with clippings of the *fauxoir*'s rave reviews.

Mercedes asked about the display and I told her how I'd been scammed by *Don* Pedro. When the book reached the bestseller lists, I bought a bottle of champagne and invited her over.

She arrived carrying a big box and said, "I've got a couple of presents for you." Inside the box was the much-vaulted Margaritanator 3000, a chrome-and-glass powerhouse of a blender. Mercedes took a sheet of folded paper out of her pocket and handed it to me. "Here's another."

"What is it?"

"It took considerable digging, but I found out that your pal *Don* Pedro isn't from the jungle. His real name is Dave Alvarez and he's from the San Fernando Valley. After his auto parts shop went under, he did a stint as a pet psychic, using the name Jasper Farswat, and from there he reinvented himself as a *Don* Pedro Nascimento. But he's just an ordinary Mexican-American like you."

I handed her a glass of champagne and raised my own. "To all the ordinary Mexican-Americans and their extraordinary imaginations."

She toasted and then said, "I read the book. It was damn good, *mujer,* aside from the fact that it's total B.S."

After Mercedes left, I sat on the pink velvet sofa and opened the *fauxoir.* After twenty pages, I realized that when I'd been channeling *Don* Pedro, I'd broken away from all the writing rules I'd imposed upon myself. His voice was loopy and florid, yes, but also fluid and touching. I began working again on my story about the girl who is taken to the underworld.

I reconnected with my old friends. The vampires and their circle kept in touch with me, although they handled me carefully. I made new friends at the local Stitching & Bitching group. They taught me to knit and I made several charming sweaters for Sam's toddler. I even invited them to my loft and fired up the Margaritanator 3000 for Rancho Sunsets.

The needlework had an unexpected but very welcome benefit: after so many hours of controlling my small motor skills, precise movement became automatic and extended to my large motor skills. I stopped having to worry about hugging someone so hard that I hurt him.

I decided to salvage the embroidered silk from my wedding tunic and make scarves. The garment was in a box on a shelf in my closet. I took down the box and when I pulled out the gown, a manila folder fell out of the box.

It was the guide to the vampire marriage ceremony. I hadn't looked at it before, but now I sat on my bed and opened it. The first sheet was written in the strange old alphabet. The phonetic translation was written on the second page along with the directions: "The groom places the braided birch wreath atop the bride's head." The wedding was consummated when the bride cut the groom and tasted his blood.

I fingered my bride's tunic, remembering how Oswald had looked in his scarlet robe. Then I turned it inside out to see how I could cut it. Parallel to my original seams were neat rows of stitches that took in over an inch on each side. Bad, bad Cornelia.

Edna and I visited whenever she was in town, but I was never able to talk about Oswald except in the most superficial ways. Once I said, "I miss the ranch the way it was . . . with all of us there. Those evenings we shared. They all blend together in my mind, but each was so wonderful. I was so happy."

"I know, Young Lady."

As the weeks went by, I found myself content to awake in the rosy light that came through the curtains of my pink loft. I looked forward to seeing my friends and I enjoyed my time alone writing, reading, or unraveling one of my knitting experiments.

Sometimes I even went out to dinner or a movie with a man, but I always went home by myself.

One night I walked to My Dive, as I did once or twice a week, enjoying the way the steam came up through the sidewalk grates. I watched a man changing the signage on a music hall and admired the gray cupola of City Hall against a dark blue sky. Mercedes had taken the lease on the little sandwich shop next door and installed Juanita's son Freddie as cook and manager of My Dive Annex.

I waved to Freddie as I walked past the doorway, but he was busy flirting with a California girl.

Lenny, the club's doorman, and I greeted each other with a hip bump. "Good show tonight," he said.

"It always is."

Mercedes was talking to the lighting guy on the balcony, so I helped the bar chick set up. As the house began filling up, I poured a cranberry and soda for myself and took a seat at a two-top.

Someone pulled the other chair out, and a man said, "May I?"

I looked up to see Ian Ducharme, but all the different things I could have said had a traffic jam in my throat. He sat, and instantly a waitress was there and he was ordering a bottle of wine.

"So here we are again, Young Lady. Should I ask how you are?"

"Please don't. All of my friends treat me like an invalid," I said. "But how are you and Ilena?"

Ian gave a bitter smile. "Do you expect me to be satisfied with another woman? I am still waiting for you."

"Ian, may I ask you an odd question?"

He smiled and said, "I hope you will."

"Are we married?"

He laughed a full, unhindered laugh and said, "Only under vampire law, which has archaic provisions for plunder and captives. I briefly entertained the notion that I could object to your marriage on the grounds that we were already married."

"That's quite flattering in a really insane way."

"I came to my senses," he said. "You would have hated me." He took my hand and my blood rose at the touch of his skin.

"What is it that we have, Ian?"

"We have our blood."

We didn't watch the show. We went back to my loft and this time we were in no hurry, slowly undressing each other, building up agonizing tension as we kissed and caressed. He didn't bring out the knife, so I was the one to ask, because I finally knew that I was my blood, and I knew that his blood was mine, too.

Our bond was something I hadn't asked for and didn't understand, and yet it was undeniable. It was like a chrysalis that held me.

Later, we opened the pink curtains and looked out on the lights of the city. I was sitting on my mattress and he was behind me, his arms around me. "Ian, I'm sorry about what happened to you with your parents. How they abused you."

He dropped his chin to my shoulder, and I leaned back against him. "Wherever did you get that idea?"

"You don't have to be embarrassed. Ms. Smith told me there were unfortunate circumstances and your sister admitted that your parents were blood addicts and used to bleed you for their own highs."

I felt the rumble of his laugh. "My parents' greatest sin is that they are very irresponsible with our estate. They wouldn't ever do such a mad thing."

"Why am I not surprised that Cornelia lied? She lied about wanting to see me happily married. I'm fairly sure she canceled my hotel reservation when I went to see the Council, and I know that she set up the 'complimentary' stay when I ran into you and Gigi."

"I'd wager Cornelia lied to appeal to your tender heart by

painting me as a victim," Ian said. "She does want to see you happily married. She's told me so many times." He reached over to his jacket and I saw a glint of something in his hand. He took my hand and slipped the beautiful red stone ring on my finger. It looked as if it belonged there, as if it had always belonged there.

"What is it exactly you do for the Council, Ian?"

"Perhaps someday, my own girl."

I took the ring off and handed it back to him. "Perhaps someday, Ian." I felt the chrysalis around me yield a little.

Epilogue

Ian was, as Ilena had said, always on the planes, and he wanted me to travel with him to whatever it was he did. I turned him down because I was busy with my own life. We established a relationship of sorts, seeing each other when he could make it to the City. We never used the word "love."

When I finished my story about Persephone, I printed it out, packed it up, and mailed it to the famous author I'd met on my trip east. I hoped he would like it, but if he didn't, I'd try not to be discouraged. After all, my *fauxoir* had outsold all of his books together and there was talk of a biopic.

I was taking a walk when I saw a brown dog with a grayish chest wandering by himself. He was skinny and dirty, but he waggled right up to me as if he knew me. After a bath and a week of food, his chest was as snowy white as Daisy's, and his chocolate fur began to shine. I tried to find his owner, but no one ever claimed him. I applied for a license and took him to the vet for his shots and an exam.

"What's his name?" the receptionist asked me.

"Rosemary."

"Rosemary is a girl's name."

"Rosemary is for remembrance," I said.

When I was walking the dog home, I said, "I'm going to tell you a story about an ordinary human *chica* who wanted to be a sincere and serious person and how she met a truly fabulous man and a nest of vampires who became her dear friends. This story has villains and heroes, madmen and con men, schemers and dreamers, urbanites and socialites. There is a beautiful and loyal dog named Daisy. There's adventure and passion and danger and love and laughter, too. She made mistakes, some foolish and some terrible, but she also tried to make amends.

"The story may be about transformation."

The dog looked up at me, and I said, "No, it's not a tragedy. For though the girl *wanted* to be sincere and serious, she adored silliness, and luckily for her, tragedy has no interest in the silly. She's going through a metamorphosis though. She doesn't know if she loves a dangerous man, or wants to win back a fabulous one. A more practical girl would dispair, but our girl believes she's ready for whatever adventures await her."

Reading Group Guide for
The Bride of Casa Dracula by Marta Acosta

Questions and Topics for Discussion

1. Milagro describes her fiancé Oswald Grant as "a fabulous man." How does Milagro's attitude toward him change as she prepares for their wedding? How does Oswald's attitude toward Milagro change during the course of the novel?

2. Why is there tension between Oswald and Milagro about their careers? Is either of them asking too much of the other? What does Milagro discover about her own writing in the process of ghostwriting *Don* Pedro's memoir?

3. Do you agree with Milagro's reasons for objecting to take the Vampire Council's loyalty oath? Do you agree with Mr. Nixon's comment that she'll never be accepted as an American? And why is it important to Oswald for Milagro to follow the Rules Committee's requests?

4. What compels Milagro to always "poke the bear" when it would be beneficial to acquiesce?

5. Why do you think Milagro persists in calling herself a normal human chica when she possesses extraordinary abilities and a taste for blood? What does Milagro like about the vampires and what about them repels her?

6. What does Ian Ducharme represent to Milagro? Why is she attracted to him when she loves her fiancé? Do you think Ian is the kind of man with whom Milagro could build a lifelong romantic relationship?

7. Does Cornelia Ducharme function as a source of good or evil in the novel?

8. What does *espiritu de cockteles* represent to Milagro? And why is it so important to her?

9. Why does Milagro welcome the arrival of Pal, the new "dog" that appears at the ranch?

10. Why is Milagro continually drawn to shady characters such as Pepper, Ian, Cornelia, and *Don* Pedro? Is charm more important to her than moral behavior?

11. Milagro's two best friends, Nancy and Mercedes, are diametrically opposed characters. What does each friendship offer Milagro?

12. Milagro has many wealthy friends—Nancy, Gigi Barton, the entire Grant family—but is she truly comfortable in upper-class circles?

13. Which of the novel's characters have the most insight into Milagro's true nature? How does each of these characters view Milagro? Is there a disparity between the way Milagro sees herself and the way you see Milagro?

14. Does Milagro make the right decision before the wedding scene?

15. Discuss the novel's ending. Were you surprised at the direction Milagro's life takes? What instances in the story foreshadowed the turn of events?

A Conversation with Marta Acosta

Is Milagro really you?

As often as people ask if Milagro is based on me, they also tell me that they completely identify with her, which makes me feel absolutely wonderful.

While Milagro and I share our ethnicity and a love of literature, she was a very conscious construct. I thought about the fictional characters I love and why I love them. I tried to give Milagro a little of Jane Eyre's loneliness and spirit, Elizabeth Bennett's sharp wit and good heart, and Bertie Wooster's cheerful nature.

It was also important to me to have a character who is a common type among real Latinas, but rarely represented by the media. Milagro is smart, affectionate, college-educated, funny, and devoted to her friends. She reminds me of all the fabulous young women I've known who are trying to figure out their place in the world.

If Milagro is supposed to be so smart, how come she does some really stupid things?

The blissfully clueless characters in Mark Twain's and P. G. Wodehouse's novels are hysterical. Milagro is gullible because she's inexperienced and hopeful. She acts impulsively and makes mistakes, but she tries to amend her errors. The reasons for the misunderstandings are twofold. They set up comic situations and drama, as well as allowing Milagro to be unaware of information that I couldn't otherwise convey to the reader.

Besides, smart people aren't exempt from fabulously stupid behavior. Just watch the news.

Why vampires? Are you obsessed by the paranormal?

I really enjoy paranormal stories, but I'm not obsessed! When you're writing humor, you try to put seemingly disparate themes together to play upon expectations. I wanted to spoof the clichés of vampires as rich, European smoothies *and* I also wanted to write a comedy-of-manners that deals with social class.

If this was a math problem, you could see the overlap between these genres: young, naive person goes off to an isolated country estate and encounters wealthy snobs. In a gothic novel, there's romance and danger. In a comedy, romance and mayhem ensue. I threw everything in the blender and hit the "frappe" button.

The vampires in my books are also a metaphor for being "other" in society. They feel as if they're outside, looking in, just as Milagro does. She feels outside for a few reasons. She's seen as "other" by virtue of her ethnicity, but she also grew up without a real family, so she doesn't understand how families relate. She was an outsider among the wealthy students at her Fancy University.

There is a subtext to the story, and I hope that readers will empathize with the characters and perhaps re-think their ideas about identity and what is normal.

Why did you decide to write the story as a first-person narrative? Isn't first-person overdone?

Since first-person narrative is a natural story-telling voice, it's true that novice writers often feel most comfortable writing in first-person. However, the device also offers a wealth of possibilities within its restrictions. Think of the story as a panorama, but the first-person narrator can only describe the view seen out of a narrow window. The reader must ascertain whether the narrator's description accurately reflects the whole. (Hint: the answer is always "no.")

It's also really fun to write in first-person when one has an eccentric character with a peculiar interior monologue. The narrator's skewed perception reveals his own character, experiences, and motivations.

Some of my favorite first-person narratives include *Lolita, Jane Eyre, To Kill a Mockingbird,* and *The Innocents Abroad.*

What is the central challenge for Milagro in each of the three Casa Dracula novels?

In the first novel, *Happy Hour at Casa Dracula,* Milagro isn't grounded because she doesn't have the stability and love that a home and a family can provide. She thinks she's looking for romantic love, but what she truly desires is a family and a maternal figure. Her relationship with Oswald's grandmother, Edna, may be the most important one in the novel.

The second, *Midnight Brunch at Casa Dracula,* follows Milagro's efforts to learn more of the vampires' secrets and also to pursue her writing career. Oswald believes that she will be safer if she is kept uninformed, but knowledge is power, and Milagro insists on learning more about the clandestine vamps and their history.

The Bride of Casa Dracula finds Milagro resisting the Vampire Council's efforts to make her conform. Although she wanted to be a part of the clan, she will not give up her own identity. She's learning to trust her instincts even when everyone else thinks she's crazy.

What are you writing now? Will there be more adventures for Milagro?

I've always found it great fun to write about Nancy, Milagro's frivolous and very chic friend from F.U., so I'm writing a novel based on her quest to establish an all-encompassing theory of style. What I love about Nancy is her crazy use, misuse, and abuse of language. You're never quite sure how serious she is. Nancy is separated from her prig of a husband and is trying to start an event-planning business. She even hires a dream assistant, a too-polished young man with his own agenda. Naturally, all her plans come crashing down.

Milagro makes an appearance in this book, but I'm saving her adventures for the fourth Casa Dracula novel. Milagro will emerge as someone who is more secure in her abilities and judgment. However, since she's still a freak magnet, unexpected craziness will come her way.

Enjoy the following excerpt from
Marta Acosta's first Casa Dracula novel

HAPPY HOUR
AT CASA DRACULA

Now available from
POCKET BOOKS

one

the intolerable lightness of being silly

If I had been a rational human being, I would have had a normal job and I never would have gotten involved with any of them. But I was not a rational human being. I was and remain a square peg in a round world.

You would think that a girl with a degree from a Fancy University would have been hired *muy rápido* by some big corporation anxious to ladle on numerous perks and a generous salary. Sadly, my F.U. education did not lead me directly into wealth and fame. All my attempts to become a worthwhile cog in the capitalist machine were met with rejection, the type that has driven many other creative souls to despair and Great Art.

Here are the results of my attempts. No response at all from the many newspapers that should have been interested in a columnist who focused on bargain gardens. A soul-killing stint at an ad agency that concluded when the art director read my sardonic copy for fortified wine. A happy stretch writing a newsletter for a nutritional supplements company that ended abruptly when the FDA raided our warehouse. Miscellaneous temporary jobs, each more wretchedly depressing than its predecessor. Also two entry-level marketing jobs terminated after "improprieties," which were not my fault.

Okay, my mother Regina would have said that they *were* my fault. My mother Regina thought that anyone with breasts as vulgar as my own induced otherwise upstanding citizens to behave badly. My mother Regina had neat, tasteful *chichis*. When she bothered to look at me, an expression of dismay almost came over her immaculately made-up face. "Almost," because medical procedures rendered her incapable of normal facial expressions.

My mother Regina believed my father had wasted his hard-earned cash sending me to F.U. because I was not a serious person. My mother Regina thought thusly because I always referred to her as "my mother Regina" and because I had not dedicated myself wholeheartedly to the reformation and improvement of my garish carcass. "You have wasted your father's money," she said, ignoring the fact that I had worked, taken out loans, and earned scholarships in order to attend F.U.

I now lived in a windowless basement flat of a nice house in a nice neighborhood of the City. My rent was low because I maintained the garden and my landlord found my bosom enchanting. While he never exactly said, "I am captivated by your enchanting bosom," he did stare a lot and that's practically the same thing. The dark flat had a cement floor, a dinky bathroom, and a gloomy kitchenette. At night, I heard scrabbling in the walls, which, I suspected, was caused by fearsome Norway rats.

My income was earned by toiling as a reading consultant to executives and society dames who were book club averse. I garnered extra cash by filling in at a local nursery. My jobs were irregular, sometimes taking only ten hours of my week and other times taking fifty, but I didn't mind. It was better than sitting in an office trying to keep my eyes from bleeding while copyediting training manuals.

I worked diligently on my novel every single possible second that was available after going out, thrift store shopping, spending quality time with my friends, and finding gyms that offered the first month free. In addition to this exhausting work/art/life regime, I tried to improve the world by writing letters to political leaders about Important Issues. I wasn't picky about the issues. The world was full of pain and injustice, and writing the letters helped me keep proper perspective.

My friend Nancy had come up with the reading consultant idea because she knew how much I liked recommending books to friends. She had given me business cards on lovely ecru stock with "Bennett" hyphenated to my last name. Underneath was "Reading Consultant," with my phone number.

"Why the Bennett hyphenate?" I had asked.

"Like Eliza Bennett, you have a fine posterior," she had said. Nancy had been my F.U. roommate freshman year. Despite her unfortunate WASPier-than-thou perkiness, we had become friends.

"Eliza had fine eyes, not a fine fanny, you cultural barbarian. You never even finished *Pride and Prejudice*. I wrote that paper for you."

"And now I am showing my tremendous appreciation for

your scholarship. Also this gives you credibility with Anglophile aspirants, my little brown *amiga*." This is how we talked to each other. We thought being silly was the height of delightfulness.

Speaking of which, my name was outlandish enough without the Bennett hyphenate, but I took the cards and thanked her.

I filled my days, but there were times when I awoke in the middle of the night, listened to the scratching in the walls, and felt afraid and lonely. I missed rooming with Nancy and hearing her gentle snoring at night. Nancy did not miss me; she had moved into her boyfriend Todd's condo and was a happy camper.

People can be divided into two distinct groups: those who desire constant companionship and those who prefer calm solitude. The unnecessary crowding in *The Brady Bunch* repelled me, but I longed for an Eliza Bennettish existence: a house filled with family and friends, the agreeable conversation of a kind and compassionate sister, and the promise of dances and engagements.

Instead I had my mother Regina, rats in the walls, and boyfriends who were like beach reads, momentary fun but nothing you'd ever bother to buy in hardcover. I worried that perhaps I, as a nonserious person, was only a beach read as well. I had just reread *Middlemarch*, and I had a deep and sincere desire to be a deep and sincere character.

Nancy had connected me with most of my reading clients, but one of my former beach reads, a Russian artist named Vladimir, introduced me to Kathleen Baker. Kathleen was one of *the* Bakers, known for their famous sourdough bread: "Did a Real Baker Make Your Sour Round?"

Kathleen was fiftyish and very chic. Like my other clients,

Kathleen wanted me more for company than guidance. Sometimes she patted my head as if I was a pet and I half expected her to toss biscuits to me and say, "Good girl, catch!" I had to constantly steer the conversation back to her reading and remind her that we had a scholarly purpose.

In her enthusiasm for literature, Kathleen decided to host a reception for hot new writer Sebastian Beckett-Witherspoon. She was absolutely thrilled when he accepted. I know because she said, "I am absolutely thrilled that Sebastian Beckett-Witherspoon has accepted my invitation to hold a reception for him. Are you familiar with his work?"

In a word, yes. In three words, all too familiar. In a few more words, why wouldn't Sebastian B-W die, die, die a grisly and humiliating death? I pulled my lips into a simian grimace that I hoped Kathleen would interpret as a smile. I told her that we had met at F.U. "Marvelous!" she said. "Of course, you will be at my reception. I'm sure he'll be delighted to see you again."

"Perhaps you overestimate my delightfulness," I demurred. I had taken up demurring like mad. I thought demurring was the last word in refinement, right behind murmuring, deferring, and suggesting.

"Don't be a silly goose," Kathleen said. "This will be a good opportunity for you to meet other literary people."

So here I was at Kathleen's soirée for Sebastian Beckett-Witherspoon, the highlight of a lackluster season of morose poets, grimy novelists, and patronizing essayists. Kathleen had a magpie's fascination with all things shiny, so the room gleamed with polished floors, glittering mirrors, and lustrous furniture. I was afraid that if I moved too quickly, I'd skitter and crash down on my sincere and serious *colita*.

I wore a simple linen shirt-dress that I'd bought at a thrift store, cream sandals, and fake pearls. My straight black hair was pulled back into a low, Grace Kellyish ponytail, and I'd used a light hand with my makeup because I wanted to look good without looking like a good time.

I did what I always do at gatherings: an initial scan of the room for people of hue. One Asian man in a pinstripe suit, an African-American couple in earth-toned natural fibers, and a mixed-race woman. No obvious Latinos except for me and one waiter. I sent him the silent message: "Right on, *mi hermano*. Power to the people."

At a real party or in a club, I knew what to do or say, but here I felt as awkward as I had my first day at F.U., hauling cardboard boxes to my dorm while almost Nordic-looking people strode confidently forward with matching luggage. The other guests seemed to know each other, but their eyes slid over me and moved on to others more important.

I was all too aware of the ecru business cards in my small pocketbook. Sometimes you seek guidance in nineteenth-century heroines and other times you find inspiration in nineteenth-century hucksters, such as P. T. Barnum and his Feejee Mermaid. If Barnum could shamelessly peddle a monkey head sewn on a fish body as a sea nymph, then surely I could try to promote my novel to an agent or publisher.

Then I saw Sebastian B-W, scion of one of the most powerful families in the country. He stood by a window, and most people would have thought it was merely a lucky accident that a shaft of light from the setting sun glowed on his golden hair. He smiled and nodded as he talked to an older man. Sebastian's skin was evenly tanned with a slight, marvelous blush of pink on his cheeks. His teeth were as pearly as ever, and he seemed to have aged very little over the last several years. He was just over six foot, slim and graceful in a navy jacket and a soft blue shirt that brought out the sea-color of his eyes.

I had thought, la, la, la, that I would come here and Sebastian would see that I had moved beyond the past, that I had matured into an urban and urbane woman, a fellow scribe, and that we could have a civil, even friendly association. But just looking at him made me panic like a hemophiliac in a pin factory.

"Yummy," said a voice nearby.

"What?" I was startled and turned to see a small, wiry redheaded waiter with a tray of petite pastries.

"Would you like something yummy?" The waiter held the tray toward me and winked. He was as gay and pleasing as a posy of Johnny-jump-ups. He had a wide smile and big green eyes to go with his shock of red hair.

"I always enjoy something yummy," I replied suggestively, unable to stop my chronic flirting mechanism. Nancy said that my need to flirt was directly linked to the lack of a strong paternal figure in my life and the dominating presence of an unloving mother. I thought it was because boys were so dang pretty.

"I certainly didn't mean him," the waiter said, tilting his head toward Sebastian. "That novel was offensive."

Of course I had read Sebastian's novel, looking for secret clues to his character in every word. "I thought I was the only one who didn't like it."

"Please, girlfriend, it was pretentious as hell," said the waiter. "His school churns them out like that." He saw my expression and said, "What's the matter?"

When I admitted that I had gone to F.U., he grinned and said, "Well, present company excepted. You aren't involved with him, are you?"

"Me, involved with him? Ha-ha, you make the funny," I said flippantly. "Does he turn your engine?"

"Not my type. I like them less evil incarnate," he said. "And also hairier."

Before we could continue our fascinating conversation, the headwaiter angrily gestured for my new friend to circulate. It was time for me to circulate, too, and the first person I had to talk to was the guest of horror. My heart was pounding faster than a flamenco dancer's feet. I grabbed a flute of champagne off a tray, downed it quickly, and grabbed another.

Moving through the crowd, I noticed that everyone was surreptitiously peeking at Sebastian, all awaiting their chance to have a clever or insightful exchange so they could relate the story at their next dinner party. He caught sight of me and his smile froze. I tried to calm myself as I walked to his side.

He continued his conversation with the older man. "Naturally," he said, "I only write about perversions to expose them to the condemnation they deserve. I am not a voyeur, not one who is titillated by the steamy, I mean, seamy underbelly."

Seamy underbelly? I guess that was my cue. "Hello, Sebastian."

He turned his head fractionally toward me. "Hullo," he said tersely without meeting my eyes.

"*Hullo*? Are we suddenly British? Lord love a duck." I didn't know what that expression meant, but I'd always wanted to use it. "In America, we say 'hello' with the accent on 'hell.'"

The older fellow said to Sebastian, "I enjoyed talking with you," then edged just far enough away to eavesdrop.

Sebastian held out his hand and actually said, "I'm Sebastian Beckett-Witherspoon. And you are . . . ?"

He won tonight's P. T. Barnum award for even trying this.

I wanted to stab him repeatedly with a tiny cocktail fork until he leaked all over like a sieve. "If you don't cut it out, Sebastian, I swear I'll make your evening here one of undiluted misery."

He blanched and spoke in a low whisper. "Undiluted misery! You have no idea how much you've caused me. What are you doing here?"

"I'm a very close and special friend of Kathleen's. In fact, I'm her literary consultant," I said, trying to sound important.

Sebastian was confused. "You mean you suggested that she have this reception?"

"Oh, be real," I snapped. "Did I like your incest-fest novel? I did not." It occurred to me that this was not the most politic thing to say if I wished to resuscitate our association.

"*You* are criticizing me? You, who write political horrors!" He snorted. "Blood and gore and monsters and tedious left-wing diatribes. Utter swill."

Why were my feelings hurt when I had no respect for him? "You said you liked my stories," I said before I could stop myself. I pushed away a memory of the early weeks of our acquaintance and how I felt seeing him strolling across campus toward me, smiling as the wind blew back his hair.

"I may have said it, but I didn't mean it."

"Did you ever mean anything you told me, Sebastian?" It was as if no time had passed since our last encounter: I was flooded by unnameable emotion, wanting to cry and shout and say all the things I'd never had a chance to tell him. I hadn't done anything wrong, yet he had cast me out of his world. What was worse, he'd done it when I was taking a course in Milton, so I'd become obsessed with finding the answer to my misery in *Paradise Lost*. I'd received an A on my term paper, but my time would have been better spent getting advice from *Cosmopolitan*.

"Why are you here, Milagro?"

The whole history of our relationship was in the knowing way he said my name. It felt too intimate, as if he knew too many of my secrets. "I'm here to make contacts. Introduce me to your agent or your publisher."

"You are still out of your tiny little mind."

Before I could retort, wheedle, or threaten, Kathleen began speaking on the other side of the room. Sebastian moved away so fast, it was like he had been teleported.

"Your feminine wiles leave something to be desired," said a deep voice so close to me I felt warm breath on my neck. I stepped away reflexively. Beside me was a somewhat fabulous man in a strange suit. Now, Nancy would tell you that I often see fabulous men, that I think more men are fabulous than not, and that I am overly generous in bestowing the description of "fabulous" on a man. Her comments have caused me to doubt my ability to judge fabulousness, and I was feeling particularly insecure right now.

I focused on this man just to center myself. Rich brown hair brushed straight back, gray eyes, a strong nose, pale, perfect skin, nice cheekbones, and a lovely, rosy curved mouth. He was medium height, lean and muscled. He smiled crookedly, which either added or detracted from his charm, depending upon your point of view. "Aren't you going to say anything?" he asked.

"As you have noted, my feminine wiles have eluded me this evening." I was still trying to figure out what was wrong with his suit. It was well made, but the cut was about fifty years out of style, give or take a century. And the smell . . . under the light, clean scent of a good aftershave was cedar. My guess was that his suit had been hanging in a closet for ages.

His smoke-colored eyes took a leisurely journey up and down my body, causing my trampy internal gears to shift of their own volition. "Perhaps I misjudged," he said. His voice was as sexy as a funky bass line on the dance floor.

My recent encounter with Sebastian had made my nerves buzz, and I had no idea if this man was flirting with me or insulting me. "So kind of you to offer your criticism gratis to strangers," was my utterly pathetic retort. Who said "gratis"? Pretty soon I'd be uncontrollably uttering "pro forma," "ipso facto," and "carpe diem" in conversation ad nauseam. As a tactical maneuver, I moved through the rapt audience to the other side of the room before I said anything else idiotic.

Sebastian was now addressing the guests, droning the usual glad to be here, happy so many devoted fans, et cetera, and opening a copy of his novel so that he could read a chapter aloud. Had I ever enjoyed his writing or had I been so flattered by his attention that I convinced myself I liked this drivel?

The other guests seemed enthralled by Sebastian's stream of blather. He used words like "luminescent," "tumescent," "iridescent," and "transcendent." Perhaps they handed out *New Yorker* vocabulary lists at every graduate writing program in the country. I wouldn't know. My mother Regina had convinced my father that liposuction on her "problem spots" was more critical than helping me through grad school. Listening to Sebastian now, I began to think that maybe she'd had a point.

The carrot-topped waiter returned and whispered, "Warm chèvre with tapenade," as he offered his tray.

"No thanks," I said.

The waiter gracelessly deposited his tray on a side table. "You seem to be attracting the attention of some of the gentlemen here," he said chattily. I wasn't surprised at his unprofessional interest in me. I have always had a symbiotic relationship with the waiter species.

"If by that you mean I imposed my company upon the guest of honor, then I guess, yes."

"No offense, but these guys aren't your type. I know what I'm talking about." Coming from someone else, his statement would have sounded like a *West Side Story* stick-to-your-own-kind, but I assumed he was offering his assessment of sexual orientation.

I wasn't going to insult his obviously flawed gaydar, so I said, "Thanks. I'll take that into consideration."

The waiter winked at me, then slipped away. I wondered why he left the tray of hors d'oeuvres. He was a nice guy, but a very bad waiter.

Sebastian finally concluded his yammering. There was hearty applause, and then I saw the fabulous man smiling in my direction. Sauntering to me, he said, "This joint is a bust. Let's scram."

Though I had come to the party to hawk my wares, this was not what I had in mind. But the room seemed too close and too crowded. I was still fantasizing about stabbing Sebastian, and I thought it was a good idea to get away before I did something legally prosecutable in front of numerous witnesses. "I don't suppose you're connected to the publishing world?"

"Why else would I be here? You're a writer?" His lopsided smile inspired parts of my body to attempt mutiny and throw themselves at him. "We'll go somewhere quieter where we can talk about your writing. I can tell you are an interesting writer, unique."

"Excuse me, but exactly how dumb do you think I am?" Men seemed to think there was an inverse relationship between bouncy bazooms and brainpower.

His laugh carried to his eyes and he said, "That did sound like a bad line, didn't it? But I'm right, aren't I?"

"Every writer wants to think that she's unique and interesting. That doesn't mean it's true." I hated the idea that Sebastian had out–P. T. Barnumed me tonight. Would Barnum have rejected a potential investor? "You haven't introduced yourself," I murmured, as if I was a proper young lady.

The fabulous man took my elbow and led me through the crowd. He escorted me down the marbled hallway, through the wood-paneled foyer, and when we were away from the chatter of the party, he said, "I am Oswaldo Krakatoa."

His name was patently absurd. I was strongly tempted to question its veracity. "I'm Milagro De Los Santos." Judging from his expression, I had just won the ridiculous-name contest.

"Miracle of the saints?"

"It's a sad little story. I'll tell you sometime when I'm feeling particularly full of self-pity. You can call me Mil."

"All right, Mil." We stepped outside. The fog had rolled in and the damp Pacific air was refreshing after the packed, over-perfumed room.

My bus stop was far down the street. My options were: talk to this handsome fellow, track down my pals for a whine-and-wine session, or go home and cry a million tears because my business cards were still in my handbag and Sebastian had frazzled me to the utmost.

A limousine pulled up and the driver stepped out, opening

the passenger door. I wondered who the lucky bastard was. Yes, I knew every drug dealer and prom kid rented these, but those tiny bottles of liquor were so amusing. Oswaldo said, "I'm staying at the Hotel Croft. We could talk there in the bar."

I loved the Sequoia Room at the Croft. They had silver bowls of salted cashews and the waitresses let you nurse one overpriced cocktail for hours while you listened to the pianist play Gershwin. It was one of the City's great old hotels, and I always liked to imagine the passionate trysts that took place there, the corrupt business deals, the after-theater dinners. "I'm not . . . ," I began, and then I saw Sebastian rushing out of Kathleen's house. He looked outraged and he was heading my way. "Sure, let's go, *now.*"